Caledon

by
Virginia Crow

CROWVUS

First Published in 2019
Crowvus, 53 Argyle Square, Wick, KW1 5AJ

ISBN: 978-1-913182-06-9

For comments and questions about
"Caledon"
contact the author directly at daysdyingglory@gmail.com

www.crowvus.com

Part One:
Caledon is Called

The Mackenzies of the Bridge

The springy heather underfoot was the only thing which coaxed on the faltering footfalls of the tartan-clad man as he stumbled forward. Occasionally, his footing would fail him, and the heather would come hurtling toward him, the solid twigs stinging as they struck. They could not injure him more than his shame, however, and that had been his sole companion these five days since the ill-fated events of Drumossie Moor. On the first leg of his retreat there had been company, unwelcome but present, but none of the scattered clansmen had attempted a journey this far north into Sutherland. At least, none that he knew of, for secrecy was essential.

He did not stop his desperate march until, at last, the lights of a small house came into view. It was a short distance from him, half a mile at best, and a sudden eagerness dragged him forward. The April sun had sunk behind the hill where the small house sat and, though it had been almost two years since he was last here, he knew and recognised it at once.

That half a mile seemed to stretch out before him, as long and painful as the rest of his doomed escapade. He felt desperation pull him onward, yet the whole world tried to drag him back. He lost track of how long it took him to finally arrived at the modestly tended troughs beside the door. He was forced to crawl the remaining distance, his arms pulling him forward when his feet refused to, only adding to his bitter shame. But whatever Highland dignity remained drove him to pull himself to his feet at the small wooden door, and he hammered upon it with a force which caused it to tremble. Only the slightest noise had been audible inside. Now it stopped. The firelight which had escaped from the corners of the doorway vanished, and darkness surrounded the house.

"For the love of God," the newcomer called, pounding the door once more. "Robert Mackenzie, if you have any love for your kinsman, James Og, open this door!" No sound ensued and with desperation, the man resorted to his native Gaelic tongue, pleading like a hound shut away from its master, trying to regain its place. There was a shuffling sound from inside and the door opened a little. A stern red face, a little lower than his own, could be seen staring out into the dim light. This was an older man, fifty years in age, but with his weather-beaten features and set jaw he might have been as timeless as the mountains around them.

"James Og?" he asked, opening the door a little wider and peering hard at the man before him. The loss of sight in his blinded left eye and the fading light gave the old man cause to reach out cautiously to the newcomer, still disbelieving that his words could be true.

"Father," came a voice from further in the house, gentle but firm. "It *is* Jamie. Let him in."

Robert Mackenzie stood back from the door and allowed James Og to enter, which he did gratefully, stumbling over his feet to arrive as quickly as possible.

"You look like you've a story to tell," observed the other man. He was a similar height to the old man but had a strength to him which, though it might once have been present in Robert Mackenzie, there was now no trace of in the head of the house. "Come, I'll rekindle the fire."

"Don't pester, Donnie," chided Robert's gentle voice and Jamie smiled to himself. "Can't you see he's weary."

"I see it more in your eyes than his," Donald Mackenzie remarked pointedly as he beheld the glowing eyes and smiling lips of the newcomer before him. "Sit down, Jamie, we'll have a blaze in no time. Mary, go for peat. Father," he added, taking the older man's arm and guiding him forward. "Here's your chair. Sit, I'll coax the fire aglow."

There could be no doubt that Donald Mackenzie was now the master of this house and he spoke with the comfortable authority which suggested he knew it. Yet there was nothing unkind in his orders. He endeavoured to show the greatest respect to his father, whom he adored, and he paid particular care to the protection of his sister, for whom he had watched several suitors come and go. He knew, of course, that Mary had pledged her love to their cousin, James Og, almost fifteen years earlier when they were all children, but the sight of the man before him only reinforced in Donald's mind that he was far from a suitable match. In fact, Donald all but worshipped his older sister and, whilst he regarded no man above James Og, he did not believe anyone merited her, for she was beyond the reach of all in manners, beauty and gentility.

"What's happened to you, James Og, that you come as a beggar to our door?" asked the old man and, though his words seemed harsh, they were spoken with a sincere care. He placed his hand upon the sodden, plaid-clad shoulder of James who now sat at his feet.

"I am below a beggar, sir," sniffed James, his eyes watering and his nose running at the sudden warmth and shelter. "I have come to ask shelter and safety of you, for which I know I have no right to beg. I went to war," he stammered. "As I am sure you know. Our clan is one divided."

"It was a fool's cause, Jamie," the old man sighed, sitting back further in his chair as Donald successfully lit the fire. Mary re-entered, her apron pulled upwards to help her carry the peats which she handed one by one to her brother, though her eyes never strayed from James Og and her father. "I recall my father talking of the '15; how your grandfather perished and they took our castle. Never were two brothers closer than they. I recall something of it myself, too. It was clear then that the Stuarts would never again sit on our throne."

"I can only hope that you are wrong, sir," James replied, a dreaminess taking his words to a distant place. This sound drew Donald's attention and the young man stepped forward at once as his cousin's head fell against the chair in a faint.

"Proud man," Donald muttered, unsure whether it was approval or annoyance which drove the words. "He is wounded, see," he continued, pulling James Og's plaid back to reveal his bloodied arm. "I'd wager he has walked all the way from Inverness like this."

It was not difficult for Donald to hoist James in his arms, though laying him in the box bed proved a little more awkward. Mary stood back, flustered and upset, wringing her apron until her father called her back.

"Mary, care for him as you can. But please maintain a quietness to your actions."

Despite her father's words she rushed to her brother as he walked towards her. "Is he well, Donnie? Will he live?"

"Aye," Donnie replied, irritation clear in his voice at the behaviour of his sister. "Of course he'll live. Just bathe his wound and keep him fed, both things he seems to have forgotten to do himself, and he'll be on his feet in no time."

Mary nodded quickly and stepped over to the bed, speaking rapid words, but so quietly that neither her father nor her brother could hear them. She went to her own bed only when she was satisfied that nothing more could be done for her beloved patient. It was only then that the two men began talking.

"She can't marry Jamie," Donald said firmly, tossing another peat onto the fire. It hissed and at once filled the room with a choking smoke. "He's an outlaw now."

"We could all have found ourselves outside the law, Donald," his father replied softly. "But love will not stop for such a boundary as the law."

"Father, you came all the way out here to build a home away from the death and destruction you witnessed in the attempts of the Stuarts to reclaim their throne. Surely you won't let that threat follow us by allowing Mary to marry Jamie."

"I rather fear our clansman, the Earl of Cromartie, has created that threat for us. We who carry the name Mackenzie are no longer safe here, and it's only a matter of time until we are driven away. Or worse. I want you to take Mary away, Donald."

"What?" asked the son with a confounded disbelief. "Father, your mind is flustered with-"

"No, Donald. James Og's arrival has only confirmed those thoughts I had already been considering. You are a Mackenzie, as true to the clan as any man, but as James said, we are a divided clan. There will be no heed given to the months you gave to the Hanoverian ranks when the soldiers hear your name."

"Father, I can't leave in such a manner. You know as well as I that if we flee, we'll be hunted all the more. Would you condemn us to that end? And you know what would happen to Mary."

"My mind is resolute. We must send James away as soon as he is able to leave. You must take Mary to Invergordon and find a boat to the continent."

"And what of you, Father? You can't believe that I'd abandon you. I respect my cousin more than any man. He's fair and honest, but I would not send him away only for us all to be forced to leave moments later."

But his father only held up his hand, the signal that Donald knew too well, meaning the conversation was over. He helped the old man to bed before tossing another peat on the fire and lying down beside it, having given up his bed for his cousin. He could not sleep, though not for the lack of a bed. He lay awake considering the words that his father had spoken. His heart raced, his stomach turned and every muscle in his body cried out that it was wrong. But he had never disobeyed his father. He had joined the army at his father's urging. Not that he had seen a great deal of action, for in his first battle he had been wounded and had withdrawn back home to recuperate. He had worked hard since then to avoid the sound of war, being a peaceful man at heart, driven to violence only in the defence of honour. He sighed heavily and rolled over but was on his feet in an instant as James gave a slight cry. He rushed over to his cousin who sat upright in the bed, panting for breath.

"Jamie, you're safe," Donald said firmly, trying to prise the sharp fingers from his arm. James did not let him go but relaxed from his nightmare back into reality.

"Donnie," he gasped, leaning forward. "It was like I was back there. Back at Drumossie."

"Well, you're not. You're safe." The calm and determined way Donald spoke these words steadied the two men for only a moment before there came the sound of dogs barking and heavy footsteps coming closer. They marched in time, beating the ground like drum strokes. "God in heaven," muttered Donnie, peering through the gap in the window shutters. "Get them out of here," he continued firmly, turning back to his older cousin.

"Don't be a fool, Donnie, it's me they've come after."

"I wouldn't be so sure of that. Take my father and Mary. There is a path that goes beyond the peak and down once more to the river. From there go towards Shin. You'll find shelter on its west side. I'll join you there." He had already begun shaking awake his father and sister, and he helped the three of them clamber through the window at the back of the house. He closed the shutters once more and walked to the door, pulling it open and surveying the thirty men who approached the house. He licked his lips nervously and, never closing the door, stepped back into the house, feeling both giddy and afraid.

"Mr Mackay of Moudale," he announced as a sombre man dismounted a tall horse. He was the only one who rode, the others following on foot, as blindly loyal as the snarling hounds which pulled back their lips as they watched Donald. "What can I possibly have done to earn such an honour."

"Where is he?" was all that the other man said. He grabbed a torch from one of his soldiers and pushed past Donald to enter the small house.

"My father?" Donald questioned, using his slight stall in time to concoct a lie with which the three escapees might be concealed. "He has taken my sister to Invergordon, to find a boat to the continent. I'm certain it comes as no shock to you that, after the events of Little Ferry, no one will deal with us."

"Whatever can you mean?" John Mackay asked in a tone suggesting he was happy to allow his opponent to stumble into a trap of his own making.

"As a Mackenzie, your order has only alienated us further. And yet you won't remember that when last I saw you it was to raise arms alongside you. In support of Hanover."

"You were never alongside me, Mackenzie, you were always beneath me. But I did not mean your father. Where is your kinsman, James Og?"

"James Og?" Donald asked, feigning surprise as best he could. "I have not seen him since he announced he was joining the banner of The Young Pretender."

"Interesting. And when did your father leave?"

"This morning. To try and reach Invergordon before nightfall."

"That is interesting," Mackay mused, emphasising his quiet words. "For I have two witnesses who swear they watched your father admit your cousin this very evening. And what a restless sleeper you must be, that you occupy three beds in the early hours of the night." He indicated pointedly to the box beds, none of which Donald had slept in, though all the bedding was crumpled and there were bloodied sheets where James Og had lain. Donald could find no words to speak but only shook his head in protest.

"Arrest him," Mackay said firmly. "Burn the house. I shall not have a lying traitor living in these lands." He turned to Donald and sneered as he added, "Especially not one with the name Mackenzie." He watched as Donald had his hands tied behind his back, before he stepped out of the house and looked with satisfaction as the flames of the torches began to take hold. They began at Robert Mackenzie's chair and spread rapidly through the house. Donald did try to resist now, cursing the man before him, swearing such vehement threats upon the Mackay clan which two hours earlier he would never have used on anyone. John Mackay ignored him until he had once again mounted his horse, at which point he fiercely lashed out with his booted foot, striking Donald in the face.

"They have not been gone long," he called, pulling the horse's reins towards the direction Robert Mackenzie had left in. "Let the dogs loose and we'll have them in no time."

A Cruel Betrayal

James Og was a graceful man; thin, tall and with an agility which was beyond compare, even amongst the nimble highland men. In his youth, he had scaled the sheer mountains of his west highland home for enjoyment and sport. But on this terrain, a low hill by comparison, he could not find his footing. Mary ran a few paces behind while Robert Mackenzie, despite his advanced years, leapt ahead finding a safe path. James watched the half-blind man with an awe which only grew as they continued. He was unfazed by the wind pouring sleet down upon them, or the crying of the dogs which denoted Donald had failed to conceal their direction.

The night was deep when, at last, the lights of Lairg came into view and all three of the travellers gave relieved sighs as the houses became more than distant lights. The buildings took shape as they continued, the stone walls creeping out from the black night. It was their mistake, a bitter mistake, to stand and gaze at this safe haven, for the baying of the hounds echoed from the glen's sides and they found themselves ensnared.

"Get up the ben," cried Robert and he leapt forward while James coaxed Mary to follow him. She had wept with tiredness an hour into their flight. Since then, however, she seemed not to notice what was happening around her but followed meekly where she was led, too tired to argue or cry. They had climbed barely twenty feet when the frighteningly familiar sound of shot filled the air, and the accompanying flash of light left James more blind than the old man.

"Father!" Mary screamed, rushing forward as the old man collapsed under the shot. James knelt next to him, trying to ease him.

"Take her away from here, James Og," commanded Mackenzie. "I'll not die at the hands of this wound, and I'll not have my daughter die because of it, either."

James looked down at the blood which spilt from the old man's side and nodded quickly. "Come, Mary. We must leave."

"I shall not leave my father," she protested, her strength returning through the terrible image before her.

"Mary, his wound is not fatal, but a nightmare awaits you if you remain to be taken by them."

To strengthen the truth of James' words Robert rose and began walking once more towards Lairg, pulling the hounds attention and waving his hand in a carefree way to dismiss his daughter's claims. He vanished away from them whilst Mary wept onto James' shoulder. Her crying stopped as another shot echoed through the glen and she turned to try and find her father, but he had fallen once more. She shook herself free from James' grasp and raced down the hillside, collapsing to her knees beside her father who now had a second wound to his chest.

"I told you to go with James," he stammered.

"Father, I couldn't leave you." She gave a small cry as the pack of hounds, which had so intently chased them, reached her and she struck at them with her hands, trying to keep them from her father. She hardly noticed their teeth, but continued to struggle against them, kicking them, hitting them, anything she could think of to keep them away.

"Back!" A strong voice commanded and, as one, the seven dogs retreated. John Mackay climbed down from his horse and looked across, shaking his head scornfully. "Is it not enough shame for you to carry the name Mackenzie?" he asked of the old man, snatching Mary's bleeding arm and pulling her from his side. "Must you also harbour an outlaw, and even resort to running." He looked around purposefully as he tossed Mary back towards the gathered soldiers who caught her with open arms. "And where is your cousin now? He has fled like the coward he is."

Robert Mackenzie, a man in whom the resolve of Highland stubbornness was never more prevalent, pushed himself to his feet. He was covered in cuts from the dogs' teeth and the two shot wounds continued to bleed. Yet for all the knowledge his own death was impending, he would not allow himself to be addressed in such a way.

"He is well safe from you, and as God knows there is no greater coward than that one known as Mackay."

In a flash of fury, John Mackay pulled the pistol he carried and, pointing it directly at Robert

Mackenzie's head, allowed the hammer to fall. Mary gave a piercing, desperate scream. The walls of the glen shook with it. She struggled in vain to reach her father, but the hold the men had on her was too great. Mackay turned and walked over to her. He placed his hand over her mouth and said firmly, "Mary Mackenzie, you should thank me. I have saved you from marrying a coward and enabled you to see your brother once more."

"Donald?" she whispered as he removed his hand.

"Yes. We shall spend the night in Lairg and tomorrow return to Golspie where you can be rejoined with your brother in Dunrobin Castle. For a time, at least, before he is hanged."

He pulled himself onto his horse, leaving instructions for the old man to be buried, and guided the other soldiers towards the welcoming lights of Lairg. Mary struggled, wept, and tried to fight against her captors, always calling out the name of her cousin in the hope he would return to save her, but James Og had already fled from the hillside and would not return to rescue her.

The Source

After the battle at Drumossie, James had not believed he could feel greater shame. But as the sky began to pale, he realised he had been wrong. All night, all the while he had been running, skidding, crawling up and down the sides of the hills towards Golspie, he had been followed by the shrieking scream of his sweetheart while he had watched in disbelief as John Mackay shot dead the wounded man. And then the repetitive wailing of his name as Mary's voice had faded. Mackay had been right in his assessment of the outlaw; he was indeed a coward. He had not always been this way. He had marched proudly under the royal banner of Prince Charles Stuart but following the sheer madness and the annihilation of so many men at Drumossie he had come to realise how rampant death was, and he was afraid to the point of terror regarding his own.

He clutched his arm and recalled, too, the skill of the shooter who had caught him with a bullet in the engulfing night. He thanked heaven that he had been more fortunate in its placing than his uncle, Robert

Mackenzie, but with this thought he was reminded once more of those terrible events and he felt bowed down with shame. He missed his footing and fell, slithering down the wooded hillside until he crashed onto the rocks at the bottom. His senses felt numbed as he lifted his hand up to his head and felt the sticky blood which rushed from it. What a foolish death he would die here, but how fitting it should be an act of shame which killed him.

Somewhere, only a short distance from him, the sound of a waterfall could be heard, both heavy and gentle in a manner which made his head throb even more. It was the hard work and efforts of these falls which had carved out the ravine where he lay. The trees which had broken his fall on his way down, clung to the sheer sides and gave the April sky a peculiar criss-cross with their branches which, though budding, had not yet come into full leaf. He realised it was no longer raining. The ground around him was dry save for the spray from the waterfall which he noticed, with interest, was coming into view. He lifted his head up and, though it spun when he moved, he was surprised to find he was able to rise. At first, he felt his eyes were betraying him, and he screwed them closed before opening them once more, but the peculiar form of the waterfall was indeed beginning to take shape. Two hands with long watery fingers reached away from the rock and rolling from side to side on wide though fragile shoulders an ever-changing head appeared. It was queer, the manner in which this form looked so alive in its monochrome appearance, and James Og gave a slight cry as two large eye sockets appeared.

He would have liked to run, to have turned away and promised himself he had only imagined the whole apparition, but he could not take his eyes from it. It had no mouth, yet as it looked at him, he could hear its liquid voice, as though a peculiar form of telepathy existed between them.

"Jamie Og," it began, its soothing voice neither male nor female in tone. "Your coming here was far from misfortune."

James looked afraid as it addressed those thoughts he had held in private counsel. "What are you?"

"More than you can comprehend," came the mystical reply. "But you must rise, Jamie Og, you have work to do."

"No," he murmured. "No man ever survived such a fall as this."

"And yet you shall." There was almost no inflection to the voice and its statements were clearly non-negotiable. "You were guided here for a purpose, Jamie Og. You are no longer the person you were when you fell into this ravine. You have purpose, and a role which has been assigned to you."

"You do not know me," James sighed and would have shaken his head if he had been given the strength to. "I've fled from all those who needed me."

"But you shall no longer. Caledon needs you now and it is for her, and her alone, that you have been saved. Already you are feeling the healing power of the spring, are you not? You are given this purpose for you have a strength, a strength that even you cannot see. But you shall not have to do this alone, Jamie Og. Men from the scattered lands of Caledon shall help you, those of both Jacobean and

Hanoverian calling. Do not seek them, Caledon shall bring them to you."

"How shall I know who to trust?"

"You will not know, you must discover. Take a little of this water, Jamie Og, for it has healing qualities. But be warned, you can use it only once, use it with care and on one you could not bear to lose, for its power is not only in recovery and healing but also protection, as you shall find."

He watched both relieved and horrified as the waterfall began, once again, to become a waterfall. "Wait!" he called out, so loud that his ears rang, and his head pounded. "How do I know what my task is?"

"To begin with, Jamie Og, you must journey westward. Your task shall find you."

There could be no further talking, for the waterfall was only that. He looked around and tried to ease his aching body, but it was too much for him and he felt the weariness of fear, disbelief and pain, pour down on him. He slipped from consciousness into a dark state where neither dreams nor rest await.

The Crusade of Caledon Begins

James was awoken by the cold, refreshing sensation of water striking his face and he struggled to open his eyes. As soon as he did, his gaze fell upon the concerned features of his cousin, Donald Mackenzie, who sighed heavily with relief as he looked down. His rosy cheeks looked sore and swollen, but there was a smile upon his face as he saw Jamie's blue-eyed gaze meet with his own. He shrugged out of the plaid which he wore and, biting the hem of his shirt, tore off a strip of fabric. He gently lifted his cousin's head and wrapped the makeshift bandage around it, tying it firmly and tightly to the side.

James did not resist. He was not sure if he was alive and, if he was, then he was unsure about his state of consciousness. His cousin never stopped in his careful tending until James' head and arm were both safely treated, at which point he leaned back and nodded proudly. James sat up with some assistance.

"We can't stay here," Donald began before James could talk. "In a moment any number of soldiers will be here. I don't know how I managed to escape, but it will not take them long, ten minutes at best, to discover where I've fled to."

"No," James answered with a clarity that surprised himself as well as his cousin. "We're quite safe here. Help me over to the waterfall and we'll be passed by, unseen."

Perhaps it was the tone which compelled Donald to do as he was ordered, perhaps it was the peculiar magic which spoke to him as it had to James, or maybe it was that the high walls of the ravine could not have been scaled, even had he wanted to. But Donald did as James commanded. He lifted him to his feet and half carried, half dragged him towards to the waterfall. Trying to get behind it proved more awkward than they had anticipated, but eventually they managed to crouch on a ledge close to the base of the falls. They had barely gained a safe position when six of Mackay's men walked up the uneven path of the gorge's side and stood at the point where the two cousins had met. There was blood which still covered the path and they stood, discussing in hushed tones what could have befallen their quarry so suddenly.

"He must have tried to climb here," one said. "Then fallen back."

James nodded slightly in agreement at this assessment of how he had hit the valley's floor.

"But then," began another. "Where is he? There must be a body."

"Look," another interrupted and the six of them turned towards the stream. One raised his hand to his mouth, and Donald and James both leaned forward to try and see what they were looking at. The stream was running red, but they could see nothing else. Mackay's men seemed content their work was finished, and they turned back and began walking towards Dunrobin.

"What happened?" Donald whispered, when he was certain the men were out of earshot. "What was in the burn?"

James only shook his head, unsure he knew, or wanted to know, the answer. He rose and stepped out from behind the fall, feeling that the peculiar dream of the waterfall had been real, for he truly did feel revived. Donald stepped out after him and they both looked down to where a dead doe was caught in the rocks. James shook his head lost in thought, but Donald gave a slight laugh, failing to acknowledge the wonder in James' mind.

"I'm not at all surprised that a Mackay would mistake a deer for a man, but that six of them should proves they're more stupid than even I believed!"

"I don't think we should stay here," James said, unsure whether he feared more the waterfall or the promise of execution at the hands of Mackay.

"You're right." Donald said solemnly, calming his laughter. "Where are my father and my sister?" James opened his mouth to speak but closed it quickly as the recollection of last night's events sped back to him. Donald's ruddy face began to pale, and he grabbed his cousin's arms firmly. "What happened? Why are you here when I was to meet you at Loch Shin?"

"We were trapped," James whispered. "You must believe me, Donnie. I only tried to do what your father asked of me."

"Where is he now?" Donnie paused before he added, "And Mary, where is she?"

"John Mackay-" James swallowed and forced himself to face up to the terrible events he had brought down upon his kin. "John Mackay killed your father, and Mary would not listen to me. She fled down the hill to him and the soldiers took her." James met his cousin's eyes and said with a firm resolve, "But we'll rescue her together."

"My father? He should not have died in such a way. He should not have died at all. I should have listened to him. And how can we save Mary? How?" Donald begged, his eyes becoming desperate. "He could have taken her anywhere."

"No," James said quickly. "They were to return to Dunrobin after a night in Lairg."

"Then they will already be on the road. What can we do to save her?"

James realised with surprise that Donald expected an answer, and with greater surprise that he knew what answer to give. "They will follow Fleet. We have to get there before they turn north to Golspie."

"I have no weapon," Donald said quickly, feeling himself being swept along with the burning anger and vengeance he felt towards John Mackay.

"If we can time it right, there will be no need of any. Mackay may have twenty men, but none will be on horseback save himself. Come on, Donnie. We have to get moving."

James pulled himself up the gorge side with comparative ease, whilst Donald was driven now by the need to find and save his sister.

Loch Fleet, which had seen the watery deaths of many of the Mackenzie clan not a fortnight earlier, seemed a fitting place to ensnare the murderer on whose hands the blood of the Mackenzies rested. Strath Fleet was a wide valley which closed at each end, and it was here James had decided to make his attack. As Donald was unarmed and all he had was his dirk, it would not be possible to attack the gathered fifteen men as they continued north toward Golspie. Instead their best plan lay in surprise. It took them until midday to reach the mouth of the strath, and in the short time they had, James helped Donald into the branches of one of the stunted trees. It looked like it might crack beneath him at any moment, but their choices were limited. James crossed over the track and crouched down in the tall grasses. Both watched the western valley and anxiously prayed their poorly conceived plan would work.

They did not have long to wait before the band of Mackay's men entered their view, and Donald pulled his feet up, which made him look only more precarious. John Mackay led the troops and there was no telling where amongst them Mary was, despite Donald's best efforts to find her. Remaining calm and waiting until the right moment was difficult for both the cousins. Donald struggled against his desire to rescue his sister whom he loved more than anyone in the world. His blue eyes narrowed in his round face as he watched the man, who had robbed him of his father and stood between him and Mary, draw closer. His hands clenched into fists and his face burnt with such a ferocious rage it was a wonder he was not seen.

For James Og, it was a different reason. He, too, loved Mary Mackenzie with all of his heart, but the newfound zeal with which he had formed this ludicrous plan was now fading, and fear returned to him. All the nonsense he had dreamed of by the waterfall was drifting from his mind and despite the strength he had felt then, he could feel himself returning to his natural cowardice. He gripped the handle of the dirk and tried to talk courage into himself. He had to do this. He could redeem all which he had failed in if he would only stand brave. He looked over his shoulder at the dome of the mountain behind him and longed to retreat to its rocky security.

When at last the men reached them, their plan was put to the test. John Mackay followed the track through the birch and elder trees, and Donald waited until the horse's head had passed beneath him before he swung his feet down and kicked the mounted man in the face, causing him to become unhorsed with the force. He did not wait to see if James was ready for his part in the plan but ran forward and snatched the bound hands of his sister pulling her with ease from the startled men.

"Kill him," shouted Mackay, spitting out a mouth full of blood and a tooth with it. "Shoot both of them."

Donald pushed his sister behind him and, for the first time, noticed he was alone. He glanced at the hummock of grasses which had concealed has cousin. But it was empty.

"Shoot, you fools!" shouted Mackay while Donald turned to his sister and frantically shouted,

"Run, run!"

He turned back to find himself staring down the long barrel of a musket, and he cursed himself and James Og for ever believing they could win this fight.

"Wait," came a voice which stilled all the movement in the strath. Donald's gaze never left the gun before him, though he did begin to move backwards, towards his sister who stood rooted to the ground. "I believe your leader would like to amend his statement."

James Og was no longer the man who had fled Drumossie Moor, nor abandoned his kin last night. He was a new figure, sitting aback Mackay's horse as though he had always known how to lead. He gripped Mackay's short hair in one hand and his dirk at Mackay's throat in the other. His bandaged head was leaning so far down that it would have been impossible for any of the men to have secured a shot without running the risk of shooting their commander.

"I believe what Ensign John Mackay," he spoke the name with a mocking tone, "wished to say was: 'March on, men. I shall rejoin you in Golspie.' Was that not it, Ensign?"

"I have no guarantee that you will not slit my throat the moment they have left."

"That is true, Ensign, but you have my word. But first, before you give the order to march, inform your men of your misguidance regarding my valour and the valour of all the Mackenzies. You can repeat what I say." There was a quality to James' voice that caused Mary and Donald to gape openly at their cousin, for though both loved him, neither had ever considered him to be such an assertive man. "I acknowledge now that I was mistaken." James waited for the repetition and when none came, he forcefully pulled Mackay upright by the hair. The soldier repeated the words through clenched teeth and James continued. "I acknowledge the bravery of the Clan Mackenzie, and of James Og of that clan." The words were repeated and finally, when he felt content with the sincerity of the words, James added. "Having recognised his bravery and valour, I order you to march on to Golspie where I shall rejoin you by midnight tonight."

The men, clearly unsure about what they should do, were forced to obey. They continued their walk without their commander or their prisoner, a confused swarm like bees without a queen. James Og waited until they vanished before pushing John Mackay forward in the direction of the mountain. There was a cave two hundred feet up that he guided the horse into, and he waited as Donald and Mary followed them in. Here, James quickly bound the ensign's hands and carefully cut the bounds Mary wore. Now the silence was broken, and Mary clung to her brother tightly.

"Keep this man away from me, Donnie," she pleaded, although there was more anger in her voice than fear. "He is a coward. He abandoned father and me to suffering and death."

"But he came back for you," Donald said softly, gently smoothing his sister's hair.

"Was it not *you* who came back for me?"

"Well," Donald mumbled awkwardly, trying to remember what had actually happened. "No, I think it was him," he added, feeling a pride in the slim men who stood close by and, for the first time, a genuine worthiness in him to marry his sister.

"You *think* it was him?" Mary demanded, spitting out each word with an unparallelled venom. "How noble you both were! Will you, my own brother, not defend me against the man who left me to die?"

"I tried to fulfil your father's last wish," James commented, although each of her words were as true and cutting as she had intended them to be. "I tried to lead you to safety."

"I would not abandon my father," she said firmly and, turning to her brother, struck Donald across the face. "And that is because you would."

She walked away from them and sat by the cave entrance, taking in the sunshine through watery eyes. These had been her hills. The hills her father had brought her to, away from the remembrance of the terrible ordeal their family had survived in the west. Now, they seemed lifeless without the old man. Donald's eyes held tears, too, though not from the force of the blow which his sister had delivered across his already swollen cheek, but from the terrible, unjust and shameful comments she had poured upon him. Was Mary right? Had he abandoned their father to his death? He had tried to conceal where they had gone, but he was not a man to whom lying came naturally.

John Mackay gave a small chuckle as he surveyed the view from where he had been thrown to the floor. The only man who remained silent was James Og. He lowered his head, ashamed of what he had brought upon himself, but sorrier for what pain he had caused his cousin. Donald Mackenzie was a man who, despite raising arms in the war, was the gentlest and most sincere soul he had ever known, and James felt enormous guilt at the hurt he had wrought.

Donald turned his burning face to John Mackay and felt torn between wishing to strike him and knowing it was not the person he was. Perhaps the person he had been, for his head and heart where spinning and churning with all the past day had thrown at him. He moved further into the cave, his back turned from the others, but as James watched he saw his mighty shoulders shaking with silent, unseen tears. James walked over to their prisoner, and looked down at him in disgust, kicking out at him.

"You will regret your actions, John Mackay. You have cost each one of us too dear not to."

"Fighting words from such a cowardly man," Mackay retorted. "I know how you fled the battle of Drumossie. I know how you turned away from your uncle and abandoned your cousin. You are lower than the dirt beneath my boots." He laughed before he added, "And by the expression on your face, you know it too."

"You are wrong about me, Ensign. And you will regret your error."

John Mackay only scoffed at his reply, but there was a hesitance which suggested he saw something new blooming within James. A silence clung to the cave now. A silence which lingered as minutes passed and each of them lost track of time except for the fierce growls of their empty stomachs, at which point James looked through the saddle pockets and pulled out a few strips of salted fish which he shared with his cousins. Mary refused to take food from him but gratefully shared anything Donald would offer her. Mackay received no food but shared in the water from the flask.

The sun was setting when James rose to his feet and pulled Mackay up. Donald held the reins of the horse onto which James was to tie the ensign, and Mary stood once again at the entrance to the cave, her arms folded and her face stern.

"I am a man of my word, John Mackay," James said firmly. "You will return to Golspie by the end of the day. But pay heed: I spoke the truth when I told you that you would regret your actions, too."

"Your words are rather too bold, James Og. You are an outlaw, a coward and a vagabond. You will be brought to justice and hanged. I only hope I am the one to find you."

"I'm no longer that man, Mackay."

"You're still that man. No more could a horse become a sheep than you cease to be those things."

James dragged him to the horse and looked scornfully across at him. "I am not James Og. I am Jamie Caledon, and it is *I* who will have justice from *you*."

Donald looked across, unable to hear the words his cousin was speaking but intrigued by the effect they had upon Mackay, for his face became as white as snow, and the April moonlight caught it in a peculiar and ghostly fashion. He was about to question it, but the sound of a musket shot rang through the air and Donald turned back to the cave entrance to meet the tear-filled gaze of his sister.

"No," he whispered, letting go of the reins and rushing over to her side as she looked down at the blood on her hand. "No, this cannot be true. This cannot be happening! Mary?" His voice became a desperate plea. "Mary?"

"I'm sorry, Donnie," she whispered. "I said those words, but I didn't mean them."

"I'm going to get you out of here," Donald promised, but as he turned back to the horse, it was to find John Mackay sat upon the saddle, and he spurred it forward, towards them. James was knelt on the floor, clearly knocked there by the escaping man. Donald leaned over his sister to shelter her from the horse's hooves, but Mackay steered the horse past them and out into the night. "Jamie," Donald began, his voice trembling. "You have to help her. You have to do something."

"Mary?" James whispered as he lifted her head, but already she was lifeless. He felt tears pull at his eyes. "I did this, Donnie. What was I thinking?

Caledon? What does it all mean but foolish dreams and hopes? She should never have been here."

"You must be able to do something. She was to be your wife, man! Jamie, please, anything." Donald snatched his cousin's wrist and gripped it so tightly James' hand became red. "I would give my life that she should live. Would you not do the same? Anything."

"Wait," James began, pulling himself free. "I was given this." He pulled out the tiny bottle he had filled at the waterfall.

"What is it?"

"At the moment it is hope, but it may be life." He brushed the hair from Mary's face and kissed her forehead softly before opening the bottle and tipping its contents into her mouth. Donald watched, unsure what was happening, whether it was witchcraft or alchemy. But he no longer cared as his sister tipped her head to one side and moaned slightly. The two cousins exchanged amazed and relieved glances before Donald looked once more down at the wound which was healing and faded almost at once.

"What was that?" Donald whispered.

"A gift which I believe will protect her."

"Have you more?"

"No. I had only enough for one dose, and cannot get any more. But I am certain I used it upon the right person."

Mary opened her eyes and looked up at James. She tried to speak but he placed his fingers across her lips, and only smiled before he rose to his feet and lifted her.

"We cannot stay here," James announced. "We have to go west."

"West?" Donnie whispered. "You mean south. If we go west, we will be hunted. We should go south and take a boat from Invergordon. The only way to be free is to go to the continent."

"And leave Scotland?" James asked incredulously. "Are you mad? That is exile, not freedom. I've been gone from my highlands in the noble cause of my king, but that pained me too greatly. How much worse would it be to be torn from this land with no noble cause? I can't do it."

"She's wounded, Jamie. We'll never make it through the hills to the west."

"Yes, we will," James said with a smile. A giddiness had seized him when he had seen the potion work, as though he was now invincible. "I have a route I must take. I want you to take it with me, for there is not a man in the world I would trust over you. But I would not blame you if you wanted to go south. Although I don't want you to."

Donald smiled slightly as his eloquent cousin fumbled for his words, before he nodded slowly. "West, then?"

"West it is."

The two of them left the cave under the light of the halfmoon which was visible at times through the drifting cloud. Neither of them spoke but, despite carrying Mary as their burden, they seemed to have returned once more to the young boys who had so easily skipped through the heather-clad mountains in their youth. Occasionally, one of them would miss a step and the other would only laugh and race to be ahead. With such uplifted spirits, it took them scarcely any time to reach the small town of Lairg. They stood on the summit of Ben Doula and looked down over the smoking chimneys and busy villagers.

"We will bring bad luck to whoever we stay with," James said, sombre suddenly.

"There is someone here who will help," Donald replied with surety. "She was a Mackenzie before she married. She will do her duty."

"Then lead the way, Donnie."

There was an uncertainty to their steps as they walked down the slope towards the stone houses. Reluctant to follow the streets, for they would attract too much attention carrying Mary, Donald led James past the rear of the houses until he reached one which looked very much the same as all the others. Without saying a word, he beckoned James forward and walked up to the shuttered windows, knocking three times, then twice, then four times. The window opened almost at once and James was surprised to see the manner of person who met them. Two brown eyes lit up within their pale face as she recognised Donald, and she hurriedly ushered him round to the door. Her brown hair was scraped from her face and she wore a gold pendant about her slender neck.

"Come in, Donald, quickly. What happened to Mary?" She ignored the two men for a time as she helped Mary sit comfortably in one of the chairs. She neither fussed nor neglected, but gave ample care to her patient, pouring some water into a basin and cleaning the blood from the healed wound. "Donald Mackenzie," she called over without taking her eyes from the woman before her. "Don't even think about eating that bread."

Donald lifted his hands up away from the food on the wide windowsill, while James laughed openly at this scene. Their hostess turned to them now and wiped her hands on the hem of her skirt before planting her fists on her hips.

"You're not bearers of any news that's good, I can see that."

James looked down at his feet and waited as Donald fumbled for an explanation. "We're going to the west, Annie."

"Are you mad?" she whispered. "Your father brought you here so you would never need to see those lands again."

"Father is dead," Donald said firmly. "This is not a decision I've come to lightly, Annie. But we are travelling west. Mary can't, though, and I knew nowhere else to take her."

"Donald," she said softly. "I'm so sorry about your father. When will this war end?" Turning to James, she asked bluntly, "And what is your story?".

"I am James Og of the Mackenzie clan."

"I realise that, or you would not be seen with one of that name. But how have you become entwined with Donald when your accent suggests you belong far to the south?"

"It is my shame that I have toppled this family and my fault they have become outlaws. I go west because I have a duty there and my cousin, I hope, will travel with me. I must ask of you to protect Mary. I am sorry to do this, but travel would be too dangerous for her."

"I will protect your bride," she whispered.

"How did you know?"

"Your cousin reveres you, Jamie Og. I have known of you a long time, though I have never seen your face until now."

"Yes," Donald whispered with a pride James felt was greatly misplaced. "This is he."

"Where is your husband?" James asked, looking about the room quickly and wishing his words had never been spoken as soon as he said them.

"He's dead, Jamie Og," came the flat reply. "Go and sit with your betrothed. She will wake soon."

James nodded and left Annie and Donald together. Donald watched him take a seat before he placed his arm around Annie's shoulders.

"I'm so sorry to put you in this position."

"Nonsense," Annie said firmly. "I shall hear no more talk like that. You and your father have always helped me since Thomas' death. I in the least owe it to you, but furthermore I *want* to help."

"I had not told Jamie about Thomas."

"Time makes these things easier, Donnie," she said softly, looking up at his ruddy face. "It never leaves you, but it becomes bearable. So you shall find with the death of your father."

"Have you not thought to go and return to your family?"

"And leave what I have here? No. Besides, they have travelled to Ireland. I sent word to them, but they had already gone. There were other reasons to stay, but they are quickly fading."

"No one here knows you were a Mackenzie. You should be safe."

"I can defend myself, Donald. It is you I'm worry for. Going west isn't safe. The prince has fled that way, and all the troops are following him. You must find another way now that you, too, have fallen foul of the law."

"I would follow Jamie with my last breath, Annie. He saved Mary."

"I am sure. But who will save you?"

Donald sighed and chewed his lip thoughtfully. "I don't need saving. But I will protect him. It is peculiar. You wouldn't understand, for you didn't know him before the war, but I have seen a change in him. He has purpose now, and it is a driving purpose to a better goal. I want to help him reach it." He looked at her amused expression before he added, "I don't expect you to understand."

"Quite the contrary, Donald, I understand well. But these causes have casualties and fatalities. Know what you are fighting for, or what he is fighting for."

Donald nodded slowly and held her close to him. He did not say anything but considered what his kinswoman had said. It was true, he did not know what James Og had planned, nor to what end. But in his heart, he felt he owed it to Jamie to follow his cause; that it was a just cause, which would free their clan and land. And he dreamed of peace above all else. He turned to look at his cousin and smiled slightly.

"We go west," he muttered, more for himself than Annie.

"Then I shall give you provisions to carry on your journey."

She left him and began sorting food and drink for them to travel with. Donald watched her work with a proud glint in his eyes. She was as dear to him as though she was his sister. But his love for her was of another kind. He sat down upon the floor, leaning back against the door frame, and felt sleep overcome his senses. James was already asleep, his head resting on Mary's lap, and Donald allowed himself to close his eyes, feeling safe for the first time since his cousin had appeared at his door.

He was awoken by Annie placing her firm hand on his shoulder, and she smiled down at him. "What a picture you made. You could have slept on the bed. It would have been more comfortable." Donnie took a moment to take in his surroundings and recall

all that had happened. "Don't worry," she laughed. "You are still safe, but John Mackay has arrived once more in Lairg. You should take your leave soon in order to stay safe."

"Mackay?" Donald jumped to his feet.

"Hush! Here," she said, offering him a package in a piece of folded cloth. "This food should last you both a couple of days. It's the best I can do, I am afraid."

"It is more than I had hoped for."

"Wake your cousin."

He nodded and stepped over to James, shaking him gently. "Mackay is in Lairg. We have to go."

Annie looked out of the door. When she was satisfied it was safe for them both to go, she turned back and nodded. "Be careful, Donald," she said softly as he stepped past her. "You must take care, for you are a rock to us all." Donald felt a smile cross his face, and he kissed her cheek before vanishing into the night.

"Thank you for your hospitality," James added. He was about to walk out of the house, but stopped as she grabbed his arm.

"Donald Mackenzie is the gentlest soul this world has ever known, yet he will follow you into the jaws of death. Whatever your glorious mission is, it cannot be great enough to result in his death."

"Quite the opposite. It is so great, all should be willing to die for it. But I love my cousin and I will not see him come to harm while I can prevent it."

Annie watched him leave for only a few seconds before she closed the door and turned back to Mary, whose eyes were now open and brimming with tears.

"They've gone, then," Mary whispered. "Thank God."

Part Two:
The Clan of Caledon

The Divided Couple

April was giving way to May when the two cousins finally gazed down on the small town of Ullapool. Their misadventure of the last two weeks had taken its toll on each of them. James' wound, never having been correctly treated, had broken open and Donald had been forced to carry him some of the distance as James slipped in and out of consciousness. It had cost them dear in time for Donald did not have the energy to carry his cousin over the hills, forcing them to follow the river system through much of the country. Here, small houses were dotted across the landscape and, unsure whether they held friend or foe, the pair had to travel only when it was dark enough to conceal them. On one occasion the chill cry of hounds had followed them, so they had taken refuge in a deserted, roofless farmstead. At this point, when Donald had almost despaired for his cousin, James Og seemed to return from the grave and gradually his strength came back, filling Donald with amazement at the luck of his blessed cousin. For a time, this awe had been enough to drive him forward but as the food became scarce, and they were forced to steal from the houses they passed, Donald's strength had faded. Now he collapsed to the ground and sat upon the heather amongst the green ferns and laughed contentedly.

"We made it, Jamie. Look out there. It's the sea, we made it to the coast."

"We should find all we need in Ullapool," James replied softly. "You need food, Donnie, and we both need rest."

"What did you plan to do now that we've reached the coast?"

"I'm not sure. I was certain we would find something along our route which would show me. Perhaps we should keep travelling west."

"To the islands?" Donald frowned as James rubbed his wounded arm and chewed his lower lip thoughtfully.

"To Ullapool first."

James would not offer any further comment but reached his hand down to Donald who took it and rose to his feet. Scarcely had he risen than James pushed him down once more and the two of them collapsed to the ferny floor. James beckoned Donald to follow him, crawling through the undergrowth which hid them completely from the people James had heard. And yet somehow the voices were getting closer as they sped down the hill. James stopped as he realised the two voices he could hear, a man and a woman, were talking in Gaelic.

"What are we doing?" Donald whispered.

"Can't you hear them?" James listened once again. They sounded loud and clear to him. With an air of guilt, James realised it was a soldier and his sweetheart. "Let's get down to Ullapool," he said quickly, rising to his feet. Almost at once there was a sound of a pistol being cocked. Whatever James had expected to see, he felt surprised to see a kilted Highlander before him who wore the red of the Hanoverian army. He was a thin man, as tall as himself with fiery hair and pale skin which was stretched over his sunken cheeks, and his large blue eyes looked too big for his head to hold. Behind him stood a young woman, her dark eyes looking fearfully at James. The pistol trembled in his grasp and James saw his finger closing on the trigger.

Donald rose to his feet quickly and stood between James and the Hanoverian.

"Please, don't shoot," he said automatically. "Peace, friend, I fought for the ranks of the king."

The man before them relaxed his hand but made no attempt to lower the weapon. "Who are you?"

"Donald Mackenzie," came the reply without any consideration for his outlaw status. "My cousin and I were looking for a surgeon. That's why we've come to Ullapool."

"He is wounded, William," the woman said softly, holding the sleeve of the Hanoverian both for protection and to stay his hand. "We should take them down to the town." She waited until William lowered his weapon and then she lifted her long heavy skirts, walking easily through the undergrowth until she reached them. "Let me see."

"Are you a surgeon?" James whispered.

"No, but my father and my brother are. You will have to convince me you deserve their help, though."

"Are you their gateman?" James laughed. At once the pistol was raised and William scowled across.

"Watch your manners and remember you would be dead already if she had not beseeched for you."

"This is an old wound," she mused and ran her soft fingers over his scar. He gave a nervous laugh as it tickled. "The musket ball is still in here. You should be dead by now. Or, in the least, a poison of the blood should have occurred."

"I'm sorry to disappoint you," James replied, taking her hand in his own causing William to take a step forward, jealousy burning in his gaze.

"How did you come by it?" she asked, pulling her hand from his and placing it over the wound once more.

James began to feel irked by the prolonged interrogation and stepped away from her. "I was wounded at Drumossie. And I did not take up arms for your king," he added scornfully, staring at William. To his great surprise the woman rose to her tiptoes and kissed his cheek.

"Then follow me," she said gently before she skipped back to William and, taking his offered arm, walked away from the two of them. Donald glanced across at James with a confusion James knew was mirrored on his own features. They followed the two lovers along the hillside and to their confusion realised they were walking north and leaving Ullapool behind. Suddenly their route changed, and they walked down the side of the mountain following a stream which rushed on towards the Broom. William was every bit the chivalrous admirer, helping his sweetheart over the rocks and down the slope. Donald and James did not receive any help and half fell, half slid down the side of the hill. The sun was at its highest point when they finally reached Ullapool, entering from the far north, and their guide led them to the first house, pushing the door open.

"Francis," she called out. "This man is wounded."

At once a young man with the same dark hair and bold features stepped into the room and looked at the four of them as they entered. "Where do you find these men, Catherine?" he asked pointedly but beckoned them forward all the same. "They do not look wounded."

"I'm not," Donald said quickly. "He is."

Francis and Catherine were clearly brother and sister. They looked alike and spoke with the same tone of gentleness, but Francis was even more determined than his sister. He sat James down and pulled up his sleeve, looking thoughtfully at the wound. But when he spoke it was not to James.

"You should not be here. Father swore he would kill you if you set foot in this house once more."

"William is here because I invited him," Catherine said sternly.

"Father is in town but if he finds you here on his return, you know he'll kill you."

William remained silent but took Catherine's hand and kissed it gently before he turned and saw himself out of the house. Donald felt suddenly uncomfortable as he realised what was dividing these two families. Looking over to the door, he began to walk sidewards towards it. He stopped as James muttered his name.

"Donnie, don't leave."

"You do realise I'll have to cut the wound open once more to retrieve the shot. Would it not be better to leave it as it is?"

James looked across as the young surgeon spoke, before he shook his head. "I have much running to do over the next few months. I can't afford to have it burst open once more. Take the ball out." He had come a long way from that fearful coward who had fled Drumossie, but he still felt a nauseous sickness take him as Francis nodded and retrieved a small sharp knife while he spoke to his sister.

"Fetch me fresh water, Catherine. And the curved needle and some gut."

James felt tears spring to his eyes as Francis began making the first incision, explaining that he would have to make two cuts to ensure that he could remove the musket ball without running the risk of pushing it further in. Donald stepped over to his cousin quickly as he gave a wordless cry, drawing away from the surgeon. Tutting in annoyance, Francis gripped James' shoulder, trying to hold him still. Donald stood behind the chair and held his cousin so tightly he could no longer move. Francis seemed content with this situation and worked quickly, ignoring the sounds of the man before him which ceased only long enough for him to sob. He picked the shot out with fine forceps and dropped it into the bowl in Catherine's hand, and at once blood rushed from his arm.

"Now we must stitch it as quickly as possible," Francis said as though he was training someone. But his words were wasted on his patient for the pain and shock had become too much for James to bear and his head fell forward. Donald never ceased his hold on his cousin but spoke frantically.

"What can I do to help? He has fainted. What can I do?"

"It is most likely for the best," Francis said casually as he took the threaded needled from his sister and tied in an anchoring knot. Donald watched with a curious fascination as the man, no older than himself, plied his morbid trade. At first James subconsciously pulled away but after a time he just sat lifeless in his cousin's arms. Donald waited until Francis tied off the stitches before he loosened his grip on James. Catherine turned as the door opened and smiled as an older man walked in.

"Father," she said with great warmth. "I was beginning to worry about you."

"And with good cause. Government troops are only three miles from us, Catherine. We must flee." He looked upon the scene before him and seemed to comprehend it for the first time. "Who are these men?"

"This is Donald Mackenzie, Father," she said proudly. "And this is his cousin."

"Mackenzies? You are not safe here, lad. Your chief's lands are forfeit and your lives will be too if you're found."

Donald looked down at James who remained unconscious. He seemed so peaceful, having attained a calm Donald had never observed within him before. Francis washed his hands in no rush and dried them on a small cloth.

"He is not fit to move. You must keep him here for a time."

"You can't leave." Donald walked forward. "Why would you wish to?"

"There was a man who used to live outside Ullapool. His name was David MacLeod." Francis' voice was as calm as it had ever been, but his manner seemed agitated now, his thin fingers twisting in the laces at the neck of his shirt. "He had a family and was loyal to his prince. He even hid him in the Catholic cell, and The Prince remained there safely for a night. Then MacLeod came under suspicion for his role, so the government troops tortured and raped his wife in front of him and his children until he relinquished the hiding place of The Prince. When he told them, they shot his wife and then each of his three children. The eldest was ten years old." Francis looked over at his sister who clung to their father as though she was only a child. "The Prince has moved on, hidden elsewhere. But MacLeod was desperate to save his family, so he told the troops the names of those who had hidden him."

"And I was one of them." The old man lifted his head high in a proud gesture.

Donald felt an anger burn within him, but it was not an anger at the people before him, it was an anger at the war: how brutal, cruel and foolish it all was. Before he could offer any words, the door was pushed open and William stepped in.

"They're coming," he panted, clearly having run the distance from town. "There is a ship waiting in Loch Canaird. It will sail at midnight for the continent. You have to be on it."

The old man glared at William and pulled the dirk from his belt. "I told you never to set foot in my house."

"Run me through if you will, but get Catherine to that ship."

Donald looked confused at this sudden interruption. He turned to the window as he heard the sound of horse's hooves and the beating of a military drum which transported him back to the ill-fated battle he had experienced. Francis took his father's arm and guided him further into the house while Catherine followed after, sharing an embrace with the newcomer during which Donald felt like an intruder. William tried to keep his face calm but he could not entirely conceal the turmoil which brewed within him.

A Cause to Believe in

James Og was walking through the halls of an old castle. There were pictures upon the walls, pictures of people and places that he did not know but beneath each one was carved the same name: Caledon. When he came to the end of the hallway, he looked at the final frame. It, too, had Caledon inscribed into the bottom of it but as he looked up to view the picture, he was surprised to find it was a mirror and that his own reflection stared back at him. Within the reflection a peculiar background appeared and, as James looked harder, he realised that it was the same waterfall where he had discovered his purpose. He turned around but all that greeted him was the cold stone of the castle. He looked back at the mirror as he heard the peculiar voice of the waterfall.

"Jamie Caledon, why are you here?"

"I have travelled as far west as I can walk. Must I walk further?"

"You must wake up. You are needed, Caledon."

"Is this where I am to fight?"

"To begin with, yes. But you may return to that person to whom you have become tied."

"Who?"

"The woman with whom you have already shared the tonic."

"She is worthy of it," James replied, feeling suddenly that he was being judged.

"It is a hope that you are right, for you will have her company for many years. But now you must wake."

If James had wished to direct any further questions to the supernatural entity it was too late. The image faded from the mirror and the entire castle seemed to melt away until he was standing with his feet resting on an empty void. He began to fall. He tried to stop himself, but there was nothing he could catch to break his fall. There was no light, so he did not know when he was going to hit the bottom, until he felt himself jolt and found himself sitting in a chair in a room which, for a moment, he did not recognise. Donald turned to him as he saw him start and James rose instantly to his feet as he regarded the anguished figure of William standing in the doorway.

"What happened?" James faltered.

"Thank God you're awake," Donald said quickly, helping him to walk. "There are troops coming, we have to get out of here."

"They are going to kill our host?" James asked, unsure where he had obtained this information from. Donald nodded quickly. "That's it! That's why we're here."

William looked up at him then. "There is a ship, *The Emerald Lady*. She is waiting to the north in Loch Canaird but she sails at midnight and the troops are almost here."

"You're not to blame for this," James said quickly. "I'll help them reach the boat, but I need you to help me."

"Name it," William replied with excitement at the belief this plan might work.

"Have they left?"

"Yes."

"Donnie," James said, looking across at his cousin. "It's time to leave. I'm sorry, William, but they'll never believe it otherwise."

William looked curiously across at him but stumbled back as James struck him across the face.

The force sent a stabbing pain up his arm, but James pulled his plaid over his head and ran from the front of the house. Donald followed him as quickly as he could, but he stopped as he looked down the road at the fourteen men in the red livery of the king's army who were barely fifty yards from them. As soon as they saw him they rushed forward, those on horseback driving the beasts with a fresh fury. Donald stumbled before chasing after James. After a short distance, he turned and ran down towards Loch Broom. He had lost sight of his cousin but ran on in the direction in which he believed James had gone. Shots echoed through the air and Donald realised he was running bent double to avoid the balls which were fired towards him. The horses were crashing through the heather and Donald began to imagine he could feel the breath of the beasts as they sped after him. Suddenly he felt a strong arm snatch him and pull him to the side. The horses, unable to stop or change their direction so quickly, plunged the ten foot down into the waters of Loch Broom. Donald did not wait to find out what had become of them but smiled across at James who grinned back before they ran away from the loch and headed north.

The foot soldiers did not catch up with them and they left the town of Ullapool behind. They stayed away from the open spaces and ran low to the ground so they would not be seen. When they were out of sight of the town James sat down and Donald sat beside him. Both were out of breath but felt invincible in their victory. They laughed foolishly and talked on any subject which took their fancy, neither considering nor caring about the comments they made until, at last, Donald sighed.

"I'm proud to have you as my cousin, James Og."

James looked at him, startled to hear such a declaration. He longed to share what had happened at the waterfall, but he dared not for fear that his cousin would think him mad, a fool, or both. Donald looked across at him and gave half a smile.

"There's something on your mind, Jamie. Speak it."

"Donnie," he sighed, distracted by the foolish explanation he was about to give. "I'm not the same man who arrived at your door. I was a coward then, shamed and beaten. Something happened and I was given a new direction."

"What are you taking about? A coward? I saw you face John Mackay. I've watched you outsmart and outrun men on horseback. There is not a cowardly bone in you."

"I've been called to a duty, Donnie. A duty of the highest calling and I don't know how to achieve it."

"Jamie, what are you talking about?"

"I'm not James Og anymore, I'm Jamie Caledon. I was protected and, in turn, was commissioned to protect this land. Look," he continued, pulling his sleeve up quickly to show the wound which Francis had tended only two hours before. It had neatly healed and only a scar and the stitches remained. "I spoke to something at the waterfall by Dunrobin. I think I spoke *to* the waterfall. It healed me and gave me a protection. That's how I saved Mary. I was granted enough elixir to save and protect one person."

"So now you are invincible? Nothing can kill you?"

"If only that were true," James laughed. "No, but I heal quicker and," he paused and shook his head unsure he wanted to tell his cousin what was on his mind. "And I know what I am expected to do, almost as though I'm being given orders. That's how I knew I should journey west. That's how I knew to wake up when I did in the house." Donald remained silent and James shook his head. "I am not mad. This happened, it truly did."

"So, you are now Caledon?" Donald mused softly. "Jamie, I don't feel I should believe you but I'm afraid it all makes sense. You are the best man I know, and I can think of none better to defend our ancient land. I'll follow your cause, I swear. I shall protect you as you protect this land. Only tell me what needs to be done, Jamie Caledon, and despite my misgivings, I shall fulfil the task."

"You cannot know how grateful I am to hear your words, Donnie. And it need not be so difficult and sad all the time. Come, we have a ship to adieu."

James felt that a great weight had been lifted from his shoulders in sharing this news with his cousin, but accordingly Donald felt burdened by it. He continued to glance sidewards at his cousin. The discovery and acknowledgement of his revelation frightened Donald. He did believe his cousin, of course he did, but he could not help but wonder what Caledon had in store for himself and those around him. He did not voice his fears but continued to follow his cousin until they stood on the crest of the hill looking down over Loch Canaird. James ran nimbly down, and Donald tried to keep up with him. At the bottom there was a small boat waiting, resting on the silver shale and moored to a stunted birch. Francis and his father already occupied it along with five other men. James rushed through and found William and Catherine a short distance away within the tree line. He did not mean to pry, but his sharp hearing picked out their words.

"You and I will always be worlds apart," William whispered. "But this way I know at least that you shall be safe. Safe from those who would harm you and safe from the harm I might unintentionally cause you."

"I will wait for you, William. Come to France and find me."

"I swear I will. One day."

Donald and James watched silently as William and Catherine clung to each other before they walked over to the boat and William helped her climb in. Donald looked confused as he whispered, "He is not going?"

"He would only bring disgrace upon the family in France. He is bound to stay."

William stood on the edge of the shore and watched as the boat was rowed out to the tall three-masted ship that stood in the shelter of the island in the loch. His shoulders were hunched, and he remained watching as the lights of the great ship began to drift away over the sea in a ghostly silence. James and Donald turned and began to climb up from the beach.

"I'm so tired," Donald whispered. "I have never thought the heather looked so comfortable."

"That is untrue," James replied playfully. "I recall a young boy who used to fall asleep on the springy heather mattress of those eastern hills."

"Whatever happened to him?" Donald laughed.

"He's still there."

They walked on in silence for a time until they had climbed far beyond the loch and then they lay down on the ground, each using their philamor as a blanket to conceal them in the bracken and ferns.

"Where do we go from here, Jamie Caledon?" Donald asked sleepily.

"East, back to Lairg. I am anxious to know how Mary is."

"As am I," Donald replied with a faint smile and a dreamy voice.

The next thing he knew was that someone close by had drawn a weapon. He had heard it through his sleep. Slowly he sat up and looked around him. There was little light, for the moon was new, and it took him a time to focus on anything. James was already sitting up and staring out into the darkness but, like Donald, he could only peer blindly forward.

"I am in your debt," a soft voice said from close by.

"William?" Donald and James asked as one.

"Indeed." The man came into view and squatted down before them. "You were easy to follow. Your snores are echoing through the glens. But I must know: Why did you help? You who fought against me at Drumossie."

James looked across and smiled. "You are a son of Caledon, and she was Caledon's daughter. I do not choose who is right or wrong, I only seek to protect the people who belong to this land."

"You are a difficult man to understand," William laughed, but there was no mirth in the sound.

"Why did you let her go?" Donald interjected. "What will you do now?"

"One day I will find her, if that is what you mean," William said defensively. "When Scotland is at peace I shall travel to France and make her my bride. Until then we cannot be together. I want to join you."

The sudden and blunt manner of the final statement caused James to choke and the sound bounced across the hills just as William had told him it would. "And you are welcome to, but why?"

"My corp will not believe it was an accident Catherine's father got away from me. Nor can I in good faith deny those vows I made to the king. But I am a true son of Scotland, and a Gael in my heart before ought else."

"Then I do, indeed, welcome your company."

"Where do we travel to?"

"Lairg," James replied with certainty. "I have someone to see there."

Donald smiled across at his words and considered how desperately he wished to see his sister.

"We can be there in three days," William laughed. "Quicker if Donald Mackenzie can maintain my pace."

"I can match your pace," Donald said with only a degree of annoyance.

"Good, for since hard times have come to these parts the hills have been run amok with thieves and cutthroats."

James and Donald were pleased to have the company of William on the day that followed. He was an excellent navigator and explained how he had been given this job when he was a child, for he was quick and could move almost silently over any terrain. William was a year older than Donald and a year younger than James, but he had a different perspective to them both, having been brought up in the coastal town of Ullapool. Neither of the other two knew what it was to live amongst so many people, how to read them and how to anticipate their words and, more significantly, their deeds. They did not discuss the events of the day before but left them on the west coast as they hurried toward Lairg.

Despite himself, Donald found that, by the end of the day, he was exhausted and simply collapsed on the ground. They had reached Loch a Bhith already and it was by its side they settled for the night.

The soft heather coaxed them to sleep and soon it was only James who was awake. William had foresight enough to have brought some food with him and James had never been so appreciative of so little. He had the feeling, as he sat there, that something was about to happen. He was about to wake his comrades as an arrow flew past his head. It must have found it's mark, for there was a cry from just in front of him. In a second Donald and William were awake and the three of them crouched down below the heather unsure what they had become caught up in. Donald turned around and found that he was facing the barrel of a musket. Almost at once another arrow was fired and the man before him spun his gun towards his assailant and fired off a shot. Donnie knew now whose side to take and he rose to his feet. As though this was the signal William and James had waited for, they rose and began to fight, too. There was a group of five men before them, none of whom seemed prepared for the fight they received. There were two other men, both of whom appeared to be archers. William was the only one of the defenders who carried a firearm, but he put it to good use.

"Enough," came a loud voice which carried across the moor. "You are beaten." The statement was true for, of the five brigands, only one remained unwounded. James continued as the four who were still alive were gathered together by Donald. "Who are you?"

"They are a group of vagrants who deserve to be shot," came a reply from behind them. "For three weeks we have tried to catch them. They deserve nothing more than to have their throats slit."

"On what grounds and to what ends?"

"This is not a court," came the bitter reply. "On the grounds that it is exactly what they did to our village when they arrived to plunder it. You are no better than Campbells."

"Hold your arm," William warned.

"Hear this. You have another chance at life. Go out and tell all those you meet, Caledon has risen. Caledon will be protected and defended. And to you who would cause her harm, be prepared. A new fight has come."

"Caledon is just a dream," came the hurt reply.

"No," James continued, and William stood amazed at the words he spoke while Donald felt his heart might explode with pride. "I am Caledon. I am here to seek justice for this land, and I will defend myself at all costs against those who threaten me and my people, whether they are Lowland or Gael, Hanoverian or Jacobite. You have been warned, tell others. Now go."

The small band, having been relieved of their guns and weapons, hurried away, leaving the corpse of their fallen comrade. Reluctant to leave this man to the carrion and elements of the hillside, Donald buried him in a shallow grave, questioning with each stone who the man was. Finally, the three of them turned to look at the other two newcomers. One of them, the youngest by appearance, was kneeling over the other.

"You have to help him, Caledon," came the plea. It caused James to step away, for there was nothing but faith and desperation in his words. He did not doubt James was Caledon, nor that he had any right to question it. "He was loyal to you."

"He will be fine if we can just get the wound clean," William said softly. "The shot has torn through muscle only."

"Have you any of that whisky left?" James asked quickly.

"A little," William replied hesitantly.

"Then use it."

William begrudgingly handed over the flask to the younger man who used it as sparingly as he could. James stood over them while Donald placed his hand on the young man's shoulder in what he hoped with a gesture of comfort.

"Who are you?"

"The last of our village."

Donald frowned as he replied. "How?"

"The banner was raised, and all the men joined. There were no Redcoats in our midst," he added pointedly as he looked across at the redcoat William was pulling on.

"Perhaps you would rather we didn't help?" James asked in a cutting tone. "I joined the banner of The Prince, but you should know that, of the three of us, I was the only one."

The young man mumbled something which William graciously took to be an apology. Donald nodded thoughtfully and encouraged the youngster to continue.

"After the retreat from England, those of us who were still alive returned home. Some of us joined the ranks at Drumossie, but Murray's heart was no longer in the fight, and many of the men knew that. The government troops came through barely a week later. They arrested all the men they could find and marched them to Inverness. God knows what became of them. Some ten of us remained hidden in barrels, but then there were only women and children left. The night after *they* arrived. I had fought and killed so many Redcoats, but these men I truly hate. They torched the buildings, plundered them, killing people who got in their way and those they did not kill were forced out into the hillsides to starve to death. Four of us followed them. Two of them have since died and now only we two remain."

"What is your name?" Donald asked softly.

"Robert MacBeath."

"And what is his?"

"Malcolm Murray." Robert looked up at James and smiled. "He is a true son of Scotland, Caledon."

"And he shall be treated as such. We travel to Lairg. You are welcome to join us." James glanced across at his cousin who took out a square of cloth and tied it as a tourniquet at the top of Malcolm's arm before hoisting him up. "We should move on," James continued, and William nodded while Robert rose and stood to attention as though he were still a soldier. They continued across the moor, having to tread in one another's footsteps for the ground was boggy and it was almost impossible to see. William guided them, his strong eyes picking out the safe paths, even in the dark.

The sun was rising by the time they stopped, having reached Oykel Bridge. The stone structure rose over the river and each of them hurried across before finding shelter on the north bank.

"We are halfway to Lairg, now," William said softly as they sat together in a circle. Malcolm had not spoken a word except in thanks and he continued to drift in and out of consciousness.

Robert tended him now, as they all sat in a circle. "Who is this man you must see?"

"Man?" James whispered. "No man. She is my betrothed, Donnie's sister. She was wounded and we were bound to leave her for her own safety."

"A woman?" William whispered. "Are you not an outlaw in these parts?"

"Yes, but I gave my word and I love her. Would you not risk that to find Catherine?"

"Perhaps," William whispered. "It is not the law that prevents me but her father."

"To my shame, I need not worry about that." James felt the pain of remorse like a dagger as he recalled watching his uncle die. Donald watched him with curiosity but remained silent. "Get some sleep, William. And thank you for bringing us safely here."

Despite their weariness all of them struggled to get any sleep in the daylight except for Donald whose exhaustion was beyond measure. William continued to turn and twist, trying to get comfortable while Robert fussed constantly over Malcolm. James, feeling he needed some time to think alone, walked a short way and sat on the rocky side of the River Oykel. The water danced below him, and he was reminded, as so often, of the peculiar waterfall in the ravine. Robert's response to being told that he was Caledon had baffled him as he considered how freely the man had accept it. Of course, the boy could scarcely be eighteen, but the people of Scotland needed to feel that their spirit lived on. Mackay had only scorned him, but perhaps he underestimated how greatly Caledon was needed.

Ensign John Mackay he held in the highest contempt, and he had promised to have satisfaction from him. But despite his deep loathing of the man, it was the tale of Robert MacBeath's village which haunted James. War may have been honourable, but such blatant murder as they had experienced chilled him. These had become his people to care for, his race to defend.

A Broken Engagement

The night of travelling which followed was done in near silence, and they continued until they stood staring down at the town of Lairg the next day. They had encountered no one else in the hills, although once they had heard gunfire carried on the wind to them. Each one of them longed to share in the comforts the houses below contained, but none of them wished to risk the dangers which waited there.

"Malcolm needs a physician. Is there a doctor in Lairg?" Robert looked at the older men with desperation. "One we can trust?"

"Not exactly, but there is someone who will help," Donald replied, a faint smile catching his features. "Follow me."

William was not happy to relinquish his role as navigator, but Donald ignored him. He was only so pleased to be returning to Annie. William sometimes laughed and sometimes cringed at what he called the coiseachd cliobach which Donald made, labelling him as an oaf as he skidded down the glen side, still carrying Malcolm.

Donald Mackenzie guided them along the banks of Loch Shin and toward the small house which belonged to his kinswoman. Using the knock James remembered from the last time they had stood before the shuttered windows, each man waited and looked about them doubtfully. Donald felt an anxious frown cross his face as he eased Malcolm down to the ground.

"I'll go and find her," he said quickly, rising once more to his feet and stepping round the side of the building but he turned to look at his cousin who snatched his sleeve.

"Have a care, Donnie. You're a wanted man here. I can't lose you."

"I'll be careful," he promised before continuing to the front of the building.

The remaining four men waited in silence until the door opened and Donnie ushered them all indoors. Each stepped in, Robert helping Malcolm.

"Where is the lady of the house?" James asked quickly.

"I don't know," Donnie whispered back. "But the door was open."

They all turned as the front door opened and Annie stepped in.

"What is the meaning of this?" she stammered, her voice trembling as her gaze rested on Robert and Malcolm.

"Annie," Donald began, and at once her face calmed, although her tone when she spoke was no less anxious.

"Donnie, what are you doing here? This is not a safe place for you yet."

"Nor is anywhere." He embraced her warmly, ignoring the other men and their words and laughter at such a gesture. "But Malcolm is injured, Annie. Can you help him?"

"Who are these men? And what happened?"

"Please, Annie," Donald begged. "Can you help him?"

"I'm not a physician, Donnie," she whispered, but observing the expression of desperation in her kinsman's face she nodded. "I will try." She threw her shawl over the arm of a chair and indicated this was where she wanted them to place her patient. "Fetch me the salve by the bed, Donnie. And draw some clean water from the well."

She did not say anything more but tended the injured man as diligently as though he were her brother. Donald, who was exhausted, lay down on the floor, wrapping his plaid about him as a blanket and fell asleep almost at once. William stood at the shuttered windows and peered out onto the world beyond through the slight opening. Robert knelt beside Annie and silently helped her as much as he could, handing her anything she needed, while he held tightly to Malcolm's hand. James watched all this and leaned against the doorpost as he considered what his next move would be. Drifting in and out of causes seemed a sure way to be caught as he lowered his guard, and furthermore it would now endanger the other four men who had sworn to assist him.

"You kept him safe, James Og."

He faced Annie as she stepped over to him, running her hands down the woollen skirt she wore.

"I love him as much as you do, Annie. I hope I might always protect him. For he is my strength."

"He is a wonderful man," she agreed. "What are you doing with these men, James Og? What are your plans which you claimed were worth the deaths of us all?"

"You would not believe me if I told you," he laughed slightly.

"Did you tell Donnie? Did you tell the others?" She watched as he nodded. "And did they believe you?" He nodded once more. "Then why do you fear I shall not?"

"I had hoped Mary would be here," James said quickly, eager to talk on any other topic.

"I'm sorry about her, Jamie," Annie said quietly.

"Sorry?" James spluttered. "What do you mean 'sorry'?"

"She left. Not long after you did." Annie folded her arms before her and sighed. "She would no longer remain, no matter how often I pleaded with her. She didn't wish to marry you, James," she said, her face becoming dark. "And she told me of how you fled from saving her father. When she told me that, I decided I should no longer hold her here. I thought you would have led Donnie to his death."

"He is very much alive," James whispered, his anger and his sorrow fighting one another. "I am not the man I was then. Was saving her life not enough to prove that?"

"It would seem not," Annie said gently. "And she has protected her interests most cunningly."

"What do you mean?" James demanded.

"She is engaged to another."

"She is still engaged to me," he snapped. "Who is this man that seeks to usurp me, and who she allows to do so?"

"Ensign John Mackay," Annie flatly replied.

"Yes," James said angrily. "She truly is protecting her interests and being foolish enough to think she will be safe in so doing."

"She is not a bad woman for doing so."

"Perhaps not bad, but blind." James looked at the four men who had followed him so readily and tried to fathom why, in light of this, he could not secure the loyalty of the woman who, for so many years, he had been engaged to marry. "He only marries her to attack Donnie and me."

"I think you are seeing this wrongly, James Og. It is that she wishes to attack you by marrying him."

"Then they are suited to one another."

Annie watched as he walked out of the house before she turned at Robert's voice.

"Where is Caledon?"

"Caledon?" Annie laughed. "If we knew that we might not live in the fear we do now."

"But he is Caledon," Robert explained as he rose to his feet and looked across at her with an expression which suggested this was obvious.

"James Og?" She looked down at Donnie who sat up quickly.

"Where is he? Where's Jamie?"

"Donald Mackenzie," Annie began with a tone of such fear Donnie stumbled to his feet and took her hands. "Tell me what this is about. Caledon? That is a myth from an ancient time."

"Where's Jamie?" Donnie asked softly, ignoring her questions. She pulled her hands free from him and stared across.

"Tell me you are not following your cousin because he has claimed to be Caledon."

"I am following my cousin because I love him, Annie," Donnie replied.

"You can't follow him, Donnie. Caledon is a lost cause. And he only claims it so you will follow him."

"I love you, Annie," Donnie said softly, leaning forward and kissing her forehead. "But you are wrong about this."

Annie watched with a mixture of emotions as he walked out. "Caledon?" she whispered, addressing William and Robert. "You are all madmen!"

Those Called to the Clan

James wasted no time in escaping Lairg. He needed time to think over everything he had just heard and had questions which none of his friends could answer. He paused as he looked down thoughtfully over the town. They were not his friends. Only Donald Mackenzie could be classed as such, for he knew little more than names of the others.

With a new burst of energy which spurred on his steps, he reached the peculiar waterfall by late afternoon. The land was full of Mackay's men but, as soon as he stood before the eternally changing falls, he knew he was safe. He stood for a time, waiting for the water giant to step away from the cliff and the two eyes to appear, but nothing happened.

"I need to know," he said flatly, trying to reassure himself that he was not mad for addressing the waterfall. "What am I to do next?"

"Caledon," the familiar voice began. The tendril fingers of the waterfall bent and tensed as it awoke.

"You need not seek me here. I shall find you wherever you might be. As I found you in Ullapool."

"I am without direction."

"Because you have been blinded. You cannot love, Caledon, for your love must be of your people."

"She is only marrying him to protect herself."

"Do you not listen to what your wisdom says? She is marrying him to injure you. Beware her, Caledon, for she will stop at nothing to destroy you."

James laughed nervously. "Mary is not wicked."

"Not bad, but blind?"

James swallowed hard as he recognised the words he had spoken only hours earlier.

"Caledon, she is blinded by her anger at her father's death and has lost faith in the cause you protect. You must stay away from her."

"What else must I do? I came here for direction."

"You came here because you did not like the direction you knew you should follow. Six is the number, Caledon. Six it has always been. You," the waterfall pointed its liquid finger at him. "You must bring them together."

"But we do not yet number six. There is Donnie, who I trust beyond compare and without whom I could not have survived. There is William, who can find anywhere even in moonless nights. And there is Robert, who is so driven by loathing and hatred I scarcely trust him. Malcolm is in no fit condition to decide whether he wishes to follow the cause. But even then, there are only four."

"There is you," the waterfall said calmly. "How do you assess yourself?"

"As a man without direction but with a madness which spurs him onward. Five, then."

"Then you have your Power, your Stealth, your Zeal, your Strength and your Nobility. You have one more to find."

"What are you talking about?" James pleaded. "Why must you speak in riddles?"

"I do not speak in riddles, Caledon. You chose to hear my words in such a way. I have seen many people with these titles. You need Wisdom. And you have it, but you will not accept it." The waterfall began to retreat back to the rock. "You must unite your clan, Caledon. Then you will be able to fight your new enemy."

"John Mackay will always be my enemy."

"There is a worse one than he."

The waterfall was once more just a waterfall. James Og stood staring at his hands and tried to take in all that he had heard. He knew he should return to Lairg, but it would take until nightfall to arrive and he felt unsure about covering the distance without William's strong eyesight to warn him of Mackay's men. He hated John Mackay with everything that he was but found the thought of a greater enemy frightening. He turned quickly, pulling free his dirk, as he heard someone behind him.

"No need for that, Jamie," Donnie said calmly, pushing the blade down. "I thought you would be here."

"Did Annie tell you about Mary?"

"What about Mary?" Donnie asked quickly, feeling his heart racing at the thought anything could have happened to his sister. "She was to journey to Invergordon and then to the continent."

"She has chosen to disobey you, for she is journeying no further than Golspie. She is to marry Mackay."

"What?" Donnie hissed. "But she is engaged to you."

"But she can't reconcile with the fact I tried to follow your father's last wish."

"And yet she can reconcile with the man who killed him? Why would she?"

"Annie claims she is protecting her interests. She will always be a Mackenzie and no doubt feels she must align herself with the one person who can release her from that shame."

"Annie is the wisest woman I know," Donnie mused, failing to notice Jamie staring at his words. "The wisest person."

"Then she is Wisdom?" James turned back to the waterfall, feeling he needed the reassurance of its agreement. But it remained a waterfall. "I can't risk her life."

"What are you talking about?" Donnie asked. "I won't let you endanger Annie. But why would you even consider it?"

"So that we are six once more."

James' contemplative tone caused Donald to falter and, unsure he wanted to discover the reason for this change in his cousin he turned the conversation back to the news of his sister.

"John Mackay?" Donnie spat. "How could she do this to you?"

"To us both," Jamie said pointedly. "Still, at least we won't be expected to attend the wedding. We shall be shot on sight."

"What is happening, Jamie Caledon?" Donnie sighed. "Where do we go from here?"

"We must ensure the others are willing to join us. I'm quite sure I must give them the option to leave with honour, or to state their intention to support us. Then the path should become clear."

Donnie, he realised, never questioned this, and the two of them returned to Lairg. The cousins trusted one another more than any other soul, and if one heard something in the hills the other would follow this example and crouch down low. It was as though they were boys once more, running through the hills and chasing dreams through the heather. The night was complete, with only a glimmer of the moon visible through the fine clouds, when they both crept toward the wall at the back of Annie's house.

"I could hear that oaf a mile away," William's voice announced softly. "You grieve me each time you attempt secrecy, Donald Mackenzie."

Donnie did not respond but frowned thoughtfully before he climbed over the wall and Jamie did the same.

"Where are the others?" James asked quickly.

"Inside. Malcolm even managed more than three words. Your friend is a great healer, I believe, Oaf."

Donnie glared at William as he walked past him and into the house. James shook his head and encouraged William to follow his cousin. Malcolm was lying on the bed while Robert sat beside him, although the young man rose to his feet as Jamie and Donnie entered. Annie glowered at the two of them, pausing in the action of kneading dough.

"Caledon," Robert began. "I thought you had left."

"And so I did. But I have returned with a greater purpose." He sat cross-legged on the floor close to the bed and invited the others to form a circle. "Caledon can't survive alone. Each time Caledon has risen it has been with the support of followers. I have to ask you all, without concern that your honour will be negated, but knowing that, from here, there can be no retreat: Will you follow me?"

"I will, Jamie," Donnie said at once, bringing an annoyed sound from where Annie stood. He turned to look over his shoulder and smiled slightly. "It's fine, Annie."

"I will follow you, Caledon," Robert said quickly. "You carry the cause which I would give my life for."

Annie made another sniffing sound and began striking the dough with more force.

"Thank you, Robert." Jamie smiled slightly. "Let us hope our cause will not lead you to such an end."

"Malcolm?" Robert said softly, taking his companion's hand. "Malcolm, are you to join Caledon's cause?"

"Caledon? Have I not already proved it in every field?" Donnie felt his eyebrows rising at Malcolm's clear English accent. "I am as loyal to Caledon as any man could be."

"You are madmen," Annie said angrily. "You will never live to see the new year, far less see

Caledon prosper. The Butcher is hacking the trunk of our land. You will all be the next to fall."

"Annie," Donald began softly as he faced her once more. "Is this not a cause worth fighting? If The Prince had not returned perhaps Caledon may have slept on. But the people of this land, of our land, deserve protecting, don't they? Whether Redcoat or Jacobite."

"You'll all be killed," she whispered as she turned once more to her task.

William offered half a smile. "I don't recall ever being indebted to a man who delivered such a strike to my face, but I owe you all the promise of future happiness I possess. I will not forget such a debt. I will follow you, Jamie Caledon."

"Then we have five." James turned to where Annie opened the door to the range at the end of the house. "What have you to say, Annie?"

"I?" she demanded, closing the door before sucking her burnt fingers and cursing the men before her for causing her to lose her concentration. "I have nothing more to add than that you are fools. All of you."

"Then you won't join us?"

"Jamie," Donald said quickly, but stopped as Annie replied.

"I am tired of Caledon. I am tired of battle. I am the widow of a baker. A man who thought he could raise arms in support of his dream of Caledon. He died in his first combat. Caledon is a doomed cause. You are fools to follow it."

"I can't make you," James began, unsure how to persuade her but knowing that he needed her in his small clan. Perhaps William understood these thoughts for he rose to his feet and kissed her burnt fingers which caused a flash of jealousy on Donnie's face.

"You do know why Caledon needs you, don't you, Annie?" William said softly. "Because no one else can keep that clumsy oaf safe. We can tell him what to do, to stay quiet, to avoid known dangers. But you truly are the only one who can protect him."

"Donald Mackenzie," Annie began, tears blooming in her eyes. "What would your father say?"

Donnie shook his head. "Father died for Caledon, Annie."

"Do you know how your father died?"

James stiffened at her words but Donnie only shook his head again. "John Mackay killed him, and I shall not stop until he has paid for it. While Mary wishes to marry him as punishment, I am inclined to think he deserves something worse."

Annie nodded slightly and gave a heavy sigh. "I shall regret this in the end, I know. But how can I trust the five of you? You," she pointed to Jamie. "You shall answer to me, James Og, if any harm befalls any one of them. MacBeath is little more than a child; Murray is as weakened as an infant; you," she continued, pulling her hand from William. "Are as sweet tongued as a bee. And James Og, any harm you wrought to these men I shall repay on you fivefold."

"Then you shall join us?" James asked eagerly.

"What choice do you believe I have? I shall have to protect you all, for you have proved you cannot protect yourselves."

"You'll be an outlaw, Annie," Donald began, unsure he wanted her to commit her life to the cause as blindly as he had done.

"I am a Mackenzie, Donnie," she said, kneeling down beside him. "I am already regarded with mistrust by people."

"Then we have a duty in the north which we must attend to," James announced, feeling the new purpose drop into his head, and ignoring the exchange between Annie and his cousin. "On the coast. The moment Malcolm is able we shall journey there. In the meantime, I have a wedding to attend, which I would not miss for the world."

Part Three:
The Wedding of
Ensign John Mackay

The Pact is Sealed

Mary Mackenzie had never thought of herself as a strong woman. She was not physically strong, though she had managed to do all the tasks running her father's house had thrown at her. But now, as she stepped down to the shores of Loch Fleet, carrying a torch for there was scarcely a moon in the sky, she felt driven by a strength of will which nothing could dissuade. She stepped onto the slippery rocks and carefully negotiated her way to the sandy shale where she had been told to wait. She carefully pushed the burning torch into the loose ground and waited.

She hated James Og. She hated the cowardice she had witnessed in him, and hated that he had done nothing to protect her father. Perhaps her choice of husband seemed odd, since he had pulled the trigger on her father, but she blamed James Og entirely for the death of Robert Mackenzie. Marrying the man James hated above all others made sense to her.

"You came, then," a voice stated as a woman appeared. She was ageless, beautiful but with hair so white it appeared almost transparent. "And you lit the Lughnsadh beacon."

"What is it that you want of us?" asked another, older voice. But she looked as radiant as the first woman.

"I was advised that you might be able to assist me," Mary began, looking at the two women who slunk toward her torch, never appearing to move their feet. "There is a man I seek to destroy."

"To kill, you mean?" began the first. "We are not murderesses."

"I need your advice, only," Mary began. "He should have died several times, but he seems blessed with an immunity to such wounds."

"As you are," the second announced, cupping Mary's chin. Her hair was like the flames of the torch, dancing between orange, red and yellow. "Did he give you this potion?"

"I believe so."

"Then we can help you, Mary Mackenzie. We shall help you against your betrothed."

"How did you know that?"

"We know all about you," the first began, laughing lightly. "You need the first harvest of the elder berries which bear the dew of the lammastide. Bring them here in four nights time and we shall give you what you seek, Mary Mackenzie."

"I am to be married three days later. Will I have sufficient time to prepare the substance?"

"Yes. Time will be your ally in this, and all things."

Mary looked about her but found she stood alone. There were no footprints in the sand, she realised, but those she had left herself. She looked about nervously, recalling with trepidation the stories of the tortures and killings of those women Scotland accused of witchcraft the century before. Snatching her torch, she returned to the house in Golspie where she had been living for the past month.

Dawn found her at the hedges close to the shore where the salty dew still rested heavy on the berries, brought in by the unnaturally quick covering of haar which had vanished beneath the scorching sun. Having collected the produce in a clay jug she returned to the house with a renewed spring to her step. She concealed the jug in the corner of the large cupboard in the pantry, hoping desperately it would not be found.

Whether it was magic or good fortune, she was not discovered and, on the night she had been instructed, she donned her cloak once more, collecting the jug and walking out to the beach. She encountered no one and saw no movement during the journey.

"Married on a Friday?" asked the old voice of the red-haired witch the moment Mary had pushed the torch into the sand. "It will be a difficult marriage."

"We can only assume you completed your challenge," the other said flatly.

"Indeed," Mary said, lifting the jug.

She watched as one of the women snatched the jug and held it over the fire. Presently, the stars in the heavens became visible and bright. The women began crying out in a strange language and the white-haired witch snatched Mary's sleeve, lashing out at her with a branch of thorn, slicing her arm. Mary gasped in pain, but the witch only caught two drops of her blood and of the tears that trickled from her eyes, before she returned the jug to the torch.

Almost at once the world became dark. The flames guttered and died. The witches had gone. The silence, after the crazed calls in a twisted language, made her head spin. Unsure what she was to do now, Mary walked forward and was about to lift the torch from the sand when the flame leapt alive, towering over her. She did not cry out but stumbled backward from the two women, who had also reappeared.

"This is what will give James Og to you," the red-haired woman began, offering the jug back to Mary, but before she could take it the woman continued. "But we need payment, do we not, Fortune?"

"Indeed we do, Beauty," the other replied.

"What is it that you want?" Mary whispered.

"Traditionally we would ask for your first child," Beauty said, still offering the jug to Mary.

"How would I conceal that from my husband?"

"You are marrying him on a lie," Fortune began. "You should have no qualms about lying to him once more."

"But my first child might not be a daughter."

Fortune placed her right hand on Mary's stomach and shook her head. "It will be a girl."

"Then she'll be yours," Mary announced, certain she would forsake anything to see James Og brought to the justice he deserved.

"It is such a time to wait, Fortune," Beauty mused. "But perhaps she shall find that out. Your daughter, then."

Mary snatched the jug and looked into it. "Have I to make him drink this? What will it do?"

"Yes," Fortune began, running her right index finger along the bloodied mark on Mary's arm which healed at once but left a long white scar. "He must drink it."

"Will it kill him?" Mary asked with more vehemence than she had meant, but uncaring who heard.

"Did we not tell you that we are not murderesses?" Beauty demanded. "It will render him helpless. What you do with him is your concern."

"Then I shall use it as I wish."

"Have a care, Mary Mackenzie," Fortune cautioned. "You owe us your daughter. If you are unable to pay, you will walk the world for an eternity bound by your debt."

"What do you mean?"

"If you kill James Og and are sentenced to death before your child is born, your spirit will know no rest."

"If I do *not* kill him my spirit shall know no rest."

"Then our pact is complete," Beauty announced and, even as Mary watched, she melted away.

"What happens if another drinks it?" Mary asked as Fortune began to fade.

"That is for James Og alone," Fortune's voice rippled.

Mary picked up the torch and stepped carefully up to the shore, trying not to spill any of the liquid. She was unsure how much of it her cousin had to drink to cause him to lose his senses. She turned quickly at the sound of a crying child, but it was within the farmhouse she was walking past. Not daring to return the jug to the cupboard she placed it beneath her bed, forbidding even the maid to enter.

While she anxiously awaited her wedding, a girlish giddiness had overtaken her. She wished each second away as she planned her revenge on the man who she hated the most in the world.

A Warning Unheeded

The sound of running water made James feel at peace. He felt he was safe, a feeling he had not known in so long. He knew, too, that he was asleep, for he had returned once more to the castle where he had last been given his direction. He walked through one of the heavy doors and looked about him. It was a large banqueting hall, with a huge table stretching down the middle, made from coarse wood. A heavy axe protruded from the centre of it. No one sat about the table, the long benches were empty, although it was laid with fine foods and fruits James did not recognise. At the end of the room stood a great mirror and, as he walked to stand before it, he found that it reflected the room as it had been in its full glory.

His own reflection stood before a host of revellers clad in all manner of clothes. Torches burnt in the brackets which should have rusted away. A minstrel sang and a dozen dogs prowled, looking for the scraps which had fallen to the ground. On the far wall where the giant fireplace should have been, ran the waterfall.

"What do you seek, Caledon?" it asked, drowning out the sounds of the room's reflection. "You are not yet ready for this castle, nor is it ready for you. You have been told to travel north."

"I have a matter I must resolve before we can journey north."

"Your clan will not remain loyal to you if you do not lead them. This wedding will undo you, should you attend."

"I have been invited. Mackay no doubt wishes to gloat that he has stolen my bride."

"Have a care, Caledon. You face a greater threat than Mackay in that hall. You must think of your people. Gain more strength before you fight this battle, for if you attend the wedding your strength will fail."

"What do you mean? I have collected my clan as you instructed me to. They have all sworn to be loyal, and I trust their word."

"You are all beyond the law, but for your wisdom. And they have not all been entirely honest with you, Caledon. Be wary."

"But surely they're a good clan, or you would not have brought them together."

"I?" the waterfall's voice echoed. "But who am I to do such a thing? They came to you. I did not bring them. You must discover who they truly are, but do so quickly for there are forces afoot which will seek to destroy your clan and use you for their own ends. You cannot allow them to do so, or you condemn Caledon into their dark hands, and they will never be compassionate to the one who showed them so little mercy. Now turn, Caledon, and fight."

James turned to find John Mackay, who lifted the axe, freeing it from the timbers of the table. Brandishing it like a madman, he ran at James who pulled out his dirk. But, turning as he did so, James' eyes rested on Mackay's reflection in the mirror to find it was Mary Mackenzie who easily wielded the enormous weapon. The revellers, the dogs, the minstrel, and the waterfall were all gone. Mary's eyes burnt with a rage such as Jamie had never witnessed in anyone. She swung the axe back to strike him but James tumbled to the side, the blow glancing away from him.

The sudden movement caused him to awake and he ran his trembling hand over his head, brushing aside the sweat which had formed there. He looked about him as he sat up. They were staying in a bothy in the hills some two miles outside Lairg. They had stayed in Annie's small house for a time, but when Mackay's men had entered the town Donald had ensured they left, unwilling to lead any harm to Annie.

He looked across at them and tried to understand all he had seen and heard in his dream. That one of these men sought to hide something from him caused him great concern and, as he watched them sleeping, he tried to unravel which one it could be. It was not Donald Mackenzie, he knew that. He had no higher regard for any man than the love he had for his cousin. Robert MacBeath was a passionate boy who had almost cost them their lives as he tried to fight Mackay's men in Lairg, but he could not believe the boy hid anything. He was impetuous and brash but with such noble intentions. Malcolm Murray had an honest simplicity to him which James could not question, he had never offered any explanation to them for his English accent but with the love and poetry which he spoke of his country, he was a true son of Caledon. William, James realised as he studied the man thoughtfully, was the person he knew the least. He scorned Donnie repeatedly for his lack of care, a curious move when he was the only other Hanoverian in the clan. James knew so much of the life William had left, but nothing of who he was now. He did not even know William's last name, nor his clan.

James rose to his feet, and now William awoke as he heard the movement. He watched James as he stepped out into the sunrise, failing to notice he had awoken the other man. William silently rose and followed him out the building.

"You woke troubled, Caledon," he stated, walking the few steps over to James.

"I had a warning in my dream. A premonition, perhaps."

"Surely you must trust yourself to discover the truth of such a thing."

"I have been advised against attending the wedding," James announced, willing himself to trust the man before him. "But Mackay has wavered his vow to kill both Donnie and myself for us to attend. We will be safe then, won't we?"

"I did not believe I should ever meet a Jacobite who would wish to befriend me. But you have proved me wrong, Jamie Caledon. But do not believe Mackay will so lightly abandon his dislike."

"Why did you choose to fight for the crown?"

"*It* chose *me*, Caledon. I would never raise arms for the Stuarts, for they seem only to bring bloodshed to the Scots."

"What is your clan, William?"

"I scarcely remember," William answered softly. "But I am of your clan now, Caledon. I will always fight for the people of Caledon before any race on earth."

James offered him a smile and nodded slowly, but it did nothing to settle his racing mind. Why did William seem intent on avoiding his questions? He was surely the man who he had been warned of and, as he and Donnie prepared to return to Lairg to visit Annie before they journeyed on to Golspie for Mary's wedding, he could not shake his mistrust of the man.

"You must promise me to stay safely hidden. You are all wanted men."

"Caledon," Malcolm said softly. "We will be safe. Just ensure you, Donnie and Annie are. I do not like this, and I don't trust Mackay at all."

"We will be safe," James said in a carefree manner. "Neither Donnie nor I trust Mackay. We'll be safe."

"See that you are," William added. "Don't trust Oaf to protect you, though he could crush an army with his colossal weight, they'd hear him coming a mile away."

Donald glared at the tall thin man and turned away rushing down the hillside, not waiting for James but trusting he would be following. James smiled across at William and bade farewell to the three men, before he followed his cousin down the slope, and they rushed on towards Lairg. They laughed and joked, feeling at once that their parley, which Mary had persuaded Mackay to offer them, made them invincible. They stumbled onto the road to Lairg and walked forward. It was strange, after four months of being forced to hide and move in secret, that they could now walk through the streets contentedly. All the same, both were relieved they encountered no troops as they walked to what had once been the baker's shop.

"We shouldn't be seen going in," Donnie said quickly. "We may have been granted a pardon for today, but there is no guarantee, when we disappear into the hills, they will not call on her."

"You really love her, don't you?" Jamie asked, laughing slightly.

"Is it really such an impossible notion to believe?" Donnie whispered, his face adopting an expression of sorrow. "Am I really as William paints me? A useless oaf?"

"No," Jamie said, trying to abate the laughter which seeped past the word.

"Then the answer is yes," Donnie replied thoughtfully.

"I don't imagine you with a wife, that's all." Jamie led him around the edge of a building a little further along the road before they walked to the rear of the baker's house. "Or if I do, she is a gentlewoman."

"Is Annie not?"

"She is as fiery as you are placid, Donnie. But she loves you entirely, of that I am certain."

"I'm not. I'm afraid she believes I'm the clumsy fool William says I am."

"She threatened me, you know?" Jamie began, placing his hand on the timbers of the door. "When we left Mary here, she told me that I had to protect you, or nothing would protect me from her."

Donald Mackenzie smiled slightly and followed Jamie into Annie's house. She turned to face them at once and gave a relieved sigh.

"I see knocking is a courtesy I no longer merit since I agreed to join your ridiculous band."

"Sorry, Annie," Jamie began, stepping over to the range and picking up one of the bannocks that rested there.

"Get your hands off those," she snapped. "I have to make a living, don't I?"

James smiled across as he began tearing chunks off the bread and eating hungrily. "Donnie will pay you."

Annie placed her hand over Donnie's lips before he could venture any words. "*You* will pay, James Og. You may claim to be Caledon, but I shall not excuse you anything as your cousin might." She spared Donnie a brief smile before she threw the cloth which was over her shoulder at Jamie. "It is a strange thing," she laughed as Donnie set a coin down on the table. "When the other three are here you are such a strong leader, Jamie. But when there is only you two, both of you behave like children."

Donald smiled. "When we ran the hills as children, we were only preparing for this. Our fathers must have known what we would become."

"Your father was the best man I ever knew, Donald Mackenzie. He would have torn his grey hair out to see the pandemonium his boy has caused." She rested her hand on Donnie's chest as she turned to James. "Nor could he guess his nephew would claim the title Caledon."

"In fairness," James began. "I did not claim it. It was placed on me."

"So you claim," she replied as she hugged Donnie's broad arm around her. "But do not set a foot wrong tonight, I beg you. Remember, John Mackay is only looking for an excuse to have you both killed."

"But Annie," James remarked as he smiled across at her. "You will be there to protect us."

"I will not walk in with you. Our safety lies in indifference, or they shall know of your haven."

"We will not bring harm on you, Annie," Donald said quickly, kissing her hand. "Now you've eaten something, Jamie, we should embark. Annie has a cart to take her, we have only our feet."

"Take a bannock, Donnie," she said softly. "You shall not be left out for being born with the manners your cousin lacks."

Donnie kissed her cheek as Jamie threw a bannock to him.

"They're good," James mumbled as he snatched another two and ran out the back door before she had a chance to rebuke him.

"See he's safe, Donald. He's going to seek revenge on John Mackay, and I'm afraid it won't end in the satisfaction he's seeking. And for God sake, Donnie, see yourself safe. I don't trust anyone there."

"You can trust me, Annie. I shall never let you out of my sight, I promise."

"Don't make promises you can't keep. Be safe."

Donald spared her a brief smile before he rushed after James and they began running in the direction of Golspie.

A Bitter Disappointment

The elation the two men shared as they fled from Annie's house, trying to eat while they ran, faded as they journeyed over the ridges overlooking Strath Fleet. Their pace lessened until each of them was walking and eventually Donald sat down among the blooming heather. James turned and looked down at his cousin before he came and sat beside him.

"What's on your mind, Donnie?"

"I was thinking about Mackay of Moudale." Donnie pulled his boot off and tipped out a collection of small stones. "That man made Father's life unbearable, even before war was announced, and he killed Father. Why would Mary marry him?"

"I should have saved your father," Jamie sighed. "That's what this is about."

"You can't blame yourself for his death, Jamie. Mackay, and Mackay alone, must carry the responsibility."

James tried to gain the courage to explain how responsible he was for his uncle's death, but he could not.

"I have never known Mary to be malicious like this."

"Sometimes I wonder what having a sister would have been like," James said softly. "Sometimes I wish I had a brother or a sister to protect and to protect me. But I swapped it for a cousin. And I know I couldn't love a brother more than I love you, Donnie."

"Don't jest, Jamie. We don't all have it in us to be Caledon."

"I couldn't do it without you. We six are a clan. It was what I was told to do, to bring you all together."

"And what were you told to do next, Caledon?"

"To journey north. And not to attend this wedding."

"Doesn't it worry you? That you were told, in no uncertain terms, you should not attend tonight?"

"If Mackay has a will to harm us, Donnie, he will do it with or without a wedding to hide behind." James shook his head as he rose to his feet and offered his hand down to his cousin. "I was also told that one of our number was concealing something."

"Who do you think it is? And what do you think it is?" Donald asked, pulling his boot on and accepting Jamie's offered hand.

"I don't believe the six of us can form a clan without loyalty. But what if one is a spy? We don't even know William's last name. I'm not sure I trust him. And he was a Hanoverian."

"So was I, Jamie," Donald said softly. "So were a good many others of Caledon's children. Mackay conveniently forgets I fought on the same side as him."

"Ensign Mackay needs to be reminded of many things."

They walked on in silence for a time before, at last, the lights of Golspie became clear in the early summer evening. The festivities were to be held in a barn close to the village, which was being used as a drill hall by Mackay's small militia, and the two cousins walked towards it. Neither one of them truly believed they would not have to fight their way into and out of the hall, but as they arrived, clad in the outlawed philamor, they were admitted, but frowned upon all the same.

Donald looked about him, his eyes focusing on each individual. He was disappointed, though not shocked, to find he knew almost no one at his sister's wedding. Mary was seated beside her groom, but upon recognising the two men who entered she rose to her feet and walked over to them. She was wearing a fine yellow gown and her dark hair enhanced the glow.

"You are radiant, Mary," Donald whispered as he kissed his sister's cheek.

"Why were you not at the ceremony?" she asked, as she smiled across at him. "Your pardons were for the full day."

"We could not get here in time, Mary," James said softly as he stared into the eyes of the woman who should have been his bride. "We had a lot of ground to cover to reach here this evening."

"Well, I'm glad you managed it," she said jovially as she led the two men further into the hall. Donald could not help considering how exposed their position was, but James spared his distaste only for the man before him.

"James Og," Mackay said flatly. "Not as much of a coward as I had believed you to be. You came for Mary, I see."

"I came because I was invited, Mackay," James replied.

"And this nonsense of Caledon. Do you still persist with it?"

"Caledon?" Mary whispered. "Donnie, what are they talking of?"

"Enough, Mackay," James said softly. "You are causing your wife to reconsider the vows she has only this day made."

"Let me make one thing clear to both of you," Mackay began, rising from his chair and staring first at James and then at Donald. "You are protected only by my word as a gentleman. Should you remain a second beyond midnight, I shall have you shot."

"John," Mary pleaded. "Enough, please. They are here on my request. James, will you come and dance with me? Donnie, our kinswoman has just arrived. Why do you not go and speak with her?" Donald turned to look at where Annie walked into the room and he allowed a smile to cross his features as he beheld her white shawl over her beige top and long brown skirt. "Go and talk to her, Donnie."

Donald nodded and walked over to Annie, feigning a pretence they had not seen one another since that terrible day when he and James had left for the west coast.

"You look stunning, Annie," he said softly taking her hand and kissing it.

"You look like you've been running through heather," Annie remarked flippantly. "But I'm glad you're safe so far. What a terrible match they make."

Donald followed her gaze and frowned slightly as he realised Annie was talking of Mary and James. "They have been promised to one another from birth. They were born within days of each other and it has always been known they were to be married."

"He is far beyond her."

Donald relinquished the hold he had on her arm and shook his head. "Mary may have disappointed me with her choice in marriage and her self-interested behaviour, but she is still my sister. She is not evil for marrying wisely instead of for love."

"I'm sorry, Donnie," Annie whispered. "But surely you can see Mary has made the wrong choice."

Donald remained silent but, after sparing her the briefest of smiles he walked through the hall and stood in the corner of the barn, staring at the scene before him.

James had felt cornered by Mary's request to dance and had accepted more through fear of the repercussions than actual enjoyment. She watched him as they danced, and in turn they were watched critically by Mackay.

"You do not wish me ill, do you, James?" she asked as they concluded their dance. "I wanted you to accept my choice. I know you and John fight on opposite sides, but can you accept it?"

"He fought alongside Donnie, yet still he has outlawed him."

"But he permitted a pardon for you both today. You can't imagine how greatly I had to beg it of him."

"That, I'm certain, is true."

"You do hate me, don't you, Jamie? I can see it in your eyes that you do."

James lifted her hand to his face and kissed it before he smiled and shook his head. "No, Mary, I don't hate you. But you must know, my resolve to hate your husband is as deep as any hatred I have ever known. Truthfully, I wish *you* every good health and happiness."

Mary's face beamed as she heard these words and she guided him over to one of the tables. James paused and looked over his shoulder as though he expected to see someone there.

"What is it?" Mary asked with a slight laugh as she handed him a clay tankard and collected a drink for herself.

"Nothing, I'm sure. Only, I've been watching my back so much in the last few months I think I am becoming afraid of such gatherings."

"I'm certain you have nothing to fear," Mary laughed. "Donnie is watching your back, see," she continued as she welcomed her brother over and offered him a drink which he gratefully accepted. "I can count on Donnie to always see the best in you, even when I could not."

"He is my leader as well as my cousin, Mary," Donnie said softly. She only smiled quizzically at him before she excused herself to return to her groom. "What is it, Jamie?" Donnie continued. "I came over because I watched all the colour drain from your face."

"I heard its voice warning me, as it warned me last night. I saw Mary try to kill me."

"What?" Donald demanded. "My sister is not evil. She has made a poor choice, I grant you, but she is still my sister."

"It has never been wrong before," Jamie whispered, staring thoughtfully into his cup. "And I can't help but wonder-"

"Enough!" Donald began, angry at the disregard both James and Annie paid to how, over twenty years, Mary had never considered herself. "If you think Mary would poison you because she chose someone else, let me prove to you that you are wrong." He snatched the tankard from his cousin and drank its contents, pausing only once to remark on the fine wine. Once he had finished, he slammed the vessel down on the table, causing the handle to snap off in his hand. "See? I'm still very much alive."

James drank from Donnie's cup and felt an overwhelming guilt as the broad figure of his cousin walked away from him to stand at the door and take in the chilly August night air. But as the night wore on, he could not escape the feeling he had been mistaken to have disobeyed his direction from the waterfall. He had thought as James Og and forgotten his duty as Caledon.

"You seem lost in bleak thoughts," Mary began as she walked over to him later in the evening.

"Why am I here, Mary? I came full of rage at John Mackay, but I cannot harm your husband."

"Then you are helpless before me?" Mary whispered.

"Not too helpless, I hope, or Mackay will be right to have me shot," he remarked as lightheartedly as he could. "But why did you invite me? When you knew I was an outlaw."

"I needed you here." She traced her finger along the lines of his palm and smiled slightly. "There is something I have longed to tell you, but I have been unable to find you in your exile." She felt her hand tighten on the hilt of the sgian dhu she had tucked

141

inside her waistline. "I was told you would be helpless to me tonight."

"I'm sorry, Mary," he replied, pulling his hand from hers and staring down in great sympathy. "But whoever told you that was as mistaken about your understanding of me as I was in my understanding of you. Congratulations and long life in your marriage, Mary, but you hold nothing over me now."

"Indeed?" she muttered, relinquishing her hold on the knife and feeling a thousand questions pouring into her head. How had the witches failed her? Why was the man before her not begging for whatever she commanded him to do? "Then I shall leave you to enjoy my feast, James Og. For at midnight you'll be an outlaw once more and by your appearance you have not eaten since the rebellion."

James watched as she walked away from him before he turned to survey the room. Red-coated soldiers filled it for the most part and, with a sickening realisation, he found that he had no idea how close he was to midnight. Nor did he wish to discover what should happen were he still in the hall into the next day. Anxiously he sought for his cousin, but amongst the drunken revellers and the spinning dancers he could not find Donald.

"I saw you talking to Mary," began a quiet voice beside him.

"Annie," James whispered as he looked down at her. "I think you were right, and Malcolm and William, and everyone who warned me not to come here tonight."

"But Mary-"

"Is not the woman I remember," James finished. "But in my ridiculous suspicions I have offended Donnie and now I've no idea where he is."

"He'll be safe somewhere. You have only a short time before midnight, but you do still have time." She took his arms and turned him to face her. "You came tonight because you believe in the best in people. That is not something to rebuke yourself for. When Donnie arrived at my door with you, James Og, your head bandaged and your arm shot, I did not believe I could ever respect you as Donnie did. But you're not the person I thought you were. Caledon? A man who sacrifices his happiness and freedom to provide for a cursed nation? Who saves souls that would long ago have perished? Who are you James Og?"

"I was a coward who believed in an idea. But then I was found and saved by a dream. But coming here has made me question only more how James Og ever thought he could become Jamie Caledon."

"You're an inspiration, Caledon. And I thank God that Donnie brought you to my door."

Donald Mackenzie sat by the door and divided his time between gazing with suspicion at the people inside the barn and admiring the clear stars of the night outside. No one paid him any attention as he sat there, thinking of the bride and groom with two very different opinions. To have come face to face with John Mackay had sparked in him, not the hatred he had expected, but a sadness which he could not believe his sister would manage to live with. Mary had been his world. He had protected her, educated her and given her every care he could, refusing to believe that, simply because she was a woman, she had any less right to learn.

"You seem greatly troubled, little brother," Mary began, as she offered down her hand to him. He took and kissed it, but made no attempt to rise. "I've never had the chance to thank you for seeing me safely to Annie's house. I'd always hoped that you and she might marry." Donnie just laughed and rose to his feet, allowing Mary to arrange the philamor over his huge shoulders. "That was why I invited her tonight."

"I saw you talking with Jamie," Donald said softly, looking into her eyes which remained perfectly calm. "Do you truly no longer love him?"

"Jamie and I have a journey to share, Donnie," she whispered. "It's true I wished more than anything to be with him tonight. But he has assured me he no longer loves me."

"Then why did you marry Mackay?"

"Has it not given me the chance to see you both once more? When you left for the west, I had no idea if you were safe, or even alive. Mackay holds the power of life over you both so, should I ever wish to see you again, I needed to form an alliance with him."

"Oh, Mary," Donnie began, hugging her close to him. "You should not have done it over such a matter. I should have taken you safely to Invergordon, as Father told me."

"We should both have done a great deal differently, Donnie. But I must learn not to lament my love for Jamie," she sighed as she turned her brother toward the door. "For he clearly has not been so lost in the absence of it."

Donald felt suddenly winded as he gazed over to where James held Annie in an embrace. After all he had told his cousin about his love for her, he could not believe Jamie's behaviour. William, Donnie realised, was right in his assessment of him. But it made sense. Donnie had nothing which set him above the greatness of Caledon. He set his face firm as he turned back to Mary.

"He's a great man," he croaked, trying to coax the words to sound. "I'm sorry you did not find him so."

"*You* are a great man, Donald Mackenzie. You owe him nothing. Remember that."

"No. He saved your life and he has become as selfless a man as any could be. Mary, he is more worthy of you now than ever."

"You don't know what happened that night, do you?" she whispered, tears blooming in her eyes as she looked up at him. "I witnessed Father die,

146

scarcely four foot from me. And where was James Og?"

"And where was Ensign John Mackay? At the other end of the gun. But I don't rebuke you for your choice to marry him, Mary. Just remember, any man might change."

"Don't you ever change, little brother, for I know I can always count on you to do as I ask. Or in the least, to do as I need."

Both of them turned as James walked over to them. He was alone, Annie having gone further into the hall. Donald forced himself to smile, while Mary offered her cousin a disapproving expression.

"I believe I owe you an apology," James began as he looked down at Mary. "I had it in my head that you sought to ensnare me tonight, for I had seen a scenario before me where you tried to claim my life."

"Jamie," she said softly, wishing more than ever to put her concealed weapon to the use she had intended it. "I could not harm you and, furthermore, I have been told you're protected."

"By Donnie?" James laughed.

"Would it be so ridiculous for me to protect you?" Donald demanded, feeling his temper fraying at the casual approach of the man before him.

"No," Mary said softly, placing her hand on Donnie's arm to restrain his words and actions. "By two ladies I encountered. But then they were the ones who told me you would be helpless to me."

"Then your soothsayers have mistaken me for another man."

Donald, forgetting for a moment all the anger and hurt he felt towards his cousin, gripped James' arm. "They've closed the doors, Jamie. How are we to leave?"

"John!" Mary began, rushing over to her husband. "What are you doing? Let them leave."

"Oh no, my wife. I offered them a parley only for one day. I cannot be blamed if they are poor timekeepers." He leaned down and kissed Mary's forehead before he shouted, "Kill them!"

There was a gunshot then, though not one of the soldiers had been given the time to load their muskets. Donald looked about him in confusion, while James wasted no time in snatching his cousin's wrist and dragging him toward the door, directly into the paths of the soldiers. They snatched at the guns of their assailants and tried to wrestle their way to the door as another shot, and another, came from the far corner of the room, striking a soldier each time. Donnie reached the beam that rested on the door and easily pulled it aside, before opening the door and ushering his cousin through.

"What about Annie?" Donald demanded, as they rushed around the corner of the building.

"She'll be fine, Oaf," William's voice announced as he stepped out of the darkness. "Be more concerned for Malcolm. He is an outlaw, a Jacobite, and still in there."

Jamie looked down at the musket he now carried, before he ran back to the door and began searching for the man to whom he was bound through an oath of loyalty. There was chaos in the hall as the ladies rushed toward the doors. James had no shot, but used the butt of the weapon to fend off the soldiers until he found Malcolm at the far end of the room. Robert was under the table, reloading the guns while Malcolm fired them.

"Caledon," Malcolm began. "I almost shot you. I'm here so you don't have to be. Get out."

The three of them upturned the table and sat with their backs against it. Robert smiled across as though he was enjoying the whole experience, but his smile slipped as one of the soldier's shots struck the wood directly behind his head.

"Fire!" someone shouted from behind them, and James looked up to see the smoke billowing from the wooden beams above him.

"We have to get to the door," James began, but Malcolm only smiled.

"We've started this fire, Caledon. Our only hope to escape is if the soldiers leave the barn."

Robert peered over the top of the table but was met with musket fire as he quickly ducked down once more. "They haven't left yet," he coughed, and peered through a hole in the table, watching the men as they retreated before closing the heavy doors. "They've gone," he called, and almost at once a thick rope was thrown down from the roof.

"You first, Caledon," Malcolm announced, and James ran to the rope, gripping hold of it as it was pulled up. Robert refused to go before Malcolm, and so the young man brought up the rear.

"They're still round the front," William announced, rejoining them as Donnie dropped the rope into the burning room below.

"Well, that was a wedding to remember," Malcolm laughed, helping Robert to his feet. "It is a good thing they weren't worried about who was invited, or you might well be dead, Caledon."

"I did tell you not to come," James began.

"And trust you to the girl you were in love with?" Robert replied, laughing slightly although he stopped as Donnie clambered down from the roof. "You would not have stood a chance in there, Caledon."

"We should leave before we're found," Donald said softly.

"He's right," Malcolm agreed.

William led the way through the heather and into the night beyond. His footing never failed him, and Donald followed, ashamed of each time he slipped and feeling the weight of William's scorn. Robert came next, glancing continuously behind them to check that Malcolm and James were following.

"Did you find the answer you sought, Caledon?" Malcolm asked, as he and James walked sedately behind the others.

"I believe so. I should have listened to each one of you who told me not to go."

"And what of Donald Mackenzie?" Malcolm asked softly, and James was surprised to find that Malcolm had a look of genuine concern on his features.

"What of him?"

"He is not the same man who walked away from us this morning. He seems-" Malcolm frowned in the direction of James' cousin. "Sad."

"His sister has just married the man who wants to kill him. I imagine that's why he's sad."

"I can understand that. I'd be vexed in that situation, too," Malcolm replied wryly. "But he seems distant from you, Caledon. I hope nothing happened which would divide you, for you are as close as brothers."

"When I first met you and Robert, I thought you were brothers," James said, trying to turn the conversation from the blame which suddenly gripped him as he considered for the first time his

152

actions with Annie. But it had seemed the most natural thing at the time, almost as though Donnie's praise of her had opened his eyes.

Malcolm's shrewd gaze took this in, and he nodded slightly. "Robert MacBeath is a loyal boy and I owe him, as I owe all of you, my very life."

"After tonight I believe Donnie and I owe *you*."

Malcolm did not respond to this except for to smile. James watched as the man, perhaps a little older than himself, walked on ahead. Turning back to admire the first glow of the early morning, James tried to consider all he had seen and heard, but never able to shake himself entirely free from the nagging doubt that Mary Mackenzie had orchestrated her wedding and party solely to inflict pain upon him. For what else could she truly hope to achieve through such a union with so cruel a man?

When they reached the bothy, the sun had risen completely and James, Malcolm and William fell asleep almost at once. Donald tried to sleep but, although he was so weary he could have wept, his mind raced over all he had seen and heard and he felt for the first time he had been wrong to follow Jamie as blindly as he had done. He had been swept along with the story and hope of salvation for Caledon, but now he was unsure he wanted anything more than the life which had been pulled from him by the arrival of Charles Stuart on the shores of Glenfinnan.

Robert witnessed his four comrades bedding down to take slumber. For his own part he prayed for the day The Prince would return and his good friend, Malcolm Murray, would be acknowledged as the person he was born to be. Caledon, he was certain, was the person to enable this.

The Power of Three

After the chaos her wedding had caused for so little in return, Mary Mackay was anxious to demand answers from Beauty and Fortune. According to the advice she had been given, though she could never again find the woman who had informed her of this, the witches met in the cover of the new moon or at certain fire feasts. This gave Mary four weeks to bottle her anger at them and, in her mind, she played through so many scenarios of what she wished to say to them.

Her marriage, she was forced to admit, was becoming a happy one. John Mackay, though calculating in his business and brutal in his warfare, was a good husband to her. He acknowledged her desire to leave behind the name Mackenzie, and sought to make her proud to carry the name Mackay. After being determined to view this marriage as the weapon it was meant to be, she found her attachment to John Mackay intensified. And though she could never acknowledge any love for him, she appreciated his adherence to duty and sought to fuel his hatred of James Og.

The fact James had escaped angered her greatly. She had been certain of success and now, as the weeks turned into September, she began to wonder whether someone had seen her down on the sandy beach. She looked over her shoulder everywhere she went and frequently remained indoors to avoid the weight of people's eyes upon her. She did concede, however, that both James and her brother had looked as handsome as any man could in the plaid, which she quietly lamented had been outlawed throughout the highlands.

Her brother was a perplexing conundrum in her plans. In him she had witnessed a loyalty toward both herself and her cousin, and she could not understand this divided allegiance, especially as this was the man who had fled from their father, leaving him to die. But the more she considered it, the more she found she distrusted Donald and suspected he may have witnessed her meeting with the witches. While she knew paranoia was overtaking her sense, she could do nothing to fight it. Yet there was a part of her, when she considered her younger brother, that wanted to protect and care for him. She knew she owed all her education to his patience and generosity. Donald Mackenzie may have been a fool in his outlook, but he was a kind fool.

So, as September arrived, she awaited eagerly the new moon and walked down the stairs of the house she shared with her husband.

"Where are you going, Mary?" he asked flatly, as she pulled a cloak about her shoulders.

"I've a mind to take the air. September is the last month before the weather turns, and I want to make the most of it before Michaelmas. There will be no late night strolls then."

"Do you want me to come with you?"

"No," she said gently. "I'll take a torch and walk up by the castle. No harm can come to me then."

He nodded, and even spared her a smile, before she collected a small lantern and walked out of the door. Mindful of the lie she had offered her husband and wishing to continue it, she walked past the window, which had its shutters closed, and on towards the castle. When she was sure no one was following her, she returned once more to the town and down to the beach. She was uncertain the lantern would work as the torch had done, but she placed it on the sandy shore and waited.

Minutes trickled by, and she huddled into her cloak as the sea breeze tried to separate it from her. Finally, the lantern flame flickered violently and in its erratic shadows she saw Fortune step toward her.

"Why are you here, Mary Mackay?"

"To deride you," she began. "And you," she added, pointing to Beauty.

"Whatever for?" Beauty said softly, collecting her burning hair in a wooden clasp. "We kept our end of the bargain. See you keep yours."

"It didn't work. James Og still lives."

"You were not honest with us," Fortune said firmly. "You did not tell us that James Og was Caledon."

"What is this?" Mary demanded. "Caledon is not a person. It is our land, a dying land as he should also have perished."

"Fool girl," Beauty said firmly, collecting a stone and drawing a circle about them before the two witches sat by the lantern, and Mary did the same. "Caledon rises when her people need her. In times of hardship or suffering she chooses one person who can lead her virtues and free her enslaved people."

"What nonsense," Mary remarked. "Jamie could never be chosen for such a role. He is a coward."

"Do not call it nonsense," Fortune snapped. "When last Caledon rose, it was against our brethren and the terrible witch hunts ensued. They were unjust and wrong. That you call it nonsense just proves you are too foolish to deal with such a man."

"I want him dead," Mary said firmly, detaching each word with great purpose. "I do not care if he is the embodiment of Caledon or of any great deity. Was that why the potion did not work? Because he is Caledon?"

"I think the potion did work, Mary Mackay," Beauty said angrily. "But that he is Caledon provides him with a certain protection. That is the same protection he imparted to you."

"What do you mean?"

"Caledon is gifted a well of healing, but is blessed only enough to protect themselves and one other. He chose you. Never before has Caledon chosen an enemy to share the healing spring, but you shall stand as a formidable foe before him."

"Who does Caledon usually gift it to?"

"Caledon calls a clan of six, each representing an ancient part of her persona. Usually, it goes to one of them."

"Let us not waste words, Beauty," Fortune said firmly. "You know, as well as I, what must happen for the potion to have an effect."

"What?" Mary asked eagerly. "What must happen?"

"Caledon killed almost all of our kind," Fortune continued, picking up the telling of the story. "But for us to be strong enough so our power may reach others, we must number three. That is why we need your daughter."

"And you shall have her," Mary said in an irked voice. "Must I wait until she is born before my plan comes to fruition?"

"Perhaps not. You are blessed with the protection of Caledon. You are seeking a justice we wish for. Why do *you* not join us?"

"To be a witch?" Mary asked incredulously. "I know nothing of your world."

"You know more than you realise," Fortune continued while Beauty smiled across. "Already you will have a bond with the man who drank the potion. You will draw from him what power he has, and through this you will grow."

"And it will give me what I want? To kill James Og?"

"It will bring you closer."

"Then I shall do it."

"Are you not afraid?" Beauty asked. "Your husband may be ordered to kill you."

"My husband does not concern me. He will be as grateful as I to see Jamie dead."

"Then this is what you must do," Fortune said softly. "Place your left hand into the fire and your right into the water and say the words: 'What I was, I am no more. Of fire and water I am reborn.' The tide is coming in, see? You must do it then."

Mary waited as the gentle lapping waves reached close enough so she could place one hand at the lantern and one hand into the foam. She repeated the words as she had been instructed and quickly pulled her hand back from the flame. She was surprised to find there was no burn there, but before she could comment on it, Beauty hushed her.

"Now place your left hand in the sand and your right in the air and say: 'What I was, I am no more. Of earth and air I am reborn.' And don't say anything else."

Mary did as she was instructed, feeling somewhat foolish in how primitive this ritual seemed to be. But the moment she uttered these final words she felt her senses heighten, and each sigh of wind or lap of waves carried a thousand messages to her. If the candle flame flickered it sounded like a gale and she felt the movement of every grain of sand beneath her.

"Now we number three, Mary Mackay." Fortune closed her eyes and listened slightly to something Mary could not hear. "You shall be Time. For that is what the elements call you, and that is what you shall control. Reach out to the stars, Time, and slow down the world."

Mary did not know what she did, nor how she had achieved it. But, as she watched the stars, she heard the waves become slower, the breeze lessened as the second split into five, ten, twenty seconds. She stared about her in amazement while Beauty only laughed.

"Now tell us, can you find Caledon?"

"What must I do to find him?"

"Think of him. Only of him. And the potion should bind him to you."

"It is not working," Mary whispered after a time. "Why is it not working?"

"Wait," Fortune snapped. "Who is this man?"

She flung a handful of sand at the lantern and the breeze collected it, whipping it into the thin image of a person. Mary sat forward and frowned as she beheld it.

"That is not James Og."

"Do you know him?" Fortune persevered.

"Yes," Mary whispered. "He's my brother."

"He will bring you Caledon. Now think of your brother."

Mary focused all her thoughts on Donald, assisted by his image before her. At once she felt a surge of energy pulse through her as though all the strength of her brother's might was given to her. She smiled as she looked at her thin hands and considered all they could now do.

"Why am I able to do this?"

"Because he drank your potion," Beauty announced.

"You told me it would work only on James Og."

"And so it would. Your brother will not fall into such a helpless state, but you will be able to draw from him whenever you think of him." Beauty paused before she added, "Do you have a love of your brother?"

"A little. Why?"

"You may have to lose it," Fortune replied. "For each time you think of him and draw from his power, he loses it."

"In essence," Mary announced. "If I wish to use my brother to kill James Og, my brother may die too?"

"Perhaps. That would depend on whether he is willing to help us or not."

Mary pushed Donnie from her thoughts but nodded slowly. This choice felt like the hardest she had ever made, for she had as much love for Donald as she had loathing for James. "He will help if I ask him to," she said with a sudden surety.

Beauty watched as Fortune's sand image of Donald Mackenzie was caught on the sea breeze and disappeared into the atmosphere. For her own part, Mary could not escape thinking of her brother, though she tried not to. As soon as she felt any of his strength, she quickly thought of someone else. Sometimes her husband, sometimes James Og, and sometimes the women before her, but always her thoughts came back to Donald.

She collected her lantern and walked once more into the town, struggling up the slippery rocks and along the sea edge. There was much for her to think on, too much for her racing mind. As she reached the top of the little sandy mound, she felt someone take her arm.

"Mary, I was becoming worried about you."

"You had no need," she panted, linking her arm through her husband's and allowing him to take the lantern. "I had to take the air, but found myself wandering a little further than I meant to."

"What happened to your hand?"

Mary looked down at her blistering left hand and frowned. "That's strange. I caught myself on the lantern when I was careless, but I don't remember it hurting at all. It's strange it's now come up so sore."

She was unsure whether he believed her or not, but neither did she care for, as the events of the evening once more played before her, she found herself thinking of her brother. The immense strength which coursed her veins made her laugh slightly and this time it became difficult to release her hold on it. As John Mackay, oblivious to her witchcraft, walked his wife back to the small house they shared, she realised with a sickening curiosity that she had no wish to relinquish the power this bond gave her.

Part Four: French Gold

Relieving Le Duc d'Anjou

As soon as Caledon's clan had recovered from the events of their foolish attendance at Ensign John Mackay's wedding, James announced it was time for them to move north. Donald spared barely a word for anyone but sat silently watching the other members of the clan. If they laughed he smiled, and if they ever required an answer he would offer it tentatively, as though he was unsure he should be talking at all. This change was noted by all of them, but it was not until a week after the wedding, as they prepared to venture north, that Malcolm expressed his concern.

"Are you sure we're doing the right thing?" He stood alone with James, staring out over the glen. Donald had walked to the summit to keep watch over the clear night. There was an almost full moon and, in the absence of any clouds, the apex of the hill was a perfect vantage point. "Should we not take Annie with us?"

"She's safer left here," James said awkwardly.

"But safer for whom, Caledon? For her? For you? Or for the poor lovelorn figure of Donald Mackenzie?" He sighed heavily and rubbed his hand over his eyes. "That is what happened at the wedding, isn't it?"

"Donald's loyalty is to Caledon. He swore it was so, and he is the most honourable soul I know. He will not impeach." James shook his head slowly. "But what you say of Annie is true. And in answer to your questions, Malcolm, I must declare it's all of them. I can't lead Annie anywhere not knowing what will befall us. I can't risk losing a member of my clan, and I can't afford for Donnie to become distracted."

Malcolm nodded slowly. "Then it will just be the five of us."

"Indeed. And though I'm unsure where we are to journey to, I am certain we'll find out on the way." Jamie paused and added softly, "Do you never worry I shall lead you into a danger you can't escape from? When I talk of having only a hint of purpose you, more than any of the others, are happy to follow me without questioning."

"Instinct," Malcolm said flatly. "My instinct tells me you intend the utmost best for Caledon, and that is exactly what I wish for, too."

This brief conversation accompanied James as the band of five began their travels north. It took them seven days to reach the north coast, reluctant to move in the daylight for fear of being seen. They journeyed through the steep sided mountains from the small fishing town of Helmsdale until they reached the more gentle terrain of Strath Halladale. Here, though, they were hindered by the vast boggy pools which often appeared without warning, so William insisted that each person trod exactly where he had.

"You follow me, Oaf," he began, taking Donnie's sleeve as though he was a child. "That way I can make sure you don't drown."

Donald had smiled slightly at this remark, but whatever the smile was designed to hide was set to remain hidden as he walked on. Robert made up for Donald's silence however for the young man never ceased talking. All night he spoke to William, Donald, Malcolm and James, on any topic which took his fancy and with an enthusiasm which spoke of his relief at being able to begin a campaign once more.

When they reached the village of Melvich they stayed some nights in a small farmstead. It had been deserted but still had enough furnishings to make it a luxury after the weeks of sleeping outdoors. During this time, they all waited for Jamie to direct them and, in turn, he waited to be given direction.

It was on their fourth day in the derelict house that James finally drifted into the dream he had been waiting for. He could tell at once it was prophetic for it began with the sound of running water. There was a strange light which seemed to shimmer and gave the impression of creating no shadows but, as he walked forward over the long bridge, he noticed an image of himself flickering before him. For the first time he looked up to take in his surroundings. He was standing before a great door which was crafted in stone, and he had to wind down a rope so it would open like a drawbridge. He was not at all afraid, being certain he had as much right to be there as anyone. As he stepped into the building he was met by the long, familiar corridor lined with pictures. The mirror at the end, however, showed him only himself in the building of stone. He turned and followed the corridor until he reached a heavy wooden door which was propped open by a tall, lanky dog. Initially he thought it was a statue but as he tried to walk into the room the animal curled back its lips and gave a long low growl. James held his palm up to it and at once it returned to its passive nature, never moving except to follow him with its eyes. This was clearly a bedchamber. An elaborately carved four poster bed dominated the room with a fireplace opposite it, but instead of a fire burning in the enormous hearth there was the familiar form of the waterfall.

"You do not belong here, Caledon. This is the room of Strength."

"The dog didn't stop me," James protested, as he turned back to the animal which remained staring at him.

"For he sees why you have come here."

"I feel that demonstrates well how I am handling my role. Even a dog knows what I should be doing better than I do myself."

"Because that dog knows its sense of loyalty and duty."

"What do you mean?" James whispered, feeling the chiding strike him as hard as a club.

"I told you not to attend the wedding of John Mackay. You should have been here a month ago."

"Here in Melvich, or here in this place? Wherever this place may be."

"This is Castle Caledon," the waterfall announced.

"Is it real?" James asked, looking around him. "I know I'm dreaming."

"Yes, it's real. Though you are here in a dream now, this place has a tangible existence. It has living space for six, as six is the number of the clan of Caledon. This is the room for Strength."

"You say strength as though it was a person."

"And so it is, James Og. There are rooms here for each person who represents the Scottish traits of power, stealth, zeal, wisdom, strength and nobility."

"Six," he whispered, realisation dawning on him. "Which of my clan is which?"

"You should know that yourself, for you called them. Tell me, what does it mean to be Nobility?"

"Not one of us is nobility."

"Then you do not know your clan."

"Do we all have dogs?" James asked, trying to deflect the criticism

"No. Only Strength. Nobility has a stag, Stealth has a marten, Wisdom has a raven, Zeal has a wildcat."

"That's only five," James pointed out. "What of the sixth?"

The waterfall remained silent as it filled the colossal fireplace, and Jamie began to suspect the conversation was over. He turned to leave but stopped as the dog began barking angrily at him. No amount of pacifying could quieten it, and nor would it allow him to pass.

"What do you want?" he demanded.

"You have angered Strength," the waterfall's neutral voice began. "I told you that you would lose loyalty if you attended the wedding, and I warned you that your strength would fail."

"Donnie?" James whispered. "He's my Strength, isn't he?"

"What happened at the wedding to so unsettle the equilibrium?"

"I took solace in the company of-" James paused and shook his head. "Donald Mackenzie is not a jealous man. What are you accusing him of?"

"I accuse no one, Caledon. But until you have resolved the failing bond you carry with Strength, the dog will continue to chase you."

"Do the others come here? Do they know what Castle Caledon is?"

"They have not done so yet, but at times the clan members have joined Caledon in these halls. You came seeking direction, did you not? You must journey west to the village of Tongue. At the kyle you will find a stricken boat. Offer to relieve them of their cargo that they might return safely from whence they came. But be cautious of your clan, for one of them may find this is to be their final run with Caledon. As I warned you once before, they have not all been entirely honest with you."

"William or Donald?"

"I do not know them by name, but by title."

James Og awoke quickly, panting for breath, and stared into the strong gaze of William.

"You called me, Caledon."

"I did," Jamie whispered. "Did I talk all the way through my dreams?"

"No," William replied softly. "But I am used to answering my name. Did you find that place from where we are directed?"

"I did. We are to meet a ship at Tongue and provide it with safe passage to return."

"I didn't know what number of habitations there were in the north," William laughed.

Nothing seemed to dampen William's spirits and James began to feel guilty for suspecting him of concealing a truth from him. They travelled on that morning, no longer having to conceal themselves in darkness for there were few people here and fewer still who would know them to be outlaws. They reached Tongue in the late morning of the second day of September and at once the ship was obvious in the kyle. It was a tall, high-masted boat and looked a great deal like The Emerald Lady, which had carried Catherine away to France. William stared at it with a wistful expression as he waited for the others to catch up with him. Donnie was close behind and stared down with a passive expression before he whispered,

"So, there's our quarry."

"What do we do now?" Robert asked James as they both stood beside the other two. Malcolm reached them and stared down at the boat for only a second before he spoke.

"That is the ship you are to intercept?"

"No," James replied pointedly. "That is the ship *we* are to intercept. Once we have assisted the removal of its cargo it will be able to return to France."

"Are they expecting us?" Robert asked eagerly.

"I'll take a boat from the village and meet it," Malcolm began. "But I have no idea how to row."

"Donnie," James said quickly. "You can row, can't you? You used to go fishing in the loch."

"Yes," Donald replied eagerly and smiled across, pleased to finally be of use to the tiny clan. "We should find a boat in the village."

"I don't know what their cargo is," James said, addressing Malcolm and Donnie. "But they should be eager to be rid of it."

"I'm sure," Malcolm replied softly. "Come on, Donald Mackenzie. Let's go and find a boat."

James watched with a curiosity as the two men walked down the incline of the hill and toward the small settlement of scattered houses. Tongue resided in the northern shadow of the giant Ben Loyal with its multiple, spiky fingers. It was a long bay down to the village and when they arrived it was to find three old men sitting around a large fishing net which they were repairing.

"Right?" one announced as the two strangers approached. "You look as lost as a fish on the shore."

"We're looking for a boat," Malcolm began, but the moment the men heard his English accent they rose as one and walked away.

"Wait," Donald pleaded. "We need a small craft for a day at most and we will pay handsomely for it."

"What kind of clansman wears a philamore but walks out with an Englishman?" one of the men asked.

"Malcolm Murray is as much a Scot as you or I," Donald said firmly. "And we are of the Clan of Caledon."

"Caledon?" another began. "Lord, we heard the rumours but did not think to find them come true. Caledon lives?"

"Indeed," Malcolm said softly. "For the first time in many years Caledon has come back."

"We are going indoors, here," one of them said as they pointed to a house close to the beach. "When you've finished with the boat, come tell us."

"Thank you," Donald and Malcolm chimed as one. Seeing what the old men were implying, that they would happily lend their craft but wanted to remain innocent in the affair, the two clansmen waited until the three had entered a small forge. Donald and Malcolm hurried down to the boat the moment they were sure no one would see them. Malcolm climbed in uncertainly and Donnie easily pushed it out into the water, clambering in as soon as he had done so, at which point he picked up the two heavy oars and directed the vessel to the middle of the kyle.

"You were quick to volunteer yourself to this task," Donnie said softly, smiling across at Malcolm who gripped the sides of the boat until his knuckles were white.

"Do you know how to swim, Donald Mackenzie?"

"Yes," Donnie replied. "And I promise I'll get you safely to shore."

"I know that ship," Malcolm said softly. "It is called Le Duc d'Anjou."

"How do you know it?"

"It's a story hardly worth telling. I'll go aboard, Donald. I shall resolve this issue alone."

Donnie nodded but remained quiet, no longer questioning Malcolm on the matter but accepting the orders he was given. He rowed the small vessel up to the side of the huge ship, feeling for once dwarfed. Malcolm called up to the boat in a series of words Donald could not understand and at once a rope ladder was thrown down. He ascended it with trepidation and stood on the broad deck.

"Can I speak with Captain Gillard?" Malcolm asked softly of the man who greeted him at the top. "My name is Malcolm Murray and I am certain he will receive me."

"As I am," the man replied with a smile. "For I am Captain Gillard. But, sir, we had almost thought to give up on you. We were told to expect you a month ago."

"My father?"

"Indeed so." Gillard said softly. "We are commissioned to get you safely to France. And we were to travel south to find your father the moment we had you safely aboard."

"This is difficult to understand, Captain, but I have not come to find safe passage. Our cause has not yet finished on these shores and, though my father may attract the attention of the English, I'm almost certain not to."

"What did you come aboard for, then, Malcolm Murray?"

"To take that which I know you carried here. I have a boat waiting below and in two journeys to the shore we should be able to carry it all from you."

"You know it is yours by right. But we lost countless livres in Arkaig, how can we return with countless more lost?"

"It's mine, Captain Gillard, and I intend to put it to use. When you see my father tell him that Caledon is risen. He will understand its significance."

The captain ordered five casks to be lowered to the boat below which Donnie easily took, but as he lined them up the boat became unbalanced and would have capsized if he did not sit as far as possible from it to equalise the weight. At Malcolm's request, he rowed the chests ashore close to the cliffs at the mouth of the inlet and returned once more to the vessel. Here, Malcolm, along with three more small chests, joined him. Donald remained silent all this while, and Malcolm seemed eager to match this mood. Whatever had been discussed on the deck of the ship, Malcolm had no intention of sharing it, and he alighted from the small rowing boat at the foot of the cliff along with the chests.

"Take the boat back, Donnie," he said softly, gazing westward towards the setting sun. "And bring some rope to the top of the cliff. We can hoist it up from there."

"Doesn't it make more sense to ferry it to Tongue?"

"No, that wouldn't be sensible." Malcolm smiled across at Donald and sighed. "This is a cargo best not observed together."

Donald pushed the boat once more out to the water, and Malcolm watched as Le Duc d'Anjou sailed out to sea before it turned westward into what remained of the setting sun. It was a strange feeling, to be offered the chance of a new life away from the war, the Stuarts and even Scotland, and he questioned as the minutes turned to hours, whether this new life might be what he was looking for.

Donald wasted no time but, the moment that the boat was ashore, he rushed into the forge to tell the men. He also enquired as to where he might purchase a goodly length of rope. He was surprised to find they found him some but insisted on no payment. In good conscience Donnie could not allow this and so left all the coin he had with him to the old men. He rushed along the top of the hillside until he reached James, Robert and William who were standing on the cliff above where Malcolm stood.

"Clattering through the undergrowth once more, Oaf," William laughed as he turned, long before James or Robert had heard him.

"Enough, William," James rebuked. "That's quite a length of rope, Donnie. Will it suffice?"

"How do you lift this?" Robert asked as Donald dropped the rope to the ground. "Much less carry it?"

"It doesn't seem too heavy," Donnie whispered, smiling in an awkward way at this compliment. "Malcolm wants us to raise the cargo one chest at a time. Is that what you think?" he asked looking at James.

"Yes," Jamie announced with a confident air which belied how he really felt. "Robert and I will go down and help him."

They measured out the rope, which was only just long enough to use.

"Do you think it will hold us?" Robert asked, trying to hide the nerves in his voice

"I'll go first," James said softly, placing his hand on Robert's arm to reassure him. "Then we will find out."

"No, Caledon," the young man answered, disgusted at himself for allowing James to suggest such a thing. "I shall go first."

Without giving James a chance to argue he tied the cord about his waist holding both the loose end and the longer section of the rope. He waited as

Donnie wrapped the other end around his body to take the strain. Taking a handful of the dry soil from the cliff top he rubbed it into his hands to increase his hold on the rope. James and William watched anxiously from the top, as Malcolm did below, while Donald gently lowered Robert down. To ensure there was enough rope he had to step to the edge of the cliff before he heard Robert's voice call up.

"I've reached the bottom. Haul it up, Donnie."

Donnie, once more, did as he was told and easily pulled the coil of rope to the top.

"My turn, now," James said jovially, wrapping the cord about him as Robert had done earlier.

"Be careful, Jamie," Donald said quickly, and with such intent that James frowned slightly. "Something-"

"What?" James asked, glancing at William before turning back to Donnie.

"I don't trust myself," Donald whispered. "I don't know why."

"I know why, Donnie," James responded. "But it is nearly a month since. I'll speak to you when I return."

"What?" Donald muttered, failing to understand what James was talking about.

"Just lower me down," James said firmly. Without waiting for Donald to tell him he was ready, he walked to the edge of the cliff and stepped over, so Donnie had to heave on the rope to hold it steady.

William watched with an anxiety which was shared by the two cousins as Donnie continued to lower James down. As the giant man walked to the edge of the cliff the rope slipped from his hands and snaked through his grasp, so William had to throw himself at the tail of the rope to catch it before it spun over.

"Are you safe?" William shouted down.

"But for a few cuts and bruises," James shouted back with more anger than hurt. "But you can tell Donald Mackenzie I will not forget this."

William turned to look at Donnie whose heavy chest rose and fell much faster than normal. He was seated on the ground close to the edge of the cliff, panting for breath and staring at his hands which he continued to tense.

"Donald?" William asked softly, and Donnie blinked in surprise to hear his name.

"Now I deserve the title 'oaf' and now you use my name."

"What happened?"

"I don't know," he said firmly, daring William to challenge him.

They did not speak anymore, but Donnie took the rope from William and pulled up each of the eight chests with an ease which belied his earlier mistake. But he could not shake the fear he felt as he considered the way in which he had lost all the strength in his broad body. It had been as though each muscle had, as one, ceased working. Still, as he hauled the eight chests over the top of the cliff, he congratulated himself on doing so. He lowered the rope once more and hoisted Malcolm, who was certainly the heaviest of the three men, safely onto the clifftop. He returned it once more and waited until Robert called up that he was ready. Being the slightest of the three men this was an easy task and Donnie heaved the rope up once more. Malcolm and William were standing by the chests talking in hushed voices. Both turned at Donald's frenzied shout.

"Take the rope!"

William took one glance at Donnie before he ran forward and snatched the cord which burnt his hands as it slipped through them. Malcolm was only a second behind, and he grabbed the end of the rope from Donnie, sliding towards the edge of the cliff as Robert clung on to the other end. The cord, which had rocked and twisted in their hands, went terribly still and James' voice called up.

"Donald Mackenzie, what have you done?"

William and Malcolm peered over the edge of the cliff, the former standing whilst the latter was laid on his front. In the presence of the new moon it was almost impossible for Malcolm to see what was happening, but William lifted his hand to his mouth as his sharp gaze rested on Robert MacBeath who lay unconscious in Jamie's arms.

"Look after him," William ordered Malcolm, pointing over his shoulder to where he assumed Donald would be, before he struggled down the cliff face. His knowledge of such surfaces, though, was restricted and it took him countless minutes before he reached the bottom.

"Is he alive?" William panted as he placed his trembling fingers on Robert's bloody forehead.

"Yes. But he struck the cliff so many times on the way down I don't understand how he is. What happened?"

"I can't tell you. I think Donnie is sick."

"He'd better find a good excuse by the time I reach him. Robert followed me, William, I can't let him die."

"He won't die, but he needs to get away from here. Somewhere warm."

"Caledon?" Robert muttered and James leaned over him, taking the boy's rope-burnt hand in his own. "Is Malcolm safe?"

"He is," James whispered as he kissed the boy's hand and watched as he slipped once more from consciousness.

The Truth Revealed

Malcolm had done as William had asked him and rushed over to the man whose catastrophic error had left Robert immobile. But Donald Mackenzie had no wish for comfort or assistance. Instead, trembling like a newborn lamb, he had pushed himself to his feet and walked away.

As the sun was rising, William clawed his way up to the top of the cliff, and he and Malcolm began hoisting up the young man who lay in a sling formed from his philamor. Seeing this, Donald had walked the short distance over to them and begun helping, making the load much easier. As they lowered Robert to the ground Donald and Malcolm stared down at the blackened and bloodied face of the young man. Donnie felt a well of guilt open beneath him.

"This is my fault," he whispered hoarsely, while Malcolm wrapped the voluminous garment about his friend.

"We all knew the dangers, Oaf," William muttered, tossing the cord down once more before

Donald heaved his cousin over the cliff edge, wishing almost at once that he had not done.

"What have you done?" James demanded, pushing Donald backward. William and Malcolm watched on silently, but neither of the cousins even acknowledged them. "Have you seen him?"

"Yes," Donnie replied firmly, taking in, too, a cut down his cousin's cheek which he was also responsible for. "I didn't mean to."

"Would it help if I said I was sorry?" James' voice made the question into a torment. "I couldn't help what happened at the wedding."

"The wedding?" Donald whispered, shaking his head slightly.

"With Annie. Must you take your jealous rage out on my clan?"

William and Malcolm exchanged the briefest of glances before Malcolm rushed over, but he was too late to pacify the giant man who lashed out as his cousin, catching him across the jaw.

"I hope you meant what happened," Donnie hissed. "For if you're unfaithful to her I will not follow you, even if you were God himself. That is not what this is about."

"Then why else did you nearly kill Robert?" James spat out a mouthful of blood from where he had bit through his tongue. "What else have I done to anger you?"

"All my life I have admired you," Donnie whispered, tears burning at his eyes as Malcolm pulled him gently away. "I've followed you around these forsaken hills, believing you could be what you promised to be."

"Then what happened?" James asked softly, overcome and uncertain by this sudden display of loyalty.

"I don't know. It was as though I could no longer make my hands, my arms, my legs do what I wanted. Like there was no strength to me anymore."

"My Strength failed," Jamie whispered, taking his younger cousin's arms and looking into his eyes. "What have I done? I didn't mean you any harm."

"What is it?" Malcolm asked. "What does it mean?"

"I don't know. I was warned, but I didn't heed the consequences." James leaned forward and kissed Donald's forehead. "I'll find a solution, Donnie."

Donald's eyes never spilt a tear, but he nodded submissively and took in a ragged breath as he watched James and Malcolm walk over to the boy he had left unconscious. William's shrewd gaze took in all that was happening as he knelt by Robert's side.

"What is in these chests?" he asked as he wiped the blood from Robert's forehead and ear. "Is it worth the life of our young friend?"

"Some people would say so," Malcolm replied. "But for me? No. A man's life is worth more than gold."

"Gold?" Donnie coughed on the word as he walked over to them. "No wonder it was so heavy. What are we doing with gold? Are we robbers now?"

"No," Malcolm said quickly. "You don't have to steal this gold." He hurriedly began building a fire which Donnie lit with a tinderbox after several attempts.

"Whose gold is it?" William asked.

"Mine," Malcolm replied, dragging his friend's litter closer to the flames so he might be kept warm.

"I'm sorry, but I haven't been entirely honest with you all."

James blinked in surprise as he heard the waterfall's voice cautioning him with almost those exact words. "Then who are you really, Malcolm Murray?"

"I'm the son of General George Murray, Lord of Atholl. And Robert MacBeath is my mother's son."

"You're brothers?" William asked in disbelief.

"Half brothers, yes. For I'm a bastard son and Robert is not. We have the same mother but different fathers. He didn't know, but I made him my sergeant for that reason alone. But he has our mother's passion and fights with an unrivalled zeal."

"Zeal?" James repeated, once more hearing the voice of the waterfall.

"Yes. His sisters, our mother, were all slaughtered by those men we were tracking when our paths collided with yours. We were to join with the ship Le Duc D'Anjou here in Tongue for my father, who saw all eventualities, wished to ensure I could journey to France and safety. The Prince's cause was lost. So, we chased those men north and resolved that, once we had killed them, we would meet the ship."

"Why did you change your mind?" James asked.

"I'm not sure I did."

"Then you mean to leave for France?" William questioned.

"I joined your war, Caledon, for it is a war worth fighting. But when the ship returns, I am unsure I'll be able to remain here. I want you to take the gold. I have no need of it, but you will need to fund your cause."

"That's not how it works, Malcolm," Jamie said softly. "What good would money do us? We have to look to the generosity and kindness of the people of Caledon. We can't simply walk into taverns and spend gold coins. We're outlaws and will continue to be with or without eight chests of gold. I understand why you wish to leave but consider this: without your commitment to the cause of Caledon, your gold is of no use to us."

"Where does this gold come from?" William asked softly.

"The French reserve. It is the second shipment of French gold my father called for. The first was lost at Arkaig. The ship came under fire and, without offloading all the money, sailed out to sea once more. Archie Cameron, he knew where it was hidden, but I don't know what became of him. I suspect the gold is sitting there still."

"Then that is what we do," James announced with a smile. "As soon as Robert is able, we shall journey south to Arkaig and seek out the French gold. And we shall leave a coin to every inhabitant of every village we journey through. That money was meant for Scotland. Let the people of Caledon use it."

"Very well, Caledon," William said, a slight smile catching his lips.

"That is noble of you, Caledon," Malcolm whispered. "I can think of no finer use."

"Donnie?" James asked, turning to his younger cousin and feeling that, after his misunderstanding of the man earlier, he sought for Donald Mackenzie's approval.

"I'll follow you anywhere, Jamie Caledon."

Robert MacBeath drifted in and out of consciousness until evening. Feeling singlehandedly responsible for his situation, but failing to understand why, Donald bound all his numerous wounds. In addition to his head injuries, his right arm had been completely skinned from shoulder to wrist from sliding down the cliff face and his right leg was grazed and bruised.

"Malcolm?" Robert whispered, reaching his left hand out to Donald.

"No, Robert. I'm Donald Mackenzie." He took the boy's outstretched hand. "You're going to be fine. Just lie still."

"I'm so cold," he muttered. "Did we find them, Malcolm?"

"I'm not Malcolm," Donnie repeated, but it was no use for Robert could not hear him.

"I don't want to leave."

"You don't have to," Donnie said flatly as he tipped William's flask onto a rag James acquired from a nearby house, arguing that if these people would not help Caledon, Caledon would not survive to help them. "You're welcome to stay, Robert."

"Do you remember Ruthven Barracks? Your father?" He pulled away as Donald dabbed the alcohol down his arm. "Was he right?"

"Lord George Murray has an unmatched reputation for always being right." In the absence of anything better Donald had removed his own shirt and torn it into several strips which he proceeded to firmly tie around the boy's arm.

Robert had once more slipped from consciousness but that evening he was able to sit up, supported by his half-brother and, though he contributed nothing to the conversation, he smiled across at each one of them as they spoke. William informed them of the easiest route to Arkaig and suggested they left at once if they were to have any chance of reaching the gold before the ship arrived.

"Robert can't make the journey as he is," William said flatly, bringing the gaze of his four companions down upon him. "There are parts of this journey which will take us along mountain sides where I would not trust his agility."

Robert turned to him and smiled across sleepily before James muttered, "He can't hear us."

Donald dropped his head into his hand and felt the guilt at bringing this down upon the young man. Robert turned at this movement and reached his bandaged right hand across to Donnie in what was meant to be a consoling gesture, but the other man did not lift his head.

"Robert," James said clearly, lifting his hand to catch the attention of the wounded man. "I need you to stay here and guard the gold." He was met once more by the same neutral smile.

"He can't stay alone," Malcolm whispered.

"Nor will he," James said, in a tone suggesting there was no way he would change his mind. "Donnie will stay with him."

"What?" Donald hissed as he lifted his gaze and glanced across at his cousin before looking at Robert's widened eyes. "Why can't I go with you?"

"You're not strong enough, Donnie. I can't trust you not to repeat your actions of last night."

Donnie offered no other response but rose to his feet and walked away. Jamie watched him go with a burden of responsibility. Until last night there had been no one he trusted more than his cousin, but the devastating injuries he had inflicted on Robert made this difficult decision the only logical solution. James had a responsibility to the people of Caledon and could no longer prioritise his cousin's emotions.

The following day, James, William and Malcolm all readied their few possessions and began journeying south. Donald did not volunteer a word to any of them beyond wishing them good luck. James met his cousin's shallow smile with a heavy heart.

"I understand," Donnie said softly. "You don't have to explain your decision."

"I will sort this for you, Donnie. I'll find how to cure it."

"Just know that I would have followed you."

James smiled and nodded. He and William waited as Malcolm and Robert parted from one another.

"Was your father right?" Robert asked as he looked across at Malcolm. "Are we really brothers?"

Malcolm nodded slightly. "And now I am going to find him. He knew to wait for the ship on the west, but I will not go to France without you."

"France?" Robert whispered, trying to follow what his brother said without being able to hear his words.

"I'm torn, Robert. But in leaving the French gold I hope I'm doing right by Caledon. Look after Donald Mackenzie. I'm afraid he'll need more help than you."

The two embraced one another before Malcolm turned to William and James, and the company divided, parting with more questions and sorrow than James would have believed possible.

Visitors on All Hallow's Eve

September drew to a dreary close and October arrived with rain and wind, so any hope Donald Mackenzie and Robert MacBeath had of remaining outside as they waited for their friends faded quickly. They were sleeping in a farmer's byre with two cattle. Robert assisted with any job which he could manage for their hosts, who were an old couple called Gow. He fed the animals and harvested the crops which still needed to be brought in. Donald helped with the heavy work, handling the cows, herding the nine sheep and repairing the farmstead in time for the onset of winter. Both of them were recovering from the incident on the cliff. Robert had removed the strips of bandaging and, though he could not bear to sleep on his right side anymore, he never complained but attacked his duty with the zeal with which he had been blessed. Occasionally Donald would lose the strength in his body and limbs, but he did not speak of it and ensured, since he could never predict when this strange weakness would take him, he worked alone as often as he could so he would not injure anybody.

"Why did I imagine valour when I followed Jamie?" Donnie sighed as he looked down at the bucket into which he tipped a shovel of cow dung.

"Caledon is a noble cause," Robert replied, stepping into the byre. He smiled across as Donald turned a surprised face towards him. "I'm not completely deaf."

"I thought you were."

"I think I was," Robert laughed and placed his hand over his left ear. "But it's only my right ear I can't hear anything in, now."

"How long have you known?"

"A few days. But I've enjoyed listening to your comments, I hadn't got the heart to interrupt you. But Caledon is a cause worth fighting for."

"I've followed James Og everywhere. I trusted him, for he's never failed me. But now he's lost faith in me, I feel like I've lost faith in myself, too."

There was no response to this statement and Donald continued to clean the byre while Robert teased hay into the iron grates on the wall. It was the end of October, the days were becoming shorter and the beasts now only walked out for two hours in the midday sun, which was barely visible through grey cloud and high hills.

"It's an unholy night," Robert remarked as the two of them sat upon the straw at the end of the byre. "The devil prowls, they say."

"Who says?" Donald hugged his arms around him, trying to stay warm. He had been given one of Mr Gow's shirts and it barely fitted him.

"Everyone. It is a night to sleep early so that you awake to All Saints in the morning."

"The devil prowls these lands every night. It's our duty to always repel him."

Robert only laughed slightly as he pulled his philamor about him and turned away from Donnie to try and settle to sleep. Sleep was a long time coming to Donald as he stared at the timbers which supported the slates of the roof he had repaired some weeks before. Was there any truth to the young man's words? For surely, as he lay there, Donald thought he could hear voices. They were women's voices and one, he was sure, was his sister's soft tone.

"He's so handsome," one said softly, and Donald sat up quickly and looked about him at the darkness as he felt a hand stroke his cheek. One of the cattle lifted its head and gave a sleepy snort, but otherwise the byre was still.

"I don't want any harm to come to him," his sister's voice said firmly.

"It is not I who drains life from him each time I consider him," the first stated, and Donnie looked down at his hand as he felt someone take it. "I'm anxious to meet him."

"His heart is no longer his own," a third voice announced, and Donald gasped as he felt a hand on his chest. "He has given it away, so he cannot give it to you."

"Annie," Mary whispered. "After all the care and devotion he has paid her, she returns it with disloyalty. She can't view him as anything but a younger brother."

"There is something strange about Donald Mackenzie," the third voice said softly, concern seeping into its tone. "A troublesome future."

"I know he will help me," Mary said firmly.

"I see your daughter born without an uncle."

"Save your predictions," Mary said angrily. "Donald would never abandon me."

"*He* abandon *you*?"

"I see," Mary muttered.

"Mary?" Donald asked into the darkness, unable to continue listening to this confusing conversation to which he seemed to be central.

"How did he shield himself?" the first voice asked, and at once he felt a hand on his cheek once more.

"A troublesome future," the third voice repeated, and Donald gave a slight cough as he felt again the debilitating weakness seize his body. He shivered as the cold penetrated each of his weakened limbs. The hand on his cheek disappeared and all the voices ceased. He was once more alone in the byre with only the cattle and his sleeping friend. The warmth of his strength returned a little, seeping into him as though he was thawing out. Lying back, he stared up at the flags and tried to make sense of what he had heard whilst simultaneously trying to convince himself it was tiredness and Robert's words which had left him so concerned. He listened to the wind as it crept under the overhanging flagstones and made strange calls as it brushed over the farm equipment outside. It was this strange lullaby of an unholy night which sang him to sleep.

"Look what they did," Mary said angrily. Donnie realised, even within his dream, that he had seen this conversation before. It had been many years ago, when Mary had been only ten, but in his dream she stood before him as radiant and beautiful as he had seen her only three months ago.

"What who did?" he whispered.

"Those crows."

Donald looked into her arms and felt disgusted as he saw a lamb with blood spilling down its face from where the crows had taken its eyes. It bleated and wriggled in his sister's arms and she sat down on the floor with it. Kneeling down, Donnie stroked its soft woolly coat.

"They are monsters," Mary continued.

"Why do they do it?"

"They single out the weakest and gentlest. Then they blind them so they can't find the rest of the flock."

"Won't the flock come looking for them?"

"Not after this. They know the lamb will die."
She looked up and met her brother's gaze. "Once
the crows have started their business, no one is
interested in saving them. And the crows will stop at
nothing to fill their stomachs."

Donnie recalled with a sickening remembrance
what the outcome had been for the young lamb so
many years ago, for he and his sister had been
unable to save it and the crows had returned some
days later. He rose to his feet and lifted his hand to
his black hair as he felt something heavy fall on his
head. He gave a cry as his fingers closed on the
silky feathers of a bird, and he realised with a
horrible sickening feeling that it was a crow. His
dream had shifted now, and the lamb was no longer
there. Mary stared across at him, repeatedly crying,

"I don't want any harm to come to him."

There were two other women standing on either
side of him and both of them watched as a second
crow flew straight at his face. He threw his arms up
to try and shield his eyes but as his gaze rested upon
the black sphere of the crow's eye, which he was
quite certain would be the last thing he would ever

see, he jumped awake and found himself back in the byre.

"Donald?" Robert said softly, placing his hand gently on Donnie's shoulder. "You are safe here."

Donnie could not stop shaking, nor did he cease rubbing his hands over his eyes to ensure they were still there.

"I've never seen anyone thrash about so much in their sleep," Robert continued jovially.

"There were crows," Donnie whispered. "I was reminded of why I hate them so much."

"It's the night, that's all." Robert lay back once more. "It plays cruel tricks on you."

Donnie nodded and looked around him, eager to see everything and frightened he should ever fall victim to this fear which had been reawakened in him. He tried to look at all his surroundings, as he contemplated both his dream and the voices he had heard before sleep took him. Failing to return to sleep again he sought the answer to both conundrums. He decided the only sensible conclusion was that Robert's words had stirred a fear within him and it was his tiredness which had given him such an unsettled night.

What the Treasure Cost

The three remaining members of Caledon's clan had travelled with great purpose at the beginning of their journey, but upon reaching Assynt their advantage quickly turned against them. They had used the tall mountains of the western highlands to conceal themselves from anyone who might be scouring the landscape for the fleeing Jacobite army. But as they arrived in Assynt it was to blizzards on the mountaintops and their progress declined rapidly. Arkaig began to feel like an unreachable dream and they each began to lament its distance as they huddled into a sheiling.

"What is it that ails Donald?" Malcolm asked, his teeth chattering as he spoke.

"I don't know," James muttered. "But I do know I shouldn't have taken him to the wedding. I was warned that Caledon's strength would fail. I thought it meant me, my own strength. But Donnie is Caledon's Strength as Robert is Caledon's Zeal."

"I don't wish to question you, Caledon," William said, as he pulled his coat about him. "But who tells you these things?"

"I'm not sure you would believe me if I told you," James laughed. "I'm not sure I believe it myself."

William smiled and nodded. "Then perhaps it's better not to tell us."

"One day I'll take you there, to the source, and you'll see what I mean."

The journey, which should have taken them a little over a week, stretched out before them and it was not until the end of October that they looked down on Loch Arkaig. With a sinking realisation, they noticed someone was already there. Amongst the stunted birches and the dying ferns there was a group of four men busily digging in the wet soil.

"Who are they?" William asked as the three of them crouched down, hiding in the bracken.

"They are not in the clad of Highlanders, nor Hanoverians," James muttered.

"They are treasure hunters then," Malcolm said quickly. "Since Archie Cameron first spoke of this wealth many have tried to discover it."

"Are they looking in the right place?" William asked.

"No."

"Then you know where it was buried?" James whispered.

"Yes. There was a reason Cameron spoke of the money. He was responsible for its concealment and instructed one of his men to hide it at Arkaig. But Arkaig is not just the loch. At Kinlocharkaig there is a river which flows north a short way. It is buried there, at the river's source."

"Then we should keep journeying west," James said softly.

Both nodded and the three of them, leaning down to avoid being seen, continued towards the location of the treasure. James glanced back over his shoulder to ensure they had not been seen, but the men in the distance continued to shovel the silt while one of them stared down at a paper which James assumed was a map. He stumbled backward as he collided with Malcolm who had stopped abruptly and, as James looked forward, he realised why.

William stood before a giant of a man who gripped the Hanoverian's throat easily in one hand. The assailant towered over them, true hatred burning in the dark circles of his eyes, and a sneer of disgust plastered on his lower face. William tried to reach the knife which hung at his waist, but James stepped forward and pushed William's hand away.

"Release him," he said firmly. "We have no quarrel with you."

"*You* may not," William coughed, as the man relinquished his hold. "But *I* do."

"Enough," James snapped.

"Who are you?" the man demanded, pointing a pistol at William.

"I am Caledon, and these are my men."

"Caledon?" His voice was now little more than a whisper. "What trickery do you hope to achieve? He is a Hanoverian. That is not the wish of Caledon."

"Then you are a Jacobite?" James asked softly. "So was I. So was he," he added, pointing back to Malcolm. "But Caledon does not differentiate for kings and politics. The men and women of Caledon are born to their title. They are chosen, they do not choose."

James gave a despondent sigh as he realised the group of men they had seen digging were rushing over. Malcolm lowered his face slightly and William shook his head, staring at the pistol which never moved away from his chest.

"Who are you?" demanded the man with the map as he reached them. "Did Lochiel send you?"

"No one sent us," James replied softly. "We move through this land without command, for this is our land."

"I know you," the man said, pointing across at Malcolm. "You're a Murray, aren't you? Son of that man who felt he could choose when our cause had ended."

"My father was Lord George Murray," Malcolm replied neutrally.

"Our cause is beyond Drumossie," James said angrily. "If you fought there, you'd be best to let us move on."

"He claims he's Caledon," the giant man said softly. "But Caledon would not keep company with such men."

At these words the newcomer's eyes rested upon William for the first time and, before anyone else could speak, he snatched a shovel from one of his workers and struck it across William's chest, causing him to collapse to the floor.

"Tie their hands and bring them back to the house," he continued, throwing the shovel down on William's crumpled form. "I don't trust Murray on account of his father, him for his ludicrous claims, and him," he kicked William's side. "No Hanoverian will be left alive at my hand."

"He is a loyal son of Caledon." James felt his hand clench into a fist, and he struck the giant man across the face as he tried to bind his hands.

"Enough!" shouted their leader and Malcolm looked about the glen, anxious of the forces who might overhear such an eruption of anger. The man drew his own gun and pointed it at Malcolm. "Come peaceably or I'll kill both your sons, Caledon."

The scathing tone of his voice bit deep into James' heart but he reluctantly offered his wrists to be bound, trusting the man before him meant every word he spoke regarding the deaths of his friends. Malcolm, no doubt with similar thoughts running through his head, submissively watched as thin cord was wrapped tightly about his wrists. William's wrists were tied so tightly his hands turned white and while James and Malcolm were escorted in the body of the small troop, William was dragged behind. Every time James turned back to look at him, he had his face lifted and a continued expression of pride filled his features. It was a pride in Caledon, James realised, and his mind raced as he tried to form a plan to free his friend from the blind malice their captor harboured for him.

They were guided to a small hut which joined onto the only house of Kinlocharkaig and all three of them looked longingly westward, knowing how close they were to the treasure and how ignorant their captors were of this fact. Malcolm and James were pushed into the dark building and James felt his stomach turn as he considered why William was not. The door was closed, and they were plunged into darkness.

"We have to help William," James hissed, trying to slip the bonds from his wrist. "These people are so foolish they will not see beyond their old battles."

"They were bloody battles, Caledon. When they see a Redcoat, they can't help but see the enemy."

"Then they're blind as well as foolish. My sgian dhu is at my waist. If you hold it, I should be able to cut this cord. It's only thin."

They both turned as a wave of light filled the building and, without offering any words, the tall man grabbed James' tether and pulled him from the room, leaving Malcolm alone once more in the darkness. The giant did not relinquish James until he stood inside the living quarters of the house, before the man he had encountered outside.

"Tell me, Caledon," the man began in the same cutting voice. "What are you doing in these parts? Are you a Cameron?"

"No," James said flatly. "But before you hear my name, I want to know yours. And I want to know what has become of my friend."

"He was your son before." Silence clung to the room and the man sat down in a chair as though it were a throne and he the king. "My name is Bruce Urquhart."

"I am James Og. A Mackenzie. But I carry the quest of Caledon, and it's for this fact alone I and my men were travelling through this area."

"Coincidence that Murray's son arrives in Arkaig?" Urquhart laughed. "No, I don't think so. You're here for the treasure, the same as I. And after spilling our blood at Drumossie we deserve it, don't we?"

"Where's my man?" James asked, ignoring the man's words.

"The German supporter? The man who stood against all which was good for Caledon, who you claim to be? We found him guilty of butchery, same as his lordly leader."

"You're not a judge. Caledon doesn't care for sides in this war but for the people who fought it. There are forces far worse than the German king to contend with, and I need my men to fight them."

"That's unfortunate. The traitor will be at the bottom of the loch by now. Let's see."

He rose from the chair and pulled open the door. James' gaze rested on three men who were loading a small raft with heavy stones and piling them about the unconscious figure of William.

"You fool," James hissed, gripping the hilt of the small knife in his hands and swinging a two-handed blow at Urquhart's face, slicing his cheek and causing him to recoil. "You blind fool. I told you who I was, I gave you the chance to help, and instead you try to kill my men." Placing his tethered hands, which still carried the knife, about his captor's neck he continued. "Either untie these bonds now, or they will strangle you." He pulled his hands back to reiterate his words.

With an angry growl the man fumbled with the knot while James left the knife resting against his chest. When he was freed, James struck him across the head, knocking him out, before he ran to the side of the house and kicked open the door to the hut. Malcolm rose quickly to his feet and James wasted no time in cutting the cord at his wrists.

"Where's William?" Malcolm asked quickly.

"Hopefully not over the loch for neither you nor I can swim. They plan to drown him."

The two of them rushed to the front of the house and James shook his head, realising that the raft he had seen some minutes earlier was no longer visible. The three men stood pointing out into the loch and laughing as though they were watching a sport rather than an execution. Both Malcolm and James ran towards the water, Malcolm trying to fight back the three men, who were all unarmed, while the strong, heavy giant returned from the loch after pushing the raft out.

"What have you done?" James demanded, striking him once more across the face. "You have tried to execute a son of Caledon."

"You are not Caledon," the man replied, snatching James' throat as he had done earlier to William.

There was a change then, subtle to observe, and James felt at once a part of the land he stood on. It was as though, through it, a great power surged. He gripped the man's arms with both hands and stared into his eyes with such vehemence the giant became unnerved and let go of his throat. They were being watched, James realised, and he turned to the four pairs of awestruck eyes as the tall man disappeared from view, dragged into Loch Arkaig by the very power he had felt.

"He is Caledon," one of the men muttered, but James scarcely heard as he splashed into the water. The raft had not travelled far out into the loch but, as the water reached his chest, he realised he would not be able to walk out to the place where he could find his friend. Taking a deep breath, he plunged his head under the water and tried to stare into the loch, but it was murky and dark. He pulled his head up once more as he felt a hand on his shoulder and turned to see one of the men pushing past him and swimming out into the loch. James stood, only his head and shoulders above the water and waited as the man returned with William's body, which he carried back to the shore.

"William?" Malcolm muttered, kneeling beside him. James splashed out of the water and took William's trembling hands. The cords which had been tied about him, dragging him down to the loch's floor, were all severed. James removed them one by one.

"Caledon?" William muttered, spitting out putrid water. "That was an experience I don't want to repeat."

"Nor will you," Malcolm assured him, helping him to sit up. "How did you cut the cords? You should have drowned."

"Sorry to disappoint you," he laughed weakly, leaning heavily on Malcolm's arm.

With a relief beyond anything James had ever felt, he returned to the house where he tethered Bruce Urquhart and placed him in his own black prison.

Malcolm and James guided the other three men to the site of the treasure. It was not easy to dig, for it had been hidden beneath rocks as well as the poor soil, and the torrents of rain which moved in from the west made the terrain slippery and uneven.

Having dug it up, he bestowed one of the chests on the three men who had unearthed it, before he and Malcolm dragged the other seven back to Kinlocharkaig. William, who had slept by the fire in the house for the remainder of the day, felt his eyes sparkle as he beheld the treasure which had almost cost him his life.

"Are we to journey north once more?"

"There is something I must do first," Malcolm muttered, and James nodded slightly, sensing that here lay the first breaking of his clan after only months.

The following day they loaded the chests onto a small hand cart Urquhart had left at the farm for this exact purpose. Following Malcolm's directions, they journeyed out to the west. It took them several weeks, hiding from the sporadic troops of men, and being forced to follow paths and passes they could take the cart through. True to their word, a coin was left at every household they passed, and more given to the people who were willing to help. When they reached the concealed bay at Arisaig it was to find Le Duc D'Anjou anchored there, and almost at once a small rowing vessel was lowered.

"They were waiting for us," William whispered as he and James watched Malcolm walk the short way down to the shoreline. They looked in silence as the once great Lord George Murray climbed from the boat and greeted his son, but they were unable to hear the conversation for the distance was too great. After a time, the two Murrays turned to James and William, and they watched as George Murray embraced his son before returning to the rowing boat and out to the French ship once more. Malcolm remained on the shale beach, watching as his father sailed out to the open sea and on to the continent, now the only safe destination for the exiled Scots. Finally, he turned to his two friends and walked over.

"My father is bound for France. And December! What a cruel time to travel."

"Why didn't you join him?" William asked, but James only smiled as he looked down at the beach where a great stag tentatively walked down to the water. Its roving eyes caught his own and he placed a hand on Malcolm's shoulder. This movement caused the animal to bolt as though it could feel the weight of his gesture.

"Nobility," he muttered before he continued with certainty. "You are Caledon's Nobility."

Part Five:
The Eile

Sharing a Burden and Discovering a Truth

January had seized the Scottish Highlands in its cold grasp by the time James, William and Malcolm returned to Tongue. The mountain passes had become impossible to cross and they had been forced to follow the coast, only increasing their chance of being caught. On four occasions they had been forced to combat government troops and on a further occasion, as they negotiated the cliffs north of Loch Ailsh, they were ambushed by bandits. But with each of these skirmishes, Caledon's legend only grew stronger and stronger so that, when they finally rejoined Robert and Donald, news of the great deeds of this mythical band had already reached them.

As they waded through the icy waters of the kyle, and on to the shore at Tongue, Robert MacBeath was there awaiting their arrival. There was no trace now of the injury he had borne in the September before. His pale features lit up to see the three men and he rushed down to meet them.

"Caledon!" he exclaimed. "We have heard great tales even in this corner of the land. A man who fights beside both Jacobite and Redcoat, and leaves a token of his love for his people."

"Was that us?" James asked as he looked from Malcolm to William.

"I don't think so," William replied seriously.

"Malcolm," Robert said softly, ignoring the teasing of the other two men, tilting his head slightly as he tried to make out their words. "Did you see your father?"

"Indeed," Malcolm's English accent announced. "He will be in France now."

"But you did not join him?"

"No. Our cause is beyond Drumossie," he said, glancing quickly at James and smiling. "But you are hearing what we say, Robert. I thought you'd never hear again."

"I can hear on my left. But not the right."

"Thank God you're well," James replied with great honesty. "Where is Donnie?"

"He's at the house," Robert said softly, and the sudden drain of enthusiasm in his voice was noted by all three.

"What is it?" William asked, glancing across at James whose expression was set but scarcely hid his concern. "How is the oaf?"

"Fine," Robert said flatly. "He's fine."

"Take me to him," James said, snatching Robert's arm and the young man nodded and walked onward. Neither William nor Malcolm followed, each perceiving they did not have a place in this initial conversation between the cousins.

"I've been sorry to have missed the adventures of which I've heard tell."

"You were with us, Robert. You are Caledon's Zeal and you alone inspired such passion in our beliefs. William almost drowned," James added, muttering these final words. "We number six for a reason. I've learnt that. Next time we go together."

"I couldn't have gone with you this time," Robert said softly. "And Donnie is a liability."

"What do you mean?"

"You'll see."

Robert walked on in silence and James followed him in a similar fashion, anxious about what he should find upon arriving at the house. It was a solid stone structure and smoke billowed from a roof hatch in a welcoming fashion. For the first time since he had been greeted by Robert, James realised how cold he was, and he felt an air of disappointment when Robert led him to the byre at the end of the house.

"Donnie!" the young man called out and James tried to encourage his eyes to focus in the dark room. The two cows, each tethered to hooks on the wall, turned to face him and one gave a long, low bellow.

"Jamie?" questioned a voice from behind him, and James spun to face his younger cousin, who he had never been more pleased to see. "I'd almost given you up. You're soaked. Here," he pulled the woollen coat he wore from his shoulders and placed it on his cousin before he had a chance to argue.

"Thank you," James whispered, and glanced at Robert who announced that he was going to fetch the others.

"Were you successful?" Donnie continued, ushering James further into the byre where it was warmer.

"Yes. We got the gold. And Malcolm decided to stay. We're still a complete clan, and I've just about established our roles. Robert is Zeal, Malcolm is Nobility, Annie is Wisdom and you are Strength."

Donald laughed slightly. "With me as Strength, Caledon is perilously weak. What of your role? And William?"

"What do you mean 'Caledon is perilously weak'? You seem in good health, Donnie."

"I am. But at times I still find myself drained. It's the strangest thing. There's no warning, I just lose my grip on whatever I'm holding, or need to support myself." He sat down in the straw which had been his bed and James sat beside him. "And I keep dreaming of a lamb."

"A lamb?" James asked, trying to recall whether the waterfall had spoken of such a thing, but sure it had not.

"It's a memory. When I was a child Mary found a lamb who had been attacked by crows, and had lost its eyes."

"What happened to it?"

"Father made us return it to the rest of the flock, then the crows would not attack another while they could eat it. They ripped it to pieces. But," Donald shook his head, thinking better of what he was about to say. "I hate crows."

"I remember," James replied with a soft smile. "It's just a dream, or a memory."

Donald nodded and gave half a smile but offered no further conversation. He introduced the three companions to their host and when Robert announced that James was Caledon the old man's eyes lit up.

"When I was a boy I knew of you," he announced as they sat around the kitchen table, huddling close to one another to find space and warmth. "Zeal, he was, the last of that clan. He was an old man, and I little more than a babe, but I remember his eyes especially."

"Robert is Zeal," James announced with surety.

"But you number only five."

"Our sixth is waiting in Lairg," James replied. "Tomorrow we'll leave you in peace and return to her."

Donald felt a bitter smile cross his face, eager to see Annie once more, but the words he had imagined his sister speaking on Hallowe'en still burnt his heart. He had spoken to no one of that peculiar conversation, wishing to explain it as the product of tiredness and fretful thoughts.

That evening Mr Gow, whose first name they never discovered, spoke long with William about how best to return to Lairg.

"Then you are Stealth," the old man remarked after a time.

"Am I?"

"Yes, and by your eyes you've already discovered that."

"What do you mean?" William asked, his usual cynicism replaced by curiosity.

"You have met your Eile, for your eyes are like his."

"My Eile? My other?"

"I've seen your eyes staring down from trees at me. Or glaring at me from beyond the chicken house. You have the eyes of the marten, the Eile of Stealth."

"I have seen a marten. I thought it was a dream."

"You are a son of Caledon. Nothing will happen to you now without it having a significance."

"I was dying, drowning, and it swam out and chewed through each of my tethers. I didn't even know they could swim."

"You will find out much about them, and yourself through them. All three of you have met your Eile, but I've not seen it in the other two. But Malcolm has the eyes of the mighty stag and Caledon has the strong set gaze of Power."

"How do you know so much of Caledon?"

"Zeal, who Robert is now to replace, was my great-grandfather. They were called to combat the trials then. Caledon alone knows what you're called now to do, but I imagine it's to save our people from this butchery which is staining our land red. It's a mighty challenge which lies before each one of you."

William did not discuss this with any of the others as he guided them on the paths Mr Gow had directed him toward. However he studied each of his companions and began to understand what the old man had meant. Their journey to Lairg took them three days moving at a leisurely speed along the banks of Loch Shin. Donald pulled the cart with ease through the snowy terrain, leaving the streaking tracks of the two wheels as they journeyed on. Twice he felt his arms weaken, but through a desire to escape pity and attention he forced himself to take each painful step until his strength returned once more. William and Malcolm headed the column and Robert's eager voice brought up the rear as he and James discussed the events of the four months they had been separated.

The Next Campaign

It was the quiet of evening when the five of them reached the small bothy which, in the late summer, had been their home. Each of them huddled in, grateful of the protection against the bitter wind which whipped down the valley. Donnie easily carried the chests into the shelter and left the small cart outside. James smiled across at him and he felt obliged to return the gesture.

"You've done remarkably well, Oaf," William said jovially. "I expected you to slip down the hillside so many times, and take the gold with you."

"One foot in front of the other," Donald said softly. "Even I can manage that."

"Where do we go from here, Caledon?" Malcolm asked, trying to turn the conversation.

"Tomorrow, we will visit Annie and ensure she's well. Then I'll travel towards the source to try and learn where our course should lead next."

Robert tilted his head slightly, trying to hear all that was being said, but turned to Donald as the broad man sat down beside him. "Can you endure a night's sleep, Donnie?"

Donnie just smiled and nodded before he rolled over facing away from the others and trying to gain some sleep.

"I'm getting tired of waiting," someone said firmly.

"What?" Donald asked, trying to sit up and look about him.

"I told you not to bring him here," rebuked another voice.

"Bring who?" Donnie asked once more, but was met with bemused expressions from the other members of the clan while William openly laughed.

"What are you talking about, Oaf?"

"Nothing," Donald replied, pulling his legs up and hugging his knees to him while Robert glanced across anxiously at James. Jamie felt the confused smile slip from his face and rose to his feet.

"Let's go outside, Donnie," he began, offering his hand down and waiting until his cousin took it and followed him out into the night. "Are you well?"

"Yes, Jamie. I think I was just dreaming."

"He's very close now," the first voice said. "This foolish tax will bring him to you."

"Did you hear that?" Donald asked, turning wide eyes to his cousin.

"Hear what, Donnie? All I can hear is the wind and the water beating the shore."

"I think I'm going mad," Donald whispered. "No, I'm just tired. I'm tired, that's all." He jumped as James took his arms.

"What is it, Donnie? What did you hear?"

"Voices. They're looking for you, I think." Donald took a deep breath and steadied his racing thoughts as he whispered, "Yes, I'm sure it's you."

"Donnie, this isn't the first time you've heard them, is it?"

"No," Donnie muttered. "Am I going mad, Jamie? What is it?"

"He'll bring Caledon to you," the second voice spoke with certainty.

"I won't," Donnie snapped, dropping his head into his hands.

"You won't what?" James asked, ignorant of the voices his cousin could hear.

"You're my leader, Jamie Caledon. I would do nothing to hurt you."

"Nor I you, Donnie. I owe you so much. You're not just Caledon's strength, you're mine. I need you to be that strength. As soon as I know Annie is safe, I'll go to the source and find out what I can do to help. I will right this wrong."

Donald only nodded. He could not hear the voices anymore and he felt too tired to venture conversation. He returned to the bothy and did not spare a word for any of the others who glanced at Jamie's eyes, which contained unshed tears. Neither of the cousins could sleep that night but rose the following morning eager to forget the night before.

The five members of Caledon's clan journeyed down the hillside to Lairg feeling like children as they threw compacted balls of snow at one another, and pushed each other into some of the deeper drifts. On one occasion Malcolm vanished into a hollow tree creating a garrison of snowballs which he proceeded to throw at the others from the security of this giant yew trunk. Their revenge came as William silently crept up and pulled him out before pushing him down the hillside.

With the exception of William, each of them was caked in snow as they reached the small town. Like playing animals who sense danger when it is upon them, they fell silent as they walked along the backs of the houses and Donnie clambered over the wall, pushing the door of Annie's house open. At once he breathed in the tantalising smell of fresh baking and a smile caught his lips, but it fell quickly as his gaze rested upon the woman who was on the bed, for she was not his kinswoman.

"Who are you?" she asked in a panicked tone, pulling the blanket about her and Donnie realised one of her arms was wrapped in a tight bandage.

"I'm Donald Mackenzie, a kinsman of Annie's. Where is she?"

"She has gone to the cobbler, for he's sick."

"Wait," Donald said quickly holding up his hand to the rest of his friends as they began entering the house. But the four of them had already stumbled in, laughing and shaking the snow from their clothes. Each stopped as their gaze fell upon the young woman on the bed, who gave a nervous squeak and huddled into the corner.

"I think we should wait outside," Malcolm said quickly, ushering them back and closing the door before Donald had a chance to follow them.

Donald offered a shy smile to the girl, blushing slightly before he muttered that he would wait in the larder so she might have some privacy. The larder was as cold as ice and he shivered as he crouched there, certain the others were warmer in the outhouse. Presently, the door to the house opened and he felt his pulse quicken as he heard the voice he had missed and longed for over the past five months.

"Moira, what's happened here?"

Donald walked to the larder door and opened it slightly to see a smile catch Annie's features.

"It's those foolish boys, isn't it? Tell me, Moira. Five of them, weren't there?" Her gaze turned to the larder door now and a smile of irrepressible relief caught her features. "Donald Mackenzie! You're safe, thank God you're safe!" She rushed over and embraced him. "I have been hearing so much of Caledon's victories, but all were of only three men. I was so worried. Is Jamie well?"

Donald felt a stab of jealousy before he nodded. "We're all well now. But Robert was wounded at my hand, so the others journeyed on alone. They are in the outhouse. Shall I get them?"

"After the mess they have made of my house?" she began, pointing to the water which covered the flagstone floor. "No, we'll leave them out there a while. Come and meet my guest. Moira, this is Donald Mackenzie, the greatest and gentlest soul to ever live. You need have no fear from him. Donnie, Moira Scott is from Golspie. She was injured when her brother was taken."

"Taken?" Donald whispered.

"There's a new tax been introduced," Annie began.

"Peter's dead," Moira sobbed. "My brother was hanged for leading men to oppose it."

"Oppose it peacefully?" Donald asked, feeling all the blood draining from his face as he recalled what the voices had said about the new tax.

"Peter has never used a weapon in his life. He is a farmer. He was a farmer," she corrected herself.

"John Mackay?"

"Yes," Annie began, but gripped Donald's arm. "Don't let it sway your judgement, Donnie. The tax is to be paid on the acreage harvested. But these farmers have to sell everything they have to cover their rent. They can't afford to pay for the privilege."

"What was Mary thinking when she married him?"

"Your sister had her own reasons, Donnie. It is not wise to try and guess them."

"I'll go and fetch the others," he muttered, kissing Annie's forehead. He turned back to her as she gripped his hand.

"There are some words I must speak to you alone, Donald Mackenzie," she began.

"No. I think you're best not doing."

"I didn't mean for it to happen. When you arrived with James Og that night in spring I was determined to hate him for any harm he might bring to you. I do love you, Donald."

"Mary was right on that, if nothing else. No matter how greatly I love you or you love me, Annie, I'll always just be that sweet younger brother to you. The gentlest man alive, but not a man to fall in love with." He lifted her hand and kissed it. "But James Og is the greatest man and, that he and you love each other, is a great comfort to me, for aside from Mary you are the people I love most in the world."

"Then you do not wish to marry me?"

Donald paused before he shook his head. "You're better with Jamie, Annie. I have a troublesome future. I'll go get the others."

Annie watched as Donald walked to the door and opened it with the gentle care she had come to expect from him. He turned back to look at her for a second, smiling beneath tear-filled eyes, before he walked out into the cold. After collecting the other four he returned to the house and they sat on the floor around the fire as Moira told her sorry story once more.

"You will help them, won't you James Og?" Annie whispered, her eyes glistening.

"How can I help when the man is dead already?" James replied with exasperation, feeling his cousin's condition required his attention far more urgently. Annie, hearing only his words and not following his thoughts, scowled across at him.

"Caledon," Robert began. "These are your people who are being oppressed."

"Of course," James muttered. "If my wisdom and my zeal are united, who am I to stand against it?"

"James Og," Annie said angrily. "I'm throwing a great deal at your feet, more perhaps than you know," she added as she cast the briefest glance at Donald who rose to his feet. "Don't make me regret it."

James watched as Donnie walked over to the low window which looked out on the premature night as it covered the snowy hilltop. There was barely a moon and somehow the snow created a mirror for the stars.

"Let me talk to you Annie," James said with a pleading tone which gave her cause only to nod. He walked over to the corner beside the great ovens and shook his head. "I haven't got the time to resolve this yet."

"The time?" she hissed, as she pointed back to the four seated people. Robert was talking quietly to Moira while Malcolm and William watched her and Jamie through curious eyes. "Those are your people.

If you were truly Caledon you would not question this."

He took her hand which still pointed at them and guided it so it pointed to Donnie. "He's my kin, Annie, and I love him as though he were my brother, not my cousin."

"As do I," she whispered.

"He needs my help, Annie. And I can't forgive myself for taking him to the wedding and all which has befallen him since."

"Do you regret what we shared at the wedding? For I have just had the kindest rebuking from Donald. I don't think I can bear to hear that you wish it didn't happen."

James did not answer her but leaned down and kissed her, bringing a cheer from William. "It's far more complicated than that," James whispered. "Donnie's ailment is not of the heart." He turned as Malcolm began talking.

"Donald?" his English tone began. "Caledon, it's happening again."

Annie watched through anxious eyes as James rushed over to his cousin as Donnie's legs gave way beneath him. Moira gave a shocked gasp and Robert helped her away from the scene while William pulled a flask from his waist and offered it toward Malcolm, who was helping James carry Donald over to one of the chairs.

"I'm fine," Donald muttered, but lifting his hand to push his friends away became too much and he panted for breath, seizing his chest as though he expected it would explode. Malcolm took the flask from William's outstretched hand and forced Donnie to drink from it.

"Donald Mackenzie?" Annie whispered as she stepped over to the chair and knelt beside him. He had his head tipped back and for a time failed to notice her until she placed his hand on his knee and repeated his name. Malcolm and James exchanged an expression which might have spoken of anything.

"Oh, Annie," Donnie whispered as he lowered his head and looked across at her. "Tell them I'm fine, Annie."

"You're not fine, Donnie. What has happened?"

"No," Donald said firmly, pushing himself to his feet as he began to feel strength in his legs once more. "I'm fine. I'll just take some air."

Annie watched as he rose easily to his feet and, though the hand he placed on the door latch trembled slightly, he walked out of the house as though nothing ailed him.

"What was that?" she whispered.

"That's what I've got to resolve," James muttered as Malcolm returned the flask to William. "At times he simply loses all his strength. But you're all speaking the truth to me," he added. "Miss Scott and her family are my people, and assisting them is where Caledon's duty lies. Tomorrow we shall go into Golspie and right this wrong which has been brought upon my people."

That evening James related to Annie all that had happened since they had parted from one another, only omitting the voices Donnie had heard last night. William, Malcolm and Donald sat playing cards while Robert, who had taken on the role of Moira's protector, sat by the young girl and regaled her with tales of Caledon's bravery, in which his half-brother featured prominently. Each of them fell asleep at different times, Moira on the bed, Robert leaning against it, while the other three men fell asleep around the dying peat fire.

Certain all the inhabitants of the room were asleep, James leaned over and kissed Annie once more, pulling her as close to him as he could. If his thoughts considered any guilt towards his cousin's heartache over the woman, who gripped him as tightly as he did her, it was short-lived. He could not help where his heart lay any more than Annie could hers.

Two Crows on the Gallows Tree

Annie stood alone in the yard staring over the mysterious pink of the sunrise on the drifted snow. She had not meant to fall in love after her husband's death and she felt, as she rubbed tears from her eyes, she had betrayed Thomas with her behaviour the night before. But what she felt for James Og was beyond what she had ever thought to feel for another man. She turned as she heard someone stepping out from the house and smiled across at Robert.

"Did you sleep well?" she asked softly, repeating the question a little louder as she recalled the young man could not hear.

"Thank you, yes. But, in honesty, I am eager to see Miss Scott's brother avenged."

"I think she would rather you helped the family who are left to her, Robert."

"But we'll do that too. She's a sweet young lady, but something worries me." He paused and looked across at Annie. "How did she know to come to you for help?"

"If that's all which worries you I can put your mind at rest immediately. Miss Scott is my niece."

"Your niece? But you don't look old enough."

"Thank you, Robert," Annie replied, blushing slightly. "But her mother was my husband's older sister, making me her family by marriage. She is a good woman, Robert, you may count on that."

"Good morning, Donald Mackenzie," Robert remarked as Donnie stepped out of the house and Annie turned to him with a guilty expression. "That's the first night in months you haven't woken me up flapping in your sleep. Annie must be a calming influence on you."

"What does he mean, Donald?" she asked as Robert walked back indoors.

"Nothing. But you look unhappy, Annie. What's wrong?"

"I know, after my behaviour towards you, I have no right to burden you."

"Annie," Donald began, accompanying his words with a heavy sigh. "Whatever has happened, I want to help you. I can't change your view of me, but neither can I alter my view of you. So let me help you."

"I love him, Donnie," she sobbed, leaning on his strong chest. "But I love Thomas, too."

"Thomas is gone, Annie," he said softly, lifting her chin slightly so he could look down into her eyes. "You remaining alone won't bring him back. And Jamie will protect you, and I need to know you'll be safe."

"I'm so sorry, Donnie."

"As am I, Annie. But today you can't think such thoughts for there's a job to be done. Today we must be the Clan of Caledon."

This brief discussion remained with Donald as he walked up to the bothy alone to collect the hand cart and he placed two chests of gold in it before returning to Lairg. Everyone was ready by the time he returned and he smiled at the pairings of James with Annie, and Robert with Moira. Malcolm offered to pull the cart but Donald dismissed him. William struck his arm in a playful manner.

"On we go, Oaf."

They walked in near silence, each one lost in his thoughts, and encountered no one, allowing them to easily follow Strath Fleet. Moira, who Robert had insisted sat on the cart, explained how all of

Mackay's men were involved in suppressing and arresting the other members of the revolt.

"We will help your father," Robert promised, as he walked behind the cart. "Won't we, Caledon?"

James nodded and smiled across. "I'll see justice is given to each of Caledon's people, Moira," he promised. "And you who live so close to the source, you are dearer to me than my heart."

"You speak silky words now, Jamie Caledon," Annie laughed. "So very different to those you spoke last night."

"I didn't know you objected to my behaviour last night," came the playful reply, to which Annie blushed and Malcolm laughed.

None of this was wasted on William or Donald who continued in silence at the front of their column, though Robert had eyes only for Moira who, in return, obliged him with a loving audience and constant conversation. When they reached the vast expanse of Loch Fleet, Moira addressed them all.

"I live on the shores of the sea. I'll part from you now for I don't want to go into Golspie and see what awaits on the green."

"We'll go into Golspie from the coast," Robert volunteered without checking with anyone else. "We will attract far less attention that way."

Malcolm smiled slightly at his brother's behaviour, for it was clear by his apparently casual nature he was saying all these things for the benefit of the woman before him. James nodded while William openly laughed.

"You might have checked with the packhorse first, Zeal. What do you say, Oaf?"

"It's little difference to me," Donald muttered.

"It's a strange thing," Moira began as they journeyed on past Littleferry and round to the coast. "But at times over the last few months there has been a light on the beach down from our house."

"Combers, no doubt." Robert smiled across.

"But we've heard voices on occasions, but there is never more than one set of footprints in the sand. But I'm certain I've heard the cries of at least three of them."

"Cries?"

"Three women, they call to one another. Sometimes they are angry, sometimes jovial, but always animated."

Donald felt a sickness seize him as he related her words to the voices he had heard, but continued to walk on in silence.

"When Caledon was last called," Malcolm mused, "was it not in defence against witchcraft?"

"Witches?" Robert muttered, unwilling to openly criticise his brother. "I thought they were found to have been false?"

"In some cases." Malcolm shrugged his shoulders. "But we're here, aren't we? Fighting and believing in something beyond sight."

Robert considered this in silence, questioning what the purpose of Caledon's Clan was. Initially he had not thought it to be against anything but the Hanoverian forces, but then he looked at William and Donald who continued to lead the small band and reminded himself they had fought on the wrong side of the war. For the first time he considered the supernatural aspect of their quest. It had never occurred to him Jamie Caledon suddenly knowing their paths and the quests they had to fulfil was unusual, and he looked doubtfully at the man beside him.

"Troops," William hissed, and as one the band dissolved into the gorse. Robert snatched Moira's hand and guided her down a small slope, under the prickly spines of the gorse bush. Concealing the cart was impossible but Donnie threw the chests down to where Malcolm crouched concealed beyond a low stone dyke.

"What are you doing, Oaf?" William began as Donald stood in the centre of the track and stared at the two soldiers who began walking towards him, lowering their guns from their shoulders.

"State your business here," one called as they walked forward.

"I'm searching for Caledon," Donald replied. "I heard of the sufferings of the people and we've come to ease their burden."

The rest of the clan stared in confusion as he walked towards the two men, his hands lifted. James tried to struggle out of the gorse, but Annie held him tightly.

"Caledon is a myth," the second soldier announced. "But I know who you are. You're the outlaw, Donald Mackenzie."

"You're wrong on both counts," James' voice announced as he appeared behind them. "Caledon is no myth. And he's Strength, a son of Caledon."

The surprise of the two soldiers was short-lived and James blinked in surprise as he heard the sound of gunfire. He looked anxiously across at his cousin who snatched at the gun of one of the soldiers but, before the other could fire at James, a shot sounded from the side of the road and Robert appeared bearing a pistol in his hand. His shot had found its mark and the soldier dropped his musket as Robert leapt forward at him. James stared on, feeling the heat of the young man's burning zeal as he watched him strike the man repeatedly. Donald stumbled away from the soldier and watched in surprise as his assailant dropped the gun and tried to grip something on his back.

"Donnie," James took his right hand and looked at the blood on his younger cousin's arm. "What were you thinking?"

"That it was better one of us was found than all of us," Donald answered honestly. "What was that?"

"That was Zeal," James said with a smile as he looked over to where Robert struck the first soldier across the face and turned towards him.

"We should kill them, Caledon," Robert replied angrily, his eyes burning. William shook his head quickly as he walked out from his hiding place.

"Your Eile. It did this." He pulled the shredded coat from the soldier.

"Just tie them up," Annie said as Malcolm helped her to the road once more.

"Caledon is above such murder," Malcolm agreed.

Robert was clearly not satisfied, but nodded and walked over to help Moira to her feet, while William secured bonds on the wrists of both the unconscious soldiers.

"Your eyes, Robert MacBeath," Moira whispered, and the others turned to the young man. "They've changed colour."

"To match his Eile," William muttered.

"His Eile?" Malcolm whispered. "His other?"

"That coat," William replied as he dragged the two bodies over to the edge of the road. "That was shredded by a far greater killer than even Zeal's blind rage."

"A wildcat," James muttered. "Yes, that's Zeal's other."

"We should keep moving," Annie said quickly, eager to continue on their course for the light was failing. "We can talk of this on the way. Donnie," she said quickly as she ran her fingers down his bloody sleeve. "You're hurt."

"No," he whispered, feeling giddy at her touch. "It only glanced my arm."

James watched his cousin's gaze light up as he regarded Annie's concern for him and now all the guilt he had expelled last night resurfaced in his mind.

"I'll take the cart," Malcolm said firmly as he returned the small chests to it.

"No," Donald began. "What use am I if I can't do this?"

William shook his head quickly as he met Malcolm's gaze.

"Very well, Donnie," Malcolm said softly. "Perhaps Miss Scott can walk from here, though."

"Of course," Moira replied.

It was only a short distance on to the farm where Moira lived and at once she rushed forward scooping up the young child who ran out to meet her. Robert felt his face harden at this, believing the child to be her own, for she embraced it with such love. He turned to face Annie as she placed her hand on his arm.

"That's her nephew," she said softly, so Robert had to tilt his head towards her to hear her. "Now an orphan, for his mother died shortly after he was born."

"Then you are not just an aunt but a great-aunt?" he said with a relieved smile on his face.

"Thank you, Robert," Annie said, her face flushing red once more.

"Come indoors," Moira called as she held the young boy to her.

"Thank you," James said warmly.

"We should keep moving," Donald persisted.

"Not until you've had a drink, surely," Moira began.

"Nor until you've had your arm cleaned," Annie added.

There was little use trying to argue with the rest of the clan and Donnie reluctantly entered the farmhouse where they were met by Moira's parents. Annie took Donnie's wrist and guided him over to a small lamp on the table while the lady of the house fussed over the other people. He let her help his bleeding arm from the tight-fitting shirt and looked across at her through his dark eyes.

"You seem unable to treat your shirts with the care they deserve," she laughed.

"It's not deep, Annie. It's fine."

"What were you thinking, Donald Mackenzie?" she began, ignoring his protest. "Walking over to those soldiers? You and James are known here, and Mackay needs no excuse to kill you."

"We would all have been found. We couldn't hide the cart."

"I've known you almost two decades, you know. I think you were seven when your father first brought you to meet me. I know when you are lying."

"I'm Strength, Annie. But each time I'm attacked by this weakness I'm left with less and less strength. I want to be useful to Jamie while I can. I want to

263

help him, to follow him, but I feel I really am the oaf William says I am. What if Jamie chose me wrongly or that he took me out of pity? I can't let him down."

Annie looked into the gaze of the gentle soul before her and felt her heart might burst. "You will never let your cousin down, Donnie."

"What if they were right? What if I am fated to lead Caledon to them?"

"Who?"

"Donnie?" James began as he placed his hand on his cousin's shoulder. "You have to stop worrying. I'll find a way to end this, I promise you."

"I don't think anyone but I can end it," Donald said firmly. "I will not lead you to them, or any danger."

"Like the danger you almost created for me today?" James began. "You can't take this campaign on your shoulders to save me. I need you to stay alive, Donnie, because what I told you is still true: you are my strength as surely as you are Caledon's."

"I've hardly any strength left."

"Strength is not just about muscle, Donnie. Strength is about willpower, stamina and heart. It's your strength in those things I value."

"I don't want to let you down."

James leaned forward and kissed his cousin's black hair before he walked back to the others. Annie, who had watched this exchange as she wiped the blood from Donald's arm, held his large hand in both of her own.

"You need some new shirts, Donald Mackenzie. As soon as we have concluded our business here, we shall have to find a tailor."

The night was complete when, at last, the clan prepared to journey the short distance to Golspie. Robert lifted Moira's hand to his lips and kissed it softly before thanking her parents and following the other five from the house. They left the cart and the gold at the farmhouse and walked hurriedly towards the town.

"Have we a plan for when we arrive there?" William asked.

"Mackay is behind this," James said flatly. "I want justice brought upon him. We must call his troops out to a meeting hall where we can contain them. But we will need bait."

"The church," Annie said.

"There is no need for bait beyond what we have," William said flatly. "You and Oaf are as much an obsession for Mackay as he is for you."

As they entered Golspie, Donald faltered, and James watched as his cousin's face became white. He followed Donnie's gaze at the same time as Annie gave a small cry, pointing over at the body that hung from the lower branch of a large tree. Two crows flew up at the sound and Donnie quickly moved over to the tree and untied the hemp rope, carefully lowering the body to the ground. Annie rushed over and knelt down beside the corpse, placing her hand on the shirt over his still heart.

"This is Moira's brother?" Robert asked as he knelt beside her. Annie nodded, and leaned against him. Robert pulled the cord from the young man's neck and glanced across at Donnie, surveying the damage the crows had already done. Donald was looking up at the birds in the higher branches. James took his cousin's arm and guided him away while Robert and Malcolm lifted the body.

"We should be going to the church," William said quickly. "I'm quite sure any element of surprise we had is now long gone." He pointed to the houses around them where shutters opened slightly.

"This was not how tonight should have gone," James whispered to himself.

At the sound of heavy footfalls they ran on to the church, reaching it amid the sound of gunfire. Malcolm and Robert, still carrying the corpse, entered behind James and laid the body before the altar. Donald turned back to the door and felt panic seize him as he realised that Annie and William were not there. James snatched his wrist.

"The troops are advancing, Donnie. If Annie has stayed away then at least she will be safe."

Pushing closed the doors the four of them began piling up any furniture they could find against them. They turned and ran to the door beyond the altar. This plan which had worked so well for them at the wedding would not work now, for the four of them faced six soldiers all armed with muskets while only Malcolm and Robert carried pistols.

"What do we do, Caledon?" Robert whispered.

"We fight," James stated with a confidence he could not feel. He watched with a numb feeling as Robert and Malcolm both fired their pistols while Donnie ran the ten paces over to one of the soldiers and wrestled with him, trying to prise the gun from his hand. James did not run. Instead he walked calmly forward to the man who stared down the barrel of his musket and tightened his finger on the trigger. For a split second, as the powder ignited a spark of light in the dark night, Jamie felt afraid, as though Caledon had fled from his blood and he was once more the coward James Og. But it was only a second before he snatched the man's musket from his trembling hands and struck him in the face with the butt of his own gun. Now holding the gun, he turned to look at what else was happening. Robert had shot one and knocked out another of the soldiers, Malcolm had shot one, and Donald had struck one and shot another. James looked down at himself as Donald rushed over to him, and stared at the blood that spilt from his shoulder.

"Honestly, Donnie," he began quickly. "I'm fine. It doesn't even hurt."

He pulled back his shirt collar and looked at the wound, but for his head spinning a little he did not feel any discomfort. Robert looked into James' face and smiled slightly.

"I've never seen a man take such a shot and keep advancing, Caledon."

"We should leave this place, Caledon," Malcolm said quickly as he ran forward. "More soldiers are coming."

These words had scarcely left Malcolm's lips than six more men appeared from around the corner of the church. James' mind raced as he tried to contrive any way in which they might escape. He glanced at the musket in his hand lifting it up but stopped as he heard the voice of Ensign John Mackay.

"Lower your weapon, James Og. You and your men are surrounded."

James only gripped the weapon tighter but turned an angry and confused expression to Donald who dropped the gun he held, raising his hands.

"What are you doing?" James demanded. "Where is the strong-hearted man who was willing to be shot for Caledon earlier?"

"I'm not willing for her to be shot for me," Donald replied, pointing to where Mackay stood. Beside him one of his men held Annie by the throat, a pistol pointing at her chest.

"Is she one of yours too, James Og?"

"No," James said quickly, feeling a look of daggers from Robert stabbing his back. "But it was her nephew you hung yesterday."

Annie's eyes met with each one of her clan members, and though her fear was evident her eyes were dry. James set his face, determined to betray no emotion to the man before him. Malcolm lowered his gun, but did not drop it, and stepped forward so he stood between his brother and the troops. It was a gesture of love and the nobility which he represented, but it was in vain for when Mackay next spoke Robert's green eyes flared.

"That's unfortunate for her, for once I've killed you my men are to go and arrest Peter Scott's father for incitement."

Robert lifted his gun once more and would have shot the man, but Donald rushed forward.

"No! He'll kill Annie." He turned his gaze to her and did not let it stray as he lifted his hands again.

"Shoot them," Mackay ordered as though the choice was a casual matter to which he offered no thought. Each of them sought any escape but none was to be found. James felt the burden of responsibility as heavy as a millstone round his neck as he looked at the three men he was condemning to death simply for believing in him.

Everyone, soldiers and clan members, turned as a huge explosion shook the ground and the night sky lit up with an enormous beacon further to the north. James wasted no time. In this moment of confusion, he grabbed Donald's wrist and pulled him away to the hedge of trees which Robert and Malcolm had already squeezed through. There were many calls in the night air including beyond the hedge as they continued to run for a time.

"What are you doing?" Donald demanded. "He'll kill Annie. You know he will."

"What was that?" Robert muttered.

"A perfectly timed distraction," Malcolm laughed. "I imagine the reason you have not mentioned William for so long, Caledon, is that you planned this."

"What a good imagination you've got," James laughed. "I need you and Robert to get down to the farm. If the soldiers reach there first Mr Scott will be shot at once. And get Annie and make sure she's safe."

"I will do that," Donald said purposefully, but stopped as James gripped his sleeve.

"I need you to come with me, Donnie. I need to face John Mackay."

"Then you'll do it alone until I know that Annie's safe." He shrugged out of James' hold.

"We'll find Annie," Malcolm said, grabbing his brother's arm and pulling him away before they could witness any further discord between the cousins.

"Then I'll go alone," James agreed, feeling suddenly the weariness of the wound at his shoulder as though, with Donald's refusal, he truly had lost his strength. Without waiting to hear whether Donnie offered any words he ducked under the hedge and stumbled forward.

The bloodied snow close to the church glistened in the bitter night and James gasped in the frozen air as this reminder caused his shoulder to throb. He had placed too much trust in his cousin, taking his gentle soul too far from where it belonged and demanding too many sacrifices from him. There was no direction to where he walked, only that he followed the footprints in the snow. Most of them led to the drill hall where there was steamy smoke swirling through the doors and the holes in the roof. There was no sign of William and any of the troops he saw did not see him. He stopped at a house a little distance from the hall and walked to the door. He could not be sure what had brought him to the door, only that there was something inside which felt familiar to him. He did not wait to knock on the door but pushed it open and walked into the room. There was no one indoors, but almost at once a maid appeared from one of the two doorways.

"Who are you?" she asked quickly, fearfully taking in his wounded shoulder and his dishevelled attire. "The Ensign is engaged and his wife has retired for the night."

"He's engaged?" James whispered, questioned once more what force had pulled him to this house. "I'm certain he will not be too busy to see me."

"Then I shall go and fetch him," she whispered.

"No need, Peggy," Mackay's voice announced as he slammed closed the door behind James. "You've got a brash and foolish courage to walk into my house, James Og. I can think of no reason to stay my hand from shooting you right now."

"I'm no longer James Og. I am Caledon."

"Ah yes, our fabled saviour. Don't take me for a fool. Caledon has faded into legend and shall never again find her place in this land. And if she did, she would never choose a coward like you."

"I didn't come here to speak petty words with a worthless man."

Mackay's eyes flashed at this and he stepped forward to James, snatching his throat in one hand and striking him across the face with the other. "Then why did you come here? To kill me?"

"I long for that day," James struggled, slashing the sgian dhu he carried toward his assailant. "But no." Mackay pushed him backward and lifted his pistol, pointing it at James' head. "Killing you will bring no respite to the people of this town, it will only escalate more deaths of innocent people. I want you to issue a pardon."

"A pardon? To an unruly mob who do not know their place? No amount of support from you can excuse them that."

James, who was far from a scheming person, tried to concoct the next move in his plan, but he had nothing to barter with this man except for his own life, and by the raised pistol he was soon set to take that. "I will not let you harm the people of Caledon."

"You're not Caledon, and these are not your people. In claiming they are, you are claiming sovereignty and that is treason. Just another reason to kill you."

There was a shot then, one that punctured the glass with a clattering crash and the musket ball trimmed the ensign's right arm, causing him to drop the pistol. Both men turned to the door as it opened. The bulky figure who stood there only a second before he walked in, did not speak a word to either of them but stepped over to the stunned Mackay and struck him across the face, before he snatched the man's wrist in a firm hold and dragged him out of the door.

"You're making a mistake, Donald Mackenzie," Mackay announced.

"It's you who has made the mistake," Donald muttered as James followed a short distance behind. "If you do not believe in Caledon, you run the risk of underestimating us. And that will cost you dear."

"As dear as your sister?" he retorted, and Donald turned on him.

"I can't imagine what gave her cause to marry you, but for any harm you bring on her I swear I will repay it five times on you."

"Your cousin is not Caledon, you fool. He is only using you for he has not the courage and strength to defend himself."

"You do not need to tell me what my cousin is, Mackay, for I know his tricks better than any man alive." He looked over Mackay's shoulder and smiled slightly at James. "But he is Caledon as surely as any man before."

When they reached the green, where the noose which had hung Annie's nephew still lay, they were joined by William who smiled as they approached."

"Where are Malcolm and Robert?" James asked quickly.

"They must be back at the house by now. And have no fear, Oaf," William added, turning to Donald. "They didn't leave alone."

William neither spoke, nor made reference to the ensign who Donald continued to drag behind him. On three occasions people tried to stop them but each time William and James fought them back while Donald maintained his rapid speed, keen to finish the night's business before the dawn. Mackay watched the exchanges between the three men with an awful shrewdness, absorbing each time James winced as the untended wound on his shoulder jarred, every time Donald stumbled, and all the numerous occasions that William addressed Donald with derision.

When they reached the farmhouse, Donald walked in without waiting to be admitted and pushed Mackay onto one of the stools around the table. William rested a knife against his throat and James pushed a blank sheet of paper before him as well as ink and a pen.

"Annie," Donald whispered as he recognised the woman who stood, leaning on the door upright. She offered him a deep smile and embraced him as he walked over to her. "I was so worried."

"You had no cause to be, Donald Mackenzie, for Caledon protects his people."

Donald smiled for the sake of everyone who watched him, but the gesture felt bitter as he considered once more the manner in which she addressed him as little more than a child, almost as Moira did her young nephew. After a time, he excused himself and stepped out into the night under the gaze of each member of Caledon's clan and Moira, who leaned on Robert's arm.

William never removed the knife from Mackay's neck until he had signed the pardon, at which point Malcolm took and read through it. He nodded slightly and William returned his weapon to his belt.

"This will not change anything, James Og," Mackay began, straightening his jacket as he rose to his feet. "The tax is still in place and, even if you kill me, it will remain there for it's the wish of the Sutherlands."

"I don't care for the tax, Mackay," James scornfully replied. "You'll find that these people are resilient and rich in ways you can't understand. But I won't ever allow you to harm my people."

"Your people," Mackay spat as he stood face to face with James and poured venom on each whispered word. "These are not your people, and I'll make you this promise, James Og. I'll have justice on you and your simple cousin for these ridiculous games you play."

"I suggest you leave, Ensign Mackay. Your men will be wondering where you are."

The Final Mackenzie

Ensign John Mackay wasted no time in leaving the house and, upon Malcolm handing the pardon over to Mr Scott, their host encouraged them all to share a quaich of whisky. James took a sip from it and watched as each of the others did the same, before he excused himself and walked out of the house. Finding what he sought, leaning against the old barn wall, he walked over and placed his hand upon his cousin's shoulder.

"I saw Mackay leaving," Donald muttered without facing James. "I can only assume it means he wrote the pardon."

"He did, indeed."

"Down there, that's Littleferry. That's where the eastern Mackenzies were killed by Mackay. He killed my father, married my sister out of the name, now there's just me. And I'm certain I won't be a thorn in his side for much longer." He turned his red face toward James and shook his head.

"It's happened again?"

"I think so," Donald whispered, turning once more to the coast. "I'm getting to the point where I don't remember anymore."

"I'm going to find a cure for you, Donnie. I'm going to find someone to help." He watched as Donald rested his head against the wall and continued to stare into the distance. "I have to thank you. Again. For coming after me and shooting Mackay. But I would like to know why you did."

"Annie didn't need me, Jamie. But you did. I believe in you. I know to Mackay and others it seems like madness, but I know you're the only man who could be called as Caledon. And for what it's worth," he added, turning back to James again. "I'm proud to call you my cousin."

"It's worth a great deal, Donnie. But you must know, if it weren't for you, I would have died tonight, and that would have cost the lives of William and Malcolm and Robert. And Annie, too. You are a crucial part of Caledon, Donald Mackenzie, and each of us need you."

"Annie doesn't need me. Occasionally I flatter myself by imagining she enjoys my company, but I know she enjoys yours more and I know she needs you."

"Donnie-"

"No," his younger cousin interrupted him. "It's true, for she told me. But it's fine, because this way I know she'll be safe. I know you'll protect her, as she knows it, too."

James nodded, but the movement made his head spin and at once the wound which adrenaline had protected him from began to throb. He screwed his eyes closed and for a split second felt himself become weightless as he soared from consciousness before he collapsed, feeling his cousin's strong arms catch him before he fainted.

"What are you doing here, Caledon?" the neutral voice of the waterfall asked, and he realised he was dreaming. "Never before has Caledon so often visited the castle."

"I need help." He looked about him and found that he was in a room with a huge chandelier in the centre, but all of the candles were unlit and cobwebs hung from it, stretching all the way to the ground. A shaft of light beamed in from the corner of the room where the waterfall cascaded down.

"Strength? I told you the wedding would cost you Strength."

"But to every ailment there is a cure," James persevered, watching with fascination the reflection in the waterfall where hosts of dancers filled the ballroom he occupied.

"There is a cure, but it is a person not a medicine. Your enemy."

"Mackay of Moudale?"

"You have a far greater enemy than he. One who is bent on your death and will destroy each member of your clan to get to you. It is this enemy who holds the cure to Strength. But have a care, Caledon. Your enemy makes ready the net to catch you and will shortly be tightening the strings. This enemy knows no restraint and will compromise everyone and everything they know to strike you down."

"What can I do?"

"Be ready to defend yourself against even your oldest friends, for you will find those who make promises are the only ones to break them."

James watched as the light from the shaft intensified and absorbed his entire gaze, before he passed from the peculiar castle into the realms of sleep.

Part Six: The Depth of Strength

Anniversary

The bitter winter stretched through March with a dampness which stabbed at James' chest as he breathed in deeply and looked at his clan. Annie had made light work of removing the shot from his shoulder and, through her wisdom, skill and care, he now only felt the pain occasionally.

"He can't understand it," Malcolm laughed. "Mackay really has no idea where this gold has come from. And now the Sutherlands are becoming angry with him for it."

"It seems a little unfair, though," William began, trying unsuccessfully to conceal his amusement. "They're still getting their money."

"I'll never feel sorry for him," James began, and all of them turned to him. "He's manufacturing his own downfall by abusing our people."

"Our people?" Donald whispered.

"We are all the Clan of Caledon. Without any one of us the others can't continue."

Robert smiled as he lined up the pistol, he held with the crude image of John Mackay they had drawn onto the side of the bothy. "How many times do you think we have to shoot this before the real man dies?"

"If Annie ever hits the target, I'm sure we'll all drop dead through shock," William replied as he smiled across at the woman who snatched the gun from Robert's hand and the men quickly ran behind her. She fired at the image, missing the picture completely.

"Keep practising, Annie," Robert said softly. "You're getting closer every time."

"You mean I actually hit the wall?" she began.

"It's a start," James said quickly, sensing that a string of words were about to be fired at his men with far more accuracy.

Malcolm drew his own pistol and shot through a tiny hole in the wall that they had all agreed was Mackay's heart. Annie watched on with a certain amount of jealousy and distrust as he walked over to talk to his brother.

"You don't need to feel inadequate because you can't shoot like Malcolm and Robert," William said softly as he walked to stand beside her. "Both of them are exceptional marksmen."

"But you and Donnie and Jamie? You are all better than I."

"Because all of us stared down the barrel of a gun to defend our lives, and to save the lives of others. That's not something you should long for, Annie."

He leaned down and kissed her cheek before walking over to James.

April was taking hold and spring was beginning to bloom when the full weight of William's words struck Annie. She lay awake for long hours considering the men who slept in the bothy a short distance from her house, and she questioned why she had ever allowed herself to become involved with such a cause. She had never shot anyone. She could not know what it was to take the life of a man and nor could she ever believe it would be right to do so. Without realising she had fallen asleep she found herself looking down at a long musket which she held in her hands. Behind her, standing at her shoulder was John Mackay, so close that as he spoke, she could feel his breath on her neck.

"Make a choice," he commanded, and she looked to find two men standing before her, each with their eyes fixed on her own. "You must shoot one of them before the sand runs out, or they'll both die."

Annie stared from James Og to his cousin, Donald Mackenzie, and back again. She felt unable to pull the trigger on either of them, but as she waited, trying to choose, the time expired and she watched as her hands, without heeding her head, shot them both. She jumped awake, sitting up quickly in her bed, relieved to be awake. But over the next week she was plagued by this dream. Sometimes they both died before her. On one occasion she tried to shoot herself or Mackay, but neither of them could die, and it only resulted in her having to watch the two men die once more. Finally, she realised a choice had to be made to break the cruel cycle of the dream.

"It's fine, Annie," Donald began softly. "I'm just happy you'll be well cared for."

"Don't shoot him," James begged, trying to reach out to her. "I'm the man who should make this sacrifice."

Annie watched as the sand trickled through the glass before she lifted the musket and fired it, sobbing as she did so.

"It's fine, Annie," Donald's voice whispered as blood spilt from the gunshot wound in his chest. "It will be all right."

But despite the fact her kinsman fell to the floor, his voice grew stronger. She was surprised to find that, when she awoke, she saw Donald sitting on the side of her bed, holding her hand and whispering words designed to comfort her.

"It's all right, Annie," he continued lifting her hand to his face and kissing it.

"I dreamed I shot you," she sobbed. "I'm so sorry."

"You don't have to apologise for a dream. I'm still here, see?"

"Why are you here?" she asked, looking about to find none of the other clansmen were in her house.

"I'm going over to The Bridge for a time," he said softly.

"Why? Your house was destroyed. There's nothing there anymore."

"Just tell Jamie, he'll understand why."

"You haven't told him?"

Donald shook his head. "But I'll only be gone a couple of days. You tell him for me, Annie. I didn't want to simply disappear, but I didn't want to explain myself to any of them, either."

"Be careful, Donald Mackenzie," she whispered, hugging him to her. "I'm so sorry."

"Don't apologise, Annie. I know you'll be safe, that's all I care about."

He kissed her cheek before he stepped out the door and into the chilled night. The waning moon shone with the final throws of winter sparkle, and he pulled the plaid about his shoulders as he walked south towards the house which had been his home. The sun was rising as he walked up the steep incline of the hillside, only stopping when he stood by the charred door. A year of absence had left the house in ruin. The roof Mackay had torched had since collapsed and, as he stepped into the building, he was able to stare up at the lightening sky which was an angry red. Decay, from exposure to a year of weather, left a ghostly effect on what was otherwise an overwhelmingly familiar room. He looked at the open hearth and sat down beside the charred remains of his father's chair. He had shared so many arguments with him over the most trivial of topics, bitter words which for twelve months he had recanted on so many occasions. All his memories of his father seemed overshadowed by his guilt at the old man's death. If he had only taken Mary at once to Invergordon to sail to the continent, as his father had requested, indeed they would have been separated but the old man would still have been alive.

"I thought you might be here today."

Donald turned quickly at this voice which intruded on his thoughts. He smiled at once as his gaze rested on Mary. She was dressed in a warm travelling cape lined with fur, so it took him the time he rose to his feet and embraced her to realise he was wrapping his arms around two people, not one.

"Mary," he whispered, his face lighting up. "Congratulations."

"Indeed," she laughed. "And if she does not make an appearance soon, I have decided to do as well-bred ladies do and take to my bed all day."

"You are a well-bred lady." He leaned down to kiss her forehead. "And how can you know it won't be a boy?"

"No. She'll be a daughter," Mary said with certainty, and at once Donald recalled the haunting conversation he had heard in the barn in Tongue.

"I'll be there when your daughter is born, Mary. I won't abandon you."

Her face paled suddenly, and he took his older sister in his arms, trying to steady her. She looked up in surprise before words poured from her mouth. She scarcely gave them any thought but continued to talk.

"You heard that, Donnie? That conversation of so many months ago? I told them you would not leave me, that you should always have a concern for me before anyone else. I knew it was true. But they have taught me such things, things I never thought I could do. John is outside, I don't want him to come looking for me, for he will kill you if he should find you, but I have so much to talk with you about. I know what happened at the beginning of the year, so I know you know where to find Scott's farm. Meet me there tomorrow night, my little brother, and we shall talk freely. An hour after sunset, I'll be there."

"I shall be there too, Mary, I promise."

She stood on tiptoes and kissed his cheek before she gathered up her cape, wrapping it around her, and ran out. Donald watched her go, peering out through a gap in the burnt door to where John Mackay welcomed Mary with a kiss. It was odd that, when this man had caused the devastation Mary had clearly come to remember, she had chosen to marry him.

He remained in the house a little time longer until, as the sun set, he walked out into the darkness and recalled with a sickening feeling what the night had brought one year ago. He tightened the laces on the shirt he wore and, positioning his plaid over his shoulder, he once more walked into the night. It took him until morning to arrive close to Scott's farm and, reluctant to draw attention to himself, he clambered down to the shore. Here, he sat in the cover of the low cliff where he settled in the dip of the rock to fall asleep.

When he awoke it was to the long shadows of the setting sun and he awkwardly rose to his feet, stumbling slightly on the uneven ground. Careful not to slip on the mossy seaweed he retraced his steps up to the farm and awaited the arrival of his sister, anxious to understand the conversations he had heard over the last six months. She arrived exactly at the time she had said, carrying a lantern which he took from her, before guiding her down to the beach at her request.

"Amazing things have happened to me, Donnie," she laughed happily. "I have been afraid to tell anyone else."

"Afraid?" he repeated.

"Watch the waves," she explained in a giddy voice.

He turned to the frothing foam and watched as it struck the shore in a steady beat. But gradually, as he watched, the waves slowed so greatly they seemed to cease altogether.

"Mary?" he whispered, and at once the waves beat with their regular rhythm. "How did you do that?"

"I don't really know," she laughed. "All I know is I've been given the title Time and, since then, I have been able to control time for those I am with. To everyone else the world appears at its usual speed. Place the lantern down and I shall introduce you to my sisters."

Donald set the lantern down, horrified and dazed by what he had witnessed. But, as Mary picked up a stick of seaweed and drew a large circle in the sand, he returned to his senses and walked over to her. Trying to escape this devilment, he heard his sister laugh lightly.

"Don't be foolish, Donnie. You can't leave the circle, it's futile to even try. Besides, we have to prove to Fortune that you shall not betray me. And I know Beauty is eager to meet you."

He followed her outstretched hand to look at the two women who now stood in the circle with them. One moved over to him and smiled up through large dark eyes as she flicked her red hair behind her.

"Donald Mackenzie," she whispered. "I had been afraid in the flesh you would disappoint me."

"And does he?" Mary laughed.

"Oh no," came the reply, and Donald leaned away from her, feeling the edge of the circle pushing against him.

"Don't touch him," snapped the other woman. She had not moved since she arrived and now she stared at the young man over the distance which separated him from her. "There is, as I have told you, something about Donald Mackenzie. Who are you truly?"

"I'm truly Donald Mackenzie," he muttered, taking a step sideward to avoid the red-haired woman.

"You do not need to play games with me, boy. I have lived over a hundred years and I well remember the last time you came looking for me." The other two watched this exchange with confusion, but it did not compare to how Donnie felt. "This man will not help you, Time. He may be your flesh and blood, but his heart owes you nothing."

"I love my sister," Donald began angrily.

"Why don't you ask him the question you wish to know, Time? Then you will discover where his loyalties truly lie."

"Donnie?" Mary began, taking his hand in her own. "Where is James Og?"

Donald faltered and looked into each of the faces which stared back at him. "That's what this is all about? About Caledon?"

"Now, who mentioned Caledon?" the other woman asked. "I wondered how you survived your sister continuously drawing from you. You're Strength, aren't you?"

Donald looked across at her before he turned once more to Mary whose eyes narrowed. "I'm a son of Caledon."

"You are a son of Robert Mackenzie," Mary began and at once Donald looked down at his hands, trying to work the strength back into them. "You said you would not abandon me, Donnie."

"It was you?" He crashed to the ground as his legs buckled and he gripped his chest as he tried to coax it to breathe. "You're doing this?"

"Wait," the red-haired woman began. "He can still be useful."

Mary shook her head and looked down at her brother. "Very well, Beauty. Donald," she continued, kneeling by his side and combing his black hair behind his ear. "I'll give you one more chance. Prove your words of earlier, that you won't abandon me in favour of that coward. Where will I find James Og?"

Donald rose shakily to his feet and looked at the three faces which stared at him. Fortune had a look of utter disgust and mistrust, while Beauty's gaze pleaded him to answer wisely. Mary folded her arms and stood directly before him.

"I'm a son of Caledon. And I will not give him up for anything."

"Make no mistake, Donnie," Mary said firmly, addressing him as a child. "I'll turn you over to my husband and he will have the truth pulled from your lips." She struck him across the face. "And then he'll have you killed."

"I have no fear of John Mackay," Donald replied. "I am a son of Caledon, and I will not give him up."

"I will not help you when you change your mind," Mary snapped. She watched as her younger brother collapsed at her feet as she felt once more his strength, the Strength of Caledon, pulse through her. "You were right, Fortune. Donald Mackenzie does have a troubled future. Troubled, but short."

She picked up the lantern and scowled down at him as Fortune and Beauty vanished, before she kicked the sand circle out of existence. Leaving the lantern as a beacon, she walked away from the unconscious form of Donald Mackenzie, never glancing back. She kept him in the back of her mind as she walked from the beach, ensuring he should remain in his current position and, as she passed two of her husband's men on patrol she at once alerted them to the presence of the outlaw on the beach. She smiled slightly as she walked onward. It could not have been better planned, for now her husband could never doubt her loyalty and he would exact revenge upon her brother, keeping her hands clean. She stepped into her house and walked over to her husband who sat by the fire. She kissed his cheek as she shrugged out of the cape she wore.

"You would not believe who I encountered on the beach this evening."

The Dog in the Burn

"Where's Donnie?"

James stirred awake and looked across sleepily at Robert who stood in the doorway. The young man's face was full of anxious concern.

"He won't have gone far," Malcolm said softly. He was sitting in the corner of the building, tying a knot in the laces of his shirt. "He's probably gone to Lairg."

"One thing's certain," William muttered as he rubbed his eyes, trying to wake up as he pushed himself up on his elbow. "He wanted to go without our knowing, for that oaf has never slipped past me before."

James rose to his feet and fastened the plaid he had used as a blanket about his waist before tossing the rest of it over his left shoulder. He watched as Malcolm rose to his feet and waited until William reluctantly did the same.

"He'll have told someone," Malcolm continued, placing his hand on James' shoulder.

"He'll have told Annie," Robert said with certainty. "He must have done."

James nodded but did not speak a word as he rushed out of the building and down into the village of Lairg. He knew the path to Annie's door so well now, but as he lifted his hand to knock, he stopped as he heard crying coming from inside. The others had clearly heard too, for Malcolm knocked quickly and pushed the door open. James, Malcolm and Robert rushed in, unsure what they expected to find, but filled with a sickening horror at what it might be.

Annie was sitting on the floor close to the large table and she turned frightened eyes towards them as they entered. Robert knelt down beside her and let her rest her tear-stained face on his shoulder, while Malcolm and James looked about the room.

"He's been here," William said flatly, as he walked in. "The gate's latched. Who else latches the gate?"

"I shot him," Annie whispered, looking up into Robert's wildcat eyes. "I shot him so many times."

"Who?" Malcolm asked, crouching down beside her.

"Donald Mackenzie."

"What?" James snapped, joining the singular conversation for the first time. "Why? Where is he now?"

"He's gone to The Bridge," she whispered.

"After you shot him?" Malcolm muttered disbelievingly.

"He's gone home?" James whispered.

"I had to make a choice," Annie replied, scrubbing the corner of her apron across her face to dry her eyes. "But I couldn't harm either of you." She rose to her feet and stood before James, holding his arms.

"It was a dream," William said flatly. "Annie, you would never hurt any one of us. Here," he pushed his flask towards her. "Take a drink and explain this in simple words. Oaf may not be here, but even I can't make sense of this nonsense."

Annie took a sip from the flask before she handed it back. Taking steadying breaths, she waited as Malcolm helped her to the chair and the four men stood waiting for an explanation. "I had a dream, it's true. But it has not left me. Each time Mackay stands beside me and orders me to shoot either

Donald or you," she said, pointing to James. "I have fought for many nights not to pull the trigger, but he and I can't die in the dream, and if I don't shoot one of you then you both die."

"But where is Donnie?" Robert asked.

"Last night I shot him," she sniffed.

"In the dream?" Malcolm ventured.

"Yes. But he was speaking words to me which awoke me, and he was sitting beside me."

"He came into the house without knocking?" William asked in disbelief. "And comforted you on your own bed? That's not like him at all."

"He said he was going to The Bridge," she continued. "And I shouldn't worry for choosing to shoot him for Caledon would be able to keep me safe. But that was not a dream. Why would he say it unless he was going to do something foolish?" She looked at James and sighed. "He said you would understand why he had gone home, and he would only be gone a couple of days."

"I do understand," James muttered, and walked over to the window under the expectant gaze of four pairs of eyes. "It's a year since it all began. And it all began with his father's death."

None of the others spoke for a time. Each took in their own thoughts and considered, as James did, how little they knew of one another. They spent the morning trying to steady Annie's shaken nerves, before she announced she had work to do. They returned to the hills which were becoming more clement with the onset of spring. Before they left, Annie took James aside and lowered her head in shame.

"This dream, Caledon. I returned to it several times after Donald left. And every time I shot him, and every time he forgave me."

"It was only a dream, Annie. You have no more control over it than I do." He leaned forward and kissed her forehead before he joined the others outside.

The following morning found Robert returning with an anxious expression before the sun was over the horizon. "Donnie is still not back. I'm worried," he conceded. "He's been becoming weaker and weaker as the weeks have passed. What if something has befallen him?"

"Annie said he told her he would be gone a couple of days, Robert," Malcolm said gently. "So far he's only been gone one."

Robert could not bring himself to discuss all he had witnessed of Donald's sufferings during the time they had shared at Tongue. He was not entirely sure what to make of such behaviour, as every thought he gave the matter, only made him believe his friend was possessed. He did not dare trust there could be any other explanation.

A cloud of dark uncertainty had fallen on the clan and none of them could settle their minds to any task. William sat a short distance from the others, staring intently down at the town, while Malcolm and Robert went in search of food. They returned empty handed in the early afternoon. James had barely ceased pacing the front on the bothy. Something did not make sense to him. He could recall clearly that night one year ago when he had witnessed his uncle's death at the hands of John Mackay. But it had taken them only hours to travel from Robert Mackenzie's house to Lairg. And yet Donald had been gone long enough to make the journey three times over.

"We'll have to rely on Annie's generosity," Malcolm muttered as he looked at the three despondent men before him. "There's no food to be had in the hills today."

He was greeted by silence.

"Shall we go after him, Caledon?" he continued.

"He said a couple of days," James replied. "But that journey should have been completed in far less time than that. He must have done something else."

"What else would he do?" William began. "His only interests are in our cause and Annie."

"And his sister," Robert ventured.

"Mary?" James whispered. "He wouldn't be foolish enough to go into Golspie. The only thing which has kept me safe from Mackay these past twelve months is that he hates Donnie more than me."

"Shall we check with Annie first?" Malcolm said, in the most light-hearted tone he could adopt. "It'll be much easier than Mary Mackay. She might even feed us."

The sun was setting as they arrived at Annie's house. She was once more composed and calm, as though the worries and tears of yesterday were long forgotten. And she was pleased to see them all.

"Annie," William began, taking and kissing both of her hands. "Tell me you have some food in that larder."

"And it's wonderful to see you all, too," she said sternly. "Help yourselves."

James, William and Robert rushed over to the larder door while Malcolm stood beside Annie and watched the three of them.

"You have a right to eat too, Malcolm," she said, smiling across at him.

"Have you had word from Donnie?"

"No. But surely you can't be worried about him yet. He's hardly been gone."

"He's not a man in the best of health," Malcolm mused.

"If he has not returned by sunrise, we'll go looking for him," James said firmly as he stepped over to the pair. "He will have had his couple of days by then."

The five clan members sat around the table, and Annie watched as they hungrily ate any food they could persuade her to place in front of them.

"Do you want to stay here tonight?" she asked as Robert stifled a yawn behind his hand. "You've eaten so much I don't think you'll be safe trying to climb those hills. Have you given any thought to where you'll live in the summer?"

"We'll live in the hills, Annie," James said sleepily. "And staying here seems like a good idea."

"When was the last time you ate?" she asked, watching as William used the final crust of bread to sop up the remnants of Robert's stew.

"When was the last time you fed us?" Malcolm replied.

"You'll be no good to anyone, Caledon, if you and your men starve."

Robert fell asleep in the corner of the room almost at once, and Annie watched as the other three sat playing cards while she was left with a table of pots to clean. The evening drew into night and, as the men fell asleep, she moved over to the window. She stared out, holding a flickering candle in her hand. She wished she knew where Donald had gone, for she felt so responsible for his current heartache. Without knowing what drove her to do so, she picked up one of the knives which rested on the table and carried it back to her bed, where she lay awake for a time before she slipped into dreams.

In his dream, James was standing before the waterfall as he had done a year earlier. The waterfall continued to pour into the gorge but at his feet the burn ran red. Curious to find out what had caused this, he walked up to its side and looked down at the animal which was trapped there. It was a huge dog, which thrashed against the river but was tethered there. Its back was covered in large cuts and it was the blood from these which had stained the burn red. James pulled it free but, by the time he had secured it on the bank, it was to find the animal was already dead. He rose to his feet and looked about him as he heard the sound of footsteps. They were heavy footsteps which pounded the ground. He turned to find six of Mackay's men who rushed forward, but as he faced them, he awoke. He could still hear footsteps and he looked across at William who was already awake and staring at him. The other three woke up quickly as there was a pounding on the door.

Annie swung her legs from the bed, gripping the knife in her hand, and walked over to the door. The timbers shook as the person outside continued to beat them and, as Annie lifted the latch, it swung open under the force of the blows. Malcolm and Robert both had their pistols pointing toward this newcomer, but Robert let the weapon fall as his gaze focused on the figure who stood there.

"Moira?" Annie said quickly, throwing the knife aside as she ushered her niece indoors. "What in heaven's name are you doing here in the middle of the night?"

Robert snatched the blanket from Annie's bed and placed it about Moira's shoulders, encouraging her over to the fire which William was trying to rekindle.

"I've run all the way," Moira panted. "Or as much of the way as I could manage."

"What for?" Robert asked.

"Is it your father?" Malcolm added. "Is it Mackay again?"

"My father's safe," she said quickly, shivering as she leaned against Robert's side. "But it is Mackay."

"What's happened?" James asked. He had not become seated around the fire as the others had, but stood with his arms folded and stared down at this woman who had saved him from his dream.

"I had put my nephew to bed, and I fancied I saw a light burning down on the beach. So, I went to look out and see what it might be. But before I could get to the beach there were any number of Mackay's men there."

"Why?" James asked firmly, uncertain where this story was to lead, but knowing he would not like whatever conclusion had brought the young woman to Annie's door in the middle of the night.

"There was a man there. I didn't see him at first and then I went back indoors to escape from the soldiers. But when they returned to Golspie I saw who it was they had found beside the lantern, for they had tied him to a pony and were taking him once more to the town. And I knew at once I had to come and find you."

William snatched James' sleeve and watched as Annie asked softly, "And who was it?"

"Donald Mackenzie."

At the sound of this name the room erupted into noise and movement. James shook off William's hand from his arm and walked over to the door, but William rushed after him.

"We'll go together, Caledon, or all that will happen is Mackay will kill you both."

"Why was he there?" James demanded from Moira, who could only shake her head. "And with a lantern? Did he plan to be seen? What have I led him to?"

"This isn't your doing," Malcolm said quickly, returning the pistol to his waist. "Whatever drove him there, we have a duty to get him back."

Robert rose to his feet and kissed Moira's cheek as she stood beside him. "Stay here, Moira. You're tired, and I'm sure Annie won't mind."

He turned to face Annie, but she did not respond. Her face had become ghostly white and, as she snatched her shawl, she felt the guilt at Moira's news overwhelm her.

"You don't have to go, Annie," William said softly.

"No," she whispered as she glanced at James. "I think I do."

Without forming a plan or contriving any way of saving their friend, the Clan of Caledon rushed out into the night, William leading the way and the others easily keeping up with him. As they ran on, James recalled with a sickening feeling what he had dreamt before Moira disturbed his slumber. The lifeless creature he had pulled from the stream. A memory had returned to him, which he could hardly bear to consider. The Eile of Strength was a dog.

A Simple Choice with the Same Result

Donald Mackenzie was woken by the bitter force of cold water striking his face and, only seconds later, the stinging pain of the back of someone's hand. He blinked his eyes open and found himself staring into the calculating gaze of Ensign John Mackay. Panic began to take him, as Mackay struck him once again and Donald realised he could do nothing to defend himself, for his hands were tied above him. His arms were stretched out so that, as Mackay nodded to someone behind where Donald hung, he felt the ropes pull him so tight he thought his arms would be torn from his body. He gripped the cords, trying to hold them back, relieved to find the strength Mary had robbed him of had now returned.

"I didn't believe it when Mary told me you had met her on the beach. And so close to Littleferry where the rest of your kin drowned. Occasionally things of theirs still wash up there."

"That's what she told you?" Donald muttered, pulling against the cords which prevented him from striking the man before him. "That's not exactly what happened."

"You have always thought yourself above me, Donald Mackenzie. It seems justice has caught up with you. Now you can beg for mercy from me."

"I've never made you beg anything from me."

John Mackay did not answer but took a step forward. He was so close, Donald could feel his breath on his face. "Where is your cousin?"

Donald remained silent, blinking tears from his eyes as the ropes once more wrenched at his body.

"It's a simple question," Mackay continued. "Where is James Og? That coward who hides behind the title Caledon."

"I wouldn't give him up to Mary," Donald spat each word. "I'd never give him up to you."

"This nonsense - Caledon - will get you all killed. Do you really believe James Og will appear to rescue you?"

"I'm a son of Caledon."

"Let me tell you something about this man you follow. This man you call Caledon and pin all your hopes on."

"I'm a son of Caledon," Donald repeated, wincing as he felt a birch cane strike his back.

"Do you recall what happened a year ago? To your father?"

Donald remained silent, but lifted his eyes so they met with those of the man before him.

"You can't have forgotten surely?"

"You shot him," Donald replied. "Not once, not twice, but three times."

"And where was your loyal cousin? Your Caledon?" Mackay grabbed Donald's hair and pulled his head back. "I'll tell you where he was, since you clearly don't know. He was not ten yards away. Hiding in the heather."

"That's not true," Donald whispered with a faltering voice, willing his words to be accurate.

"That's how I know he's not going to come and save you. Because he's a coward."

"It's not true."

"So why don't you cease this one-sided loyalty and tell me where I can find him?"

Donald Mackenzie let his head drop to his chest as Mackay let go of his hair. He felt his breath catch as the birch struck his back once more and he set his face in firm resolve as he lifted his gaze.

"I'm a son of Caledon."

"As you wish," Mackay sighed. "I've been ordered to Tain, and can't leave after midday. I'd hoped to conclude this business before then."

"I'm a son of Caledon," Donald repeated, but he realised with a nauseous feeling that Mackay had not been talking to him but to the man behind.

"I'll make you a promise, Donald Mackenzie. The moment you tell me where to find James Og, I shall cease this torment. But if you have not spoken by midday, you will accompany me as far as the gallows tree, and then you'll hang there until I return in two weeks' time."

"I'm a son of Caledon."

"And so you say," Mackay said, turning his back on the young man and walking out of the room. He did not look back once.

Donald fought against each tightening of the rope, gripping to the tethers and pulling them towards him. Every time the birch struck his back, causing blood to trickle from the fine cuts, he tried to focus on distant images of the past, or imagine what the others would say about how he had once more ruined his new shirt. He tried to count the number of times he had been forced to find new garments since he had joined Jamie on this ill-fated crusade. Had Mackay spoken the truth? Was his father's death really on the hands of his cousin? Mary had tried to warn him of it that first day, but Donnie had been too blinded by pride in his cousin to believe her.

His thoughts, which he attacked with ferocity to combat the pain, considered each of the five members of the clan in turn, beginning with James Og. He had always believed in Jamie, at times far more than the man believed in himself. It was strange he had believed Mary too good to marry him, for Mary had delivered Donald far more hurt than James had. But if what Mackay said was true, was she justified? Finding no answer there, he turned his thoughts to Robert. A dangerous and blind passion fuelled everything the boy did. And yet, as Donald tried to imagine the past Malcolm had told them of, he found he was pleased not to have witnessed his own father's death, although he rebuked himself for failing to protect the old man.

Donald's own mother had died when he had been seven, and the heartache of standing by her bedside as her soul fled, returned to him now after almost two decades of absence.

Desperate to turn his thoughts he considered Malcolm and all the man had laid aside to assist the cause of Caledon. That a man, who knew nothing of James Og, should be willing to throw away a life of safety in France to join him surely spoke louder than the betrayal Mackay had spoken of. The man was the epitome of manners and Donald could not believe that any such man would follow a coward or a traitor. Next, he considered William and realised with a curious surprise that he knew nothing more of this man than his name. He had sacrificed a chance at happiness too, with the woman he loved, allowing her to sail to France and safety while he lingered, now a fugitive from both sides of the war. Each one of those men had lost and given far more than he had. Perhaps this was the justice Mackay had spoken of, that it was his turn to offer himself to the cause of Caledon. Finally, he considered the sixth member of the clan and a wearied smile crossed his lips.

"Annie," he muttered, and almost at once the pain ebbed and he felt himself slipping out of consciousness, dropping down from his tethered arms.

He jumped awake once more as his head was pulled back and he stared up at John Mackay. He clutched something in his hand and, seeing that Donald had returned to consciousness, he held it up. It was his own shirt, Donnie realised, shredded and bloodstained.

"He's still not here," Mackay stated. "And I am running out of time. Which means *you* are running out of time."

"I'm a son of Caledon," Donald muttered.

"And so you've been saying for the last four hours. But your fictitious father is as useless at defending you as your real father was."

"I'm a son of Caledon."

"And who is Annie?"

Donald stared vehemently across at him but spoke nothing. Mackay shook his head.

"Mary wants to talk to you."

"She won't like what I have to say."

"I don't think you'll like what she has to say, either. I believe it can be summarised in one word: Goodbye." Mackay dropped the shirt at Donald's feet and walked over to the door, which he pulled open and Donnie beheld the figure who stood there.

He tried to view her as his sister, who he had loved and adored every day of his life, but he could only see the witch who had cruelly used him to try and reach their cousin. She stepped into the room, never taking her brimming eyes from her younger brother who could not believe this appearance was anything more than an act.

"Can I talk to him alone?" she asked, glancing at her husband. "I swear I shall not do anything to allow him to escape."

John Mackay looked torn as he looked from brother to sister and back once more, before he nodded. He and the other man walked out the room and Mary closed the door before she turned once more to her brother and pressed herself against it sliding the bolt into the lock.

"It seemed strange to me, Donnie," she muttered, as she walked forward and did not stop until she stood directly before him. She placed her hand on his broad chest. "That you would side with the man who left our father and me to be torn to pieces by dogs. He hid that night. He hid and he ran."

"He saved your life after you were shot."

"There isn't a rescue coming for you, little brother. He won't appear with your little band of criminals to save you. You are Caledon's lamb, you see. The weakest and the gentlest."

"I'm a son of Caledon."

"I thought you were the Strength of Caledon," she mused as she ran her fingers along his wide arm. "Fortune seemed certain that was why you had survived. And you have seen what I can do, Donnie."

"Strength is more than brawn," he whispered back. Mary's eyes flashed, and he felt at once the crippling weakness seize him while she, with all of his strength, pulled on the ropes which bound him.

"Just as well, for now you have not even that," Mary snapped as Donald dropped forward, his left shoulder dislocated. "They know you are going to die, Donnie. That's why there will be no rescue. Why will you not give him up?"

"I'm a son of Caledon."

"You've seen what I can do, Donnie. I can give you a death so swift you will not even feel it, or I can cause you a death so prolonged no man should endure it."

"I'm a son of Caledon."

Mary produced a small knife and rested it against his pounding heart. "Just tell me where he is, Donnie, and it all ends quicker than you could believe."

He collapsed, whimpering against the pain in his left shoulder as he felt more of his strength drain from him.

"Why did you drink that cup?" Mary casually asked. "That cup at the wedding was meant for James Og. That's why this is happening to you. I was to be bound to him. He was my prey."

"He knew," Donald whispered, rising to his feet once more in a great defiance which burnt at his limbs. "He didn't trust you, even then. I wanted him to see you were not trying to poison him."

"The irony." Mary barked a laugh. "And I recall he took something of yours that night, too. Annie."

"Annie was never mine."

"Twelve years you've loved her and now she's nothing to you?"

"She has a right to make her choice. And I have a duty to Caledon."

"Last chance, little brother," Mary snapped, her temper fraying with the calm determination of the man before her. "Where is James Og?"

"I'm a son of Caledon."

Mary scowled at her brother and slashed the knife across his chest before she walked to the door, unbolted it and left. Little by little, Donald felt the strength return to his body and the stinging pain of the wound his sister had inflicted on him ebbed slightly. He lifted his gaze as another man entered and, releasing him, proceeded to bind his hands before him, dragging him from the chamber and out into the fine rain of the April morning. Mackay was there, pulling large leather gloves over his hands and talking to Mary, who never spared her brother a glance as he stumbled into the daylight.

Donald looked at each house he was pulled past, all had their shutters closed or heavy curtains pulled across the windows. The streets were silent despite the hour and, but for the twenty men who marched behind Mackay and Mary, he was alone. Arriving at the tree where three months earlier they had found Annie's nephew, the company halted and Mackay turned to Donald for the first time as the younger man swallowed hard, his gaze resting on the noose which hung there.

"It's quite simple, Mackenzie," Ensign Mackay said softly, as he drew the pistol from his belt. "All you need to do is tell me where I can find your cousin and I'll give you the same courtesy I paid your father."

"A shot?" Donald whispered.

"An instant death."

Mary stepped forward to Donnie and whispered, "The crows are waiting, little brother."

Donald turned to the tree and felt an uncontrollable fear creep through him as he noticed two crows walking sideward along the branch, anticipating the events which were about to take place. Mary stepped away from him to stand beside her husband.

"Where is James Og?" Mackay repeated.

Donald looked from the pistol in Mackay's hand, to the crows and the noose on the branch, before looking once more at the pistol. Had he really believed a rescue would come? Had he thought anything could save him from this ending from the moment he had been captured? He lifted his gaze from the pistol and looked into the faces of Ensign and Mrs Mackay.

"I am a son of Caledon. And I will never betray him."

"As you wish," Mackay replied. "He wouldn't have survived five minutes for you what you endured five hours for him. Consider that."

Donald felt two men dragging him over to the tree, but he kept his gaze on his sister while the noose was tightened about his neck. Mackay climbed into the saddle of his horse and looked down at Mary.

"Don't watch what is about to happen, Mary."

"I warned him his time would stretch as well as his neck. But I shall not stay here to witness it." She turned to her brother for a moment as Donald felt once more the peculiar motion of time slowing down.

"Wait," Mackay said suddenly. "Get rid of his plaid. I'll not have even a hanging man wearing such an outlawed garment."

There was no more speaking. The cord was tightened, and Donald gasped for breath as the rope hoisted his feet from the ground. He slotted the fingers of his right hand beneath the cord, but it was impossible to prise it from his neck. Terror seized him as the two birds he had witnessed earlier landed on him, one on his crippled left shoulder and the other on his head. But there was nothing he could do to free himself and, as Mackay had predicted, no rescue came. The repeated words which he tried to speak became frantic in his head but were barely audible from his breathless lips.

"I am a son of Caledon."

A Loyal Son of Caledon

There was an unnatural quiet to the town of Golspie as the Clan of Caledon ran towards the barracks. Annie hung back a little and tried to regain her breath while the four men rushed in. Malcolm and Robert both had their pistols drawn and she expected to hear gunfire as they entered, but the unnerving silence only continued. She stood in the rain, grateful of it, for it was refreshing after the hours of running she had just done. Looking up she found William returning. In his hands he carried a shredded and bloodied cloth and, as he handed it to Annie, she realised, with a terrible nausea, it was a shirt.

"Is he dead?" she whispered, hugging the garment to her as the other three walked from the barracks. Malcolm had lowered his pistol, but Robert still clutched his.

"He's not there," William replied. "Not now."

"But where else would he be?" she whispered. "This is his shirt. I know because I bought it for him."

"Mackay has journeyed to Tain if the papers in there are to be believed," Malcolm began. "He may have taken Donnie with him."

"That's not the sort of thing he would do." James rubbed his hand over his eyes before frustration and anger overcame him, kicking one of the stones on the road, trying to vent his rage.

"Someone here must know what happened," Malcolm began.

Annie clutched the shirt to her and tried to imagine that the man who had worn it was there with her. Clenching her eyes closed she could almost believe her gentle kinsman stood before her. She jumped slightly as James spoke.

"We have to find him."

"I'll go," Annie said quickly. "Everyone here will be looking for you. No one will be looking for me."

"I don't like it," Robert muttered. "Everything is too quiet."

"Then go, Annie," James said softly. "We'll follow you along the backs of the houses. If you need us, we'll be there."

"I'll enquire from the first person I see," she promised and watched as the four men rushed to the track which ran parallel to the road she walked down.

Everything in Golspie was frighteningly quiet. But for occasionally seeing her comrades down thin pends, the only movement to be seen was the blowing of heavy curtains which were all closed over windows. No sound came from the houses. The rain was no longer refreshing but chilling as it plastered the thin strands of hair to her face. As she walked past the gable end of one of the houses she stopped abruptly. She did not know what she had expected to find as she walked through the empty streets of the town, but she felt winded by the scene before her. Two uniformed soldiers stared across, unmoved and unflinching as she collapsed to the floor.

Almost at once the four men of the clan rushed between the buildings towards her. Annie tried to wave them back but, though they were unheeding of the gesture, it alerted them enough so that Malcolm and Robert already had their pistols ready to fire upon the two soldiers. James rushed over to Annie.

"Are you hurt?" he began quickly. "What happened?"

"Caledon," William whispered and, driven by the tight tone of the man's voice, each of the clan turned to look at what the soldiers had been guarding.

"No," James muttered as he took a moment to recognise the figure suspended from the thick branch of the tree. Annie rose to her feet and stared across at the two crows which perched on the lifeless body of Donald Mackenzie.

"He was afraid of crows," Robert whispered.

They all watched in a numb silence as a heavy raven landed on the branch, stretching its wings wide. The two crows, which were dwarfed by its presence, flew beyond the houses while the raven watched down over the scene, standing protectively over the hanging corpse. Annie could not bear to see anymore. She clung to Malcolm, burying her head in his woollen plaid. Donald's plaid rested beside his stripped form, and James walked forward towards where it hung down.

"Get him down," he whispered hoarsely, and watched as William rushed to the knotted cord while Robert mercilessly fired a second shot at one of the soldiers. Untying the knot was easy for William's agile hands, but the giant weight of Donald

Mackenzie was too great for him to hold and the man's body fell heavily to the ground, the rope of the noose snaking around the tree and settling on his still chest. James pulled the plaid from the branch and placed it over his cousin, trying to return the dignity which had been taken from him. He reached up to the cord above Donald's neck and teased out the pin which had been thrust there. It bore the crest of the Mackenzie clan, now dead in the east with the passing of his cousin.

"What have I done?" James muttered as he looked across to Malcolm, who knelt on the other side of the body. Annie gently coaxed Donald's lifeless fingers from the cord on his bruised neck, and ran her trembling fingers along the long wound across his chest.

"This was not your doing, Caledon," Malcolm replied.

"It was not his, either."

Robert felt heavy tears fall from his eyes as he looked at the sleeping face of Donald Mackenzie. It bore several scratches from the claws and beaks of the crows. He turned once more to the raven which still sat in the tree. Its sharp eyes matched the black, tear-filled gaze of Annie, and he realised it was no coincidence the great bird stood watching over them. William struck Robert's shoulder in a consolidating gesture, but he was clearly shaken by the events.

"What do we do now, Caledon?" Malcolm asked. "Where can we take him?"

"Wait," James whispered. "The water. The healing spring. It worked for Mary, surely it will work for him."

This spark of hope felt too thin for the others to share in, but all the same they placed the body of Donald Mackenzie on his philamor, and Robert and Malcolm carried it through the street as they followed James. The people of the houses had emerged and now lined the route through the village, their heads bared, and their faces lowered as the small procession passed through. It was a mark of their deep regret at the passing of this great man.

Trying to reach the waterfall was difficult for there was not always a bank to the stream, and at times they had to wade through the burn itself. Finally, James Og stood on the spot where he and Donald had stood almost exactly a year ago, and he looked expectantly at the waterfall. Relieved to have reached this peculiar destination, Robert and Malcolm lowered Donald's litter, and all of them stood waiting, unsure what they were looking for but never wishing to question their leader.

After a time, the waterfall stretched its long fingers out and pulled itself from the rock. Malcolm bowed his head slightly but did not seem surprised by this revelation, while Annie and Robert openly stared at the translucent and elongated form of the figure before them. William knelt beside Donald and looked across as a long-legged dog walked down the sheer side of the gorge and began licking the dead man's face.

"Why are you here, Caledon?"

"Donnie's dead," James said in a voice which shook only a little. His clan watched him thoughtfully, unable to hear the other side of the conversation.

"I warned you what would happen if you attended that wedding."

"You can still heal him," James pleaded.

"You were told, when the healing spring was gifted to you, only one other person could be offered it's assistance. You chose Time."

"Time? What does that mean?"

"Caledon," William called. "His Eile is warming him."

"You can still save him," James pleaded, but was met with the same silence the others heard. "Mackay will pay for this."

"You have a far greater enemy in Time than you have in Mackay."

"Then why was it Mackay who hung Donnie?"

"There is an enemy here who you have not seen. You must seek the truth of what Strength died for or his sacrifice will have been in vain. But I know why you are here. I know what you want. Even now, while his body is warm, there is a chance of life. That is why the wolf stands over him. But to find this life there is a price to pay. And it is a price you may not be able to accept."

"My cousin lies dead because of this crusade. It was my duty to protect him."

"Are you willing to pay such a price?"

"I will do anything which is asked of me."

"It is not you it shall be asked of, but the one who has travelled through death's veil. Then, place him in the pool."

James turned to Robert and Malcolm.

"Place him in the pool," he ordered, a giddy feeling taking him as he considered this might wake and revive the cousin he had failed to protect. The two brothers lifted the litter once more and carried it out into the stream before stepping back to the shore. At once the pounding waters beat down upon the body of Donald Mackenzie and the burn turned a terrible red as it had in his dream. The dog had vanished, though none of them had seen it leave and there were no tracks but their own in the soft ground. William helped Robert and Malcolm from the river as it splashed Donald's blood downstream.

"I'm a son of Caledon."

Each member of the clan looked at one another at the sound of Donald's voice, and Annie clung to Jamie's arm as she pointed to the pool where they had placed Donald. There was no sign of the man's body anymore but instead they were forced to witness with a brutal accuracy the final hour of their friend's life in the suddenly calm surface of the pool. People came and went from the image, but all were faceless and impossible to identify. But it was Donald's repetition of his defiant words which struck James' heart. Annie cried uncontrollably as she saw it, the tears streaming from her large black eyes as her kinsman tried to pull the noose from his neck. Malcolm watched through brimming eyes as someone thrust the pin into the hemp rope, and he carried a silent admiration for Donald Mackenzie's brave loyalty. In turn, Malcolm comforted his brother as the young man witnessed these final moments, cursing himself for failing to share with Caledon the full extent of Donnie's sufferings. Robert winced as they saw, through the fading eyes of the dying man, the crows coming toward them, and he looked up at the trees overhead as the birds flew from their roosts, unsettled by this image.

Once the waterfall had shown all its macabre secrets and Donald Mackenzie's fading voice whispered its final syllable, Malcolm shook his head.

"There is nothing here now, Caledon. Even his body has gone."

"You said you would give him life!" James shouted, staring at the waterfall, but it had returned once more to the rocks and could no longer hear nor speak.

"Why did we have to see it?" Annie wept. "Why should we witness such an end?"

"So that we could appreciate the strength he had," Malcolm replied, swallowing hard in an attempt to deflect his tears.

"It was not solely his physical strength," James whispered as he clutched Annie to him. "He had a depth of strength which Caledon, and the world, will not see again. Annie, what have I done?"

"We should return to Lairg," Robert muttered numbly. "Moira will be afraid, and after risking so much she deserves to know our sad outcome."

"Come, Caledon," Malcolm agreed. "There's nothing to be done here."

He took James' hand and guided him along the path they had taken to arrive there, so full of hope which now seemed so vain.

"I swore to hate you," Annie whispered, grasping James' sleeve in one hand and gripping Donald's stained shirt in the other. "If any harm came to him,

I swore I should hate you. But I have come to respect you, James Og. Not as Caledon, but as the man Donnie so admired and almost worshipped."

"I'm not sure I can be Caledon anymore, Annie, for I have caused an outcome I can't reconcile with. I loved him. Not as a cousin, but as a brother. And I needed him more than I can explain."

"You've no need to try," Annie whispered. "For I feel it, too."

"I must tell Mary," James muttered, as they turned a slight corner in the ravine and a sudden gust of wind struck his chest. "There's a chance she does not know."

William watched them walk away, before he leaned down and picked up the skilfully crafted pin which had been dropped. A fine tear streaked down his right cheek as he ran his thumb over the Mackenzie crest.

"Goodbye Oaf," he whispered as he straightened to his feet. He looked at the waterfall which, only a few minutes earlier, had been a man, and felt his breath catch. His hand tightened upon the pin, so much so that a thin trickle of blood ran from his palm, and he stared hard at the sight before him.

Emerging from the waterfall came the unmistakable figure of Donald Mackenzie. He was clad only in his philamor and strong leather boots. His hands were still bound, and the noose still adorned his neck. He gave his usual apologetic smile as his eyes met William's gaze, and William opened his mouth to speak, turning to call to the others. But they had vanished from sight and he turned back to the waterfall in confusion once more.

Donald Mackenzie was gone.

Part Seven:
The Uncertain Future
of Caledon

The Clan Fractures

Despite Robert's intention to return to Lairg, and Moira who waited there, the remaining five members of the clan spent the night on the side of Ben Bhraggie. There was an absolute silence to them all. William stood a short distance away, a look of confusion on his face every time he regarded the pin he held in his hand. Robert, whose emotions ran so close to the surface, had wept until he had no tears left to cry and had fallen asleep, exhausted by grief. His half brother watched the clan with bright eyes, but could find no words to speak to them. Annie still gripped Donald's bloodied shirt to her, but her eyes were dry and her face set in resolve.

James stared down on the lights of Golspie and tried to escape the thought of what had happened earlier in the town. He had been unable to shake free from Donnie's words and they still rang in his ears.

"I'm going," he announced suddenly, the noise startling the rest of the clan.

"Going where?" Malcolm asked softly.

"To find Mary. She has a right to know."

"Don't you think she already knows?" Annie whispered.

"I have a duty to tell her. But I'll be back before sunrise."

"Then we should all go," Annie said firmly.

"Robert has only just fallen asleep," James began, glancing across and searching for any excuse to be free of them. "Leave him to sleep."

Malcolm and Annie exchanged an anxious glance as James pulled his boots on and rose to his feet. He did not speak to them but walked down the hill, feeling he had to escape the terrible reminder each of them placed on him. They were no longer a clan, they were only a collection of people united in their grief and situation. No amount of time or distance seemed able to separate him from that pain-filled and desperate voice that continued to announce,

"I am a son of Caledon."

"Donnie?" he whispered as he turned around at a sound close behind him, but there was no one there. Instead, he heard a rustling in the undergrowth as a hidden creature made its way through the night, disturbed by his presence.

Continuing down the hill he walked into the square at Golspie. There were puddles now, but the rain had stopped. He looked at the broad, strong branches of the gallows tree and swallowed hard as he recalled the image which had awaited him here earlier. Turning, he walked north, staying close to the buildings so he could use their shadow. But he had no need to worry. There were no people about in the town and the small militia had journeyed to Tain with John Mackay. He stopped at the house he had last visited at the start of the year, when he had forced a pardon from the ensign, and placed his hand on the latch. Donald had saved him then, and James felt once more the excruciating guilt at how he had responded, by leading his younger cousin to the most torturous death he could imagine. Lowering his head into his free hand he tried to dispel the picture from his mind and jumped as he felt a hand prise his fingers from the door. Without consideration he grabbed the dirk from his waist and spun to face this intruder.

"Careful, Caledon," William said quickly. "It would be careless to lose two of your clan in one day."

James felt his eyes flare at this apparently flippant remark but before he could answer, Malcolm placed a hand on his shoulder.

"Annie didn't want you going alone and her reasoning, as you would expect, was sensible."

"Really," James snapped back. "And what reasoning was that?"

"That if your cousin were in Golspie today," William replied, "she could never have missed this event. Her husband clearly spent a long time with Donnie before he had him hanged. And before he left her to travel south for a time." William watched as James stared back blankly. "She either knew or is away. Either way, you should not be here alone."

"Someone's in," Malcolm said softly. "I can smell cooking, and it smells almost good enough to rival Annie's."

"I won't tell her you said that," James whispered, forcing a smile.

William moved James' hand from the latch and pushed the door open. He walked in first, unwilling to allow James to risk his life doing so. James followed, and Malcolm carefully closed the door before turning to face the ashen features of the lady of the house.

"What is this?" Mary whispered, snatching a knife that rested on a long wooden sideboard. "Jamie? What is this?"

"Mary," James began, lifting his hands peaceably. "Have you been here all day?"

"Yes." She backed away towards the fire. "Why are you here? If John finds you, he will kill you."

"John Mackay will be in Tain by now," William said.

"How do you know?" she muttered, lowering the blade and allowing Malcolm to steer her away from the fire.

"Because we read through his dispatch notice," James said softly. "So you have remained here all day?"

"Yes," Mary replied, her mind racing to try and find a way to overpower the three men before her, but she realised, with her maid gone home and her husband away, she was alone in the house. "I was asleep this morning," she continued, building her wall of lies to defend herself, unsure how much her cousin knew of her involvement in her brother's death. "The baby is so tiring. I'm certain she will have her uncle's strength and build, for she feels far heavier than I could imagine any normal child."

"Her uncle?" Malcolm whispered as William muttered, "Donnie?"

"What has happened, Jamie?" Staring from the two men to her cousin. "Why is Donnie not with you? When he loved you beyond anyone else? Is he hurt?"

"Mackay shares nothing with you, then?" James asked, helping Mary over to a chair and kneeling before her. "Donnie was caught last night. On the beach."

"On the beach?" Mary repeated. "Who told you so? Did they see?"

"It doesn't matter who it was, Mary," James continued while William stared down at the woman, his brow creasing. "But he was caught and, while you slept, Mackay had him-" he stopped and shook his head as tears sprang into his eyes.

"Lord, Jamie, are you telling me that John has taken Donnie to be tried? Is that why he is in Tain?"

"Mrs Mackay," Malcolm said softly, seeing his leader was unable to answer beyond shaking his head. "Donald Mackenzie is dead."

"Dead?" Mary gasped. "What do you mean dead? Why did you not protect him? He would have followed you anywhere." She flung herself at Jamie, beating him with her fists before Malcolm grabbed her and pulled her back.

"I - we - came as soon as we discovered what had happened," James began, choking back tears. "But he was already dead."

"Did he suffer?" she met his eyes, recalling the events of the day and, through them, wishing to enhance the suffering of the man before her. "Or was it like when John killed Father?"

James faltered but turned to look at William who glared down at the woman.

"Yes, he suffered. In pride and pain. He was stripped and hanged." William folded his arms across his chest and glared at the scene before him. "But you can be content knowing he never disgraced his name and clan, for he didn't betray us."

James and Malcolm watched as William handed the pin he had taken from the waterfall to Mary. She took it uncertainly and stared down.

"And you hid," she began, pointing it towards James. "As you did when Father was shot. You gave him no help, you left him to die. He was Caledon's lamb who you were willing to sacrifice. Get out of this house James Og, and take your criminals with you."

"Mary, I came to offer my condolences."

"You can't bring him back, Jamie. Make no mistake, whoever tied the noose about his neck is no more responsible than you are." She rose to her feet and reached once more for the knife which rested beside her but, as she stretched for it, she stumbled and put her hands out to the sideboard, trying to steady herself. She began sobbing uncontrollably and James glanced across at the two men as she clutched her stomach.

"No," William began. "This isn't a good thing. Either she is as clumsy as her brother or there will shortly be five people in this room."

"What?" Malcolm and James asked in chorus.

"Her child is about to make an appearance, Caledon, and it would not end well for any of us if we were here when it did."

"No," Mary whimpered. "I was told I would be tended. Where have they gone?"

"We should go, Caledon," William repeated, an urgency driving his words.

"Don't leave me," Mary pleaded. "James Og do not leave me as you left my father and my brother."

"Bring her with us," James said quickly.

"No," Malcolm began. "She can't run up the mountainside like this. She needs a nurse, a woman to help her."

"We don't know any women here, Malcolm," James began. "We hardly know any women at all."

"Annie," Mary panted. "Fetch Annie."

William stepped forward and caught her as she swayed slightly. "Go find Annie," he said quickly. "I'm certain she has a better idea of what to do than any of us."

Malcolm and James both leapt at the door, but Malcolm reached it first and slammed the door closed behind him, trapping James in the room.

"I don't understand," Mary whispered repeatedly. "They said they would be here. Where are they?"

William helped her over to the chair but no sooner had she sat down than she rose once more to her feet. Mary was inconsolable as she walked backward and forward, cursing the people who had abandoned her before she turned her anger on James. When Malcolm returned with Annie and Robert, James could not leave the house quickly enough. He and Robert stood outside while Annie tended to Mary, assisted by Malcolm. William walked over to where the Mackenzie pin rested on the floor, discarded by Mary in her anguish, and he picked it up once more, recalling the image of Donald he had witnessed at the waterfall.

"You betrayed him," Mary hissed as Annie pushed her down onto the bed. "He would have given his life for you."

"I have enough guilt on this matter, Mary. You've no need to rebuke me further."

"He spoke of you," Mary continued, the pain driving her words with no consideration for them. "He loved you for fifteen years and you repaid him with scorn. You left him to the crows."

"I've come to help you," Annie whispered, tears blooming in her eyes. "But if you continue to behave like this, I'll leave you."

Malcolm handed Annie a towel and watched as the two women spoke such bitter words to one another, trying to remind himself this situation was as a result of the love they both shared for his departed friend.

"They said they would be here," Mary wailed as she clutched to Annie's arm so tightly her fingers left white marks on her kinswoman's flesh. Annie barely noticed but listened as Mary continued. "Fortune, Beauty, they promised. And Donnie said he would be here. He lied to me. He chose Jamie over me."

"Good fortune will favour you, I have no doubt, Mary. And there is nothing more beautiful than a newborn child. But you must not think of Donnie. He's gone."

"He chose Jamie over me and swung for it. Why did he choose such a coward? I needed him to live. I need his strength now, but I can't reach him."

"Caledon is no coward," Malcolm interjected.

"He allowed my father to die. Left me to the mercy of dogs and soldiers. And he abandoned my little brother, his own cousin, to the most painful and degrading death. He is a coward."

Malcolm walked from the room without another word and rejoined the other three men around the fire. None of them spoke to one another but, as the sun began to rise, a new sound filled the house. The unmistakable shrill cry of a newborn child.

James rose to his feet as Annie walked out of the room where the child's cries had been clear minutes earlier. She looked exhausted, tears stained her cheeks and she stumbled as she walked. Supporting her in his arms, James smiled down.

"Well done, Annie."

"She will not be a Mackenzie," she whispered. "But she is a strong baby."

"Donnie would be an uncle," James laughed. "I struggle to imagine that."

"I don't," Annie replied softly. "She wants to talk to you, James Og. But be careful, she's talking about things she shouldn't be."

"What do you mean?"

"I'm quite sure she knows exactly what happened to her brother."

James watched as Annie sat down on the chair while William offered her a bottle which sat beside the knife on the sideboard. Swallowing back the thought Mary could be in any way linked to the death of her own younger brother he placed his hand on the door and walked in.

Mary was lying on her bed, holding her child to her. Her eyes were barely open, and her face was pale, making her eyes appear even darker. Turning this gaze toward him she waited as he walked over to her.

"Congratulations, Mary," he said softly.

"This should have been our child, James Og," she began. "I waited so long for you."

"You're far too sensible to have married me, Mary."

"You speak flippantly, Jamie, but your words are true. I would have taken that knife tonight and killed you for what you have brought on my family. This child has saved your life."

"Then I'm very grateful to her," James said with a smile which only angered Mary more.

"I'm going to give you a head start, James Og. You have until my husband returns to vanish from these lands, taking your little band with you, before I hunt you down. And neither my daughter nor my brother will save you then."

James nodded slightly and placed his hand over the head of the infant. "I understand why you hate me, Mary. I hate myself for the same reason."

"Am I to feel pity for you? You never even told Donnie what you did that night. Or what you did not do."

"I know I was wrong to leave you. And your father. But I was honest with Donnie and I did as much as I could to protect him."

"I told him." She stared into his eyes with such vehemence that James faltered.

"When? When did you last see your brother?"

"I visited our father's house on the anniversary of his death. The anniversary of your arrival. Donnie was there, hugging the burnt remains of what had been our father's chair. Like a child. He was always like a child. Frightened, pitiful and uncommonly slow witted." She kissed her child's cheek as it began crying. "And we talked. I explained to him what had happened. And he didn't believe me. He would not believe you would ever do such a thing."

"I never lied to him," James whispered, disgust and heartbreak gripping him as he listened to the words she spoke of his beloved cousin.

"He lied to me. He told me he would be here when my child was born. And he told me he loved me, too."

"He did love you."

"But not as much as he loved you. He defended you to my face. You who left me to the mercy of the hounds' teeth and the soldiers' wants."

"Did you turn him in?"

"My husband waited for me outside the house. I can't tell you whether he had my brother followed. But you, I hold you personally responsible."

"Frightened, pitiful and uncommonly slow witted?" James muttered. "You didn't know your brother at all. He was strong, loyal and uncommonly kind-hearted. But I'll take your promised head start, Mary, for I do believe Caledon will not last long without your brother."

He walked out of the room and looked at the four faces which turned to look at him.

"We should be going. The town is waking up and it's hard to hide in daylight."

"Caledon?" Robert began. "She is grieving. Whatever she told you, you're no more responsible for Donnie's death than any of us."

"That's not true, however much I wish it were."

James walked out of the house and the others followed in a thoughtful silence as they trudged up the hillside, where only yesterday they had raced down. They did not stop until Golspie was hidden from sight, then James turned to them all.

"I have to go."

"Go?" Malcolm repeated. "Go where?"

"Away from this place. Mary spoke some acutely truthful words, and among them she highlighted that I should leave this place; her; Mackay; all of it behind. She was right. And I can't be Caledon anymore. The waterfall, the source, whoever it was chose me made a great error. And it was an error which cost Donald Mackenzie his life. I won't see that happen to any of you."

"James," Annie said quickly. "You can't leave behind this quest. We're all bound to it. Donnie would not see you do such a thing."

"Nor will he," James replied coldly. "He's dead."

"Caledon," Robert whispered but stopped as Malcolm placed his hand on his shoulder.

"Then you must go, Caledon," Annie said softly. "You know where you'll find us if you need us."

"I'm sorry." James turned from the four of them and began walking north toward the burn that would eventually feed the falls where he had begun this foolish quest. His feet found their own way and he trusted them to guide him, for his heart and his head conflicted so greatly. He did not look back at his clan but felt he had to be free of them, free of all the events of Caledon.

He walked on until nightfall, pausing only to drink from fast-moving streams, and stood looking down on the Ord as it ran through the deep valley hundreds of feet below him. Here, as the sun set and the razor sharp moon rose, he curled up amongst the ferns and wrapped his plaid around him.

"What are you doing, Jamie Caledon?"

James turned around and found he was standing on the heavy drawbridge of Castle Caledon. It was the waterfall who spoke as it cascaded down the opening, as he knew it would be for its voice was unique.

"You made a mistake," James replied. "You chose the wrong person to become Caledon. Mary was right. I have been a coward, and I've only enhanced my cowardice by failing to speak truthfully."

"Time manipulates you and you allow it to happen. Turning from your clan is the greatest cowardice you have shown."

"Donnie is dead. He would have lived if I had not begun this foolish quest. Or if you had healed him."

"That's not true."

James felt his breath catch at the sound of the voice which had haunted his thoughts for the last two days, and he watched as Donald Mackenzie walked through the gateway, the waterfall teeming down upon him. His hands were still bound, and the noose wrapped about his throat, the long hemp cord stretching behind him like a tail.

"I would have died long ago if you had not arrived at our door."

"*That's* not true," James began, looking into the cut and scratched face of his younger cousin.

"John Mackay wouldn't stop until I was dead. His kindest offer was of a shot."

"I'm so sorry, Donnie."

"What for?"

"For this," James began, pointing to his cousin's bound hands and then the noose on his neck. "And all of it. I owe you far more thanks and appreciation than I ever did before. We saw your final moments, your courage in the face of fear and pain. Your strength, Donnie. But now you've gone I have no strength left."

"You can't give up, Jamie. If you give up, I died for nothing." Donnie tried to take his cousin's hand, but the cords restricted him. "I didn't endure this so you would turn your back on Caledon. I did it so you were free to pursue it."

"I told Mary."

"What?" Donnie whispered, so quietly James was unsure he had heard it.

"I told her of your demise, for she had a right to know. She has a child now. A daughter. Donnie?" He looked across at his cousin to see blood spilling from the long wound across his chest, and his face had become as pale as when he had found him hanging.

"Leave Mary, Jamie. Please, I beg you, leave her."

"I did leave her. She has a hatred of me."

"I loved her, Jamie," Donald panted, collapsing to his knees and trying to pull the cord from his neck, but he could not. James knelt beside him, trying to help free him from the noose but it only became tighter and tighter until Donnie's gaze became unseeing. James hugged the younger man's body to him feeling once more the sickening guilt at his death.

"You should heed his plea," the emotionless voice of the waterfall began. "Leave her until you are stronger once more."

"I've lost my strength," James replied, rising to his feet. As he looked down, it was to find his cousin's body had gone, though the splash of blood still marked the ground.

"Return to your clan, Jamie Caledon. They are not safe without you, and neither are you safe without them."

"They are far safer."

"As Donald Mackenzie was? Those who are loyal to Caledon will be hunted throughout their lives by those who oppose you. Will you leave them to the death you witnessed for your cousin? You need to command, Caledon. For fear of what the repercussions might be, what answer you might give, one of your clan has not told you something. And it weighs heavily on their mind."

"You told me Donald Mackenzie would live."

"Have you not seen him before you, Caledon?"

"In dreams," James retorted. "I trusted you-"

"As he trusted you, Caledon. You must return to your clan. They need you. Enemies of Caledon are closing in around you. You cannot afford to allow these enemies to tighten their hold. Each of you must be vigilant. And do not presume to undermine and usurp your clan. They have been called for their own strengths, as you were. This is a journey you cannot flee from."

James awoke abruptly as he heard a deep, groaning sound from the valley beneath him. Everything fell silent and still once more and he rubbed his hand across his sweating forehead. He stopped as he looked down at the blood on his hand.

He had no wound, there was no cut on his body. He lifted his other hand to his face as the dream flashed before him and he realised that it was Donnie's blood.

Rising to his feet, James turned from north to south, torn between the two directions. Finally, he took a step forward and allowed his feet to follow their course.

What the Raven Saw

Eight days had passed the clan without sight or sound of their leader. Robert's sadness had turned to indignation before, by the sixth day, he had returned to a melancholy which isolated him from his other companions. The only person he spoke with now was Moira, who had remained in Lairg for a time.

"I don't understand it," Robert sighed as he helped her up the hillside before they sat together and looked down over Lairg. "What could he hope to achieve by abandoning us?"

Moira had no answer to offer, understanding far less of the situation than Robert did, but she hugged his arm and leaned over to kiss his cheek. Robert spared her the briefest smile before he turned and stared at the town once more, but saw nothing.

His brother's pensiveness weighed heavily on Malcolm. He carried his own concerns regarding James Og's absence, not least because he missed the open discussions he had been able to share with him. He could not talk with Robert for the young man was as half blinded by passion as he was half deaf to the sounds of the world. While Malcolm commended the zeal of his brother, it did not make him a safe man to confide in.

"Come and get some food, Malcolm," Annie began, pulling a chair out from the table.

"Thank you," he mumbled in reply.

"He'll come back," Annie said softly. "I know he will."

"I could be in France," Malcolm said. "I could have left all this behind and been safe, free to live within the law. I understand what Donald Mackenzie meant to him, but he only cheapens his sacrifice by leaving."

"He'll come to see that," Annie whispered, trying to dispel the lump that formed in her throat at her kinsman's name. "He needs to grieve for him, that's all. And, for what such a statement is worth, I'm pleased you didn't leave for France." She reached across the table and placed her hand on Malcolm's arm.

"Have you spoken to William?"

"No." Annie shuffled awkwardly. "I'm less certain he'll return."

"Because you don't know him," Malcolm said softly. "In his own way he laments Donald Mackenzie's passing."

"Through guilt, no doubt."

Malcolm gently pushed the plate away and took Annie's hand in both of his. "What words have you shared with him? What caused you to feel this way about him?"

"He never spoke to Donnie without insult. And yet now we are expected to believe he mourns him? I do not believe it."

"They were as different as two men could be, Annie. But it didn't mean they hated one another. I've never observed William as quiet as he has been since we found Donnie."

"He's hiding something," Annie said with a certainty which surprised her. "I don't know what it is, but I'm sure of it."

Malcolm nodded slowly. "He spoke harsh words when we visited Mary Mackay, even by his cutting standards. But what can he be hiding? He has nothing to rebuke himself for. No more than the rest of us."

"Mary Mackay," Annie muttered. "She isn't innocent in this. She spoke of the crows. How would she know of the crows if she had not seen Donald? Her own brother, Malcolm. You would not do that to Robert, would you?"

"I would not do that to my enemy, far less my brother."

They both turned as Robert and Moira stepped into the house and each pair smiled across at the other.

"Did you see William?" Annie began, and watched as Robert tilted his head slightly.

"No," Moira said quickly. "We didn't see William."

Robert nodded his agreement and sighed heavily. "He is probably far away now. Maybe he returned west to his home."

"Do we even know where his home is?" Annie asked.

"He was raised in Ullapool. That much I know."

"Wait," Annie began, her voice trembling as she lost sight of the room before her. Instead, she felt she was high in the clouds, looking down over the world. "He's gone south."

"South?" Robert muttered. "How do you know?"

"I don't. I just thought I saw him."

"Why would he go south?" Malcolm asked, never questioning how she knew.

"Oh no," Annie whispered, realising the only cause he would have to journey in that direction, towards habitation and danger. Her vision had returned once more to the room before her and she turned her gaze to Malcolm. "He's gone to find Ensign John Mackay."

"What?" Robert, Moira and Malcolm all asked at once.

"He'll be killed," Robert began. "Why has he gone?"

"I don't know," Annie replied. "I just saw him walking towards the midday sun."

"What can we do?" Malcolm asked. "He left two days ago. He could have reached Tain by now. We can't catch up with him."

"We have to try," Robert began. "He may be a Hanoverian, but he's still a part of our clan. Whatever that means now."

"It means a great deal," Annie said firmly. "James Og will return. I know it."

"What do we do in the meantime?"

"We go after William," Malcolm announced. "We're still a clan, and Caledon would not survive another loss so soon after Donald Mackenzie."

Robert nodded and kissed Moira's forehead before he snatched up the pistol he had abandoned on the wide windowsill. Malcolm rose to his feet and looked down at Annie.

"You should come, too."

"No. I came with you last time and slowed you all down. Donnie might not have died."

"Donald Mackenzie had died long before we reached him, Annie. It's not your fault. And we need your eyes."

"My eyes?" Annie whispered.

"Yes. You saw where he was going."

"I might have been wrong."

Malcolm just smiled and shook his head. He looked from Annie to Robert and felt a great regret at how the clan, which two weeks earlier had been twice as numerous, had shrunk to only three.

All of them turned as the front door opened and Malcolm instantly pointed his pistol towards it. He lowered it as he recognised the man who stood there.

"Caledon," he whispered. "You came back."

"Yes," James replied, just as quietly. "But you look like you're all going somewhere."

"I knew you'd come back," Annie muttered with a smile.

"I almost didn't. I made it as far as Olrig, and was hoping to find a boat there. But I couldn't bear to fail him."

"Fail who?" Robert asked.

"Donnie." James shook his head as he closed the door and leaned against it. "Every night I ran I held him as he died." He lifted his hand to his throat and tried to escape the image which had haunted his dreams and the terrible panic it created in him. The four people in the room watched him with expressions of pity and concern, but remained silent.

"Where's William?"

"That's where we were going, Caledon," Robert replied. "He's gone south to find Mackay."

James felt his features set in a stern expression as he pulled open the door, uncaring of who should see him. Robert and Malcolm did not waste a second in rushing after him, though Robert kissed Moira's cheek before he left. Annie followed slowly behind. Unsure her accompanying the three men was wise, she watched them walk through the street as she stood at her door.

"Annie, what are you doing?" James called back.

She turned to Moira and smiled slightly. "Be careful returning, Moira. There is more evil in Golspie than has so far revealed itself. I must ask something more of you, for I can't believe Donald Mackenzie would so recklessly allow himself to be seen. Look out whenever you see a light on the beach and tell me anyone you see there."

"What if I'm seen?"

"You need only watch from your nephew's window, and don't have a candle. I have a most terrible feeling Mary arranged Donnie's capture, but I can't understand how or why."

"Annie!" Malcolm called.

"Be careful," she repeated as she kissed her niece's cheek and hurried after them.

The night was deep when James finally stopped. Each of them was exhausted, and they had found no sign of William. They were not far from Tain now, and the likelihood William had not already reached the town was slim. With this came the heavy burden of knowledge their friend had almost certainly suffered the same fate as Donald Mackenzie. James was not entirely sure this had not been the man's plan.

"That was the homestead of Robert Mackenzie," Annie whispered as she pointed to a house on the hillside above them.

"Donnie's father?" Malcolm asked.

"Yes," Jamie said firmly, in a tone which ended all conversation. "There'll be no shelter to be found there now."

"What made you come back, Caledon?" Malcolm asked later while Robert and Annie were talking a short distance away.

"Donald Mackenzie," James whispered. "Even in his death he's my strength. He told me he had died so I was free to pursue the dream of Caledon. It must seem foolish to you that I should trust a dream, but that's all I have left of him now."

"A year ago I might have called it foolish. But you have shown me such things, Caledon, I hardly know what is truth and what is make-believe."

James laughed slightly. "We're living in a time of dreams and nightmares, Nobility. But I've realised, through it all, this is a quest I am bound to. I mean to see it succeed."

James walked down to where a small burn ran into the firth, and he knelt at its side to fill their water flasks. He had a contentment within him which he had bought at so high a price, yet he knew now what he was expected to do.

Having filled the four flasks he began splashing water onto his face, trying to remain awake so he might guard his clan while they slept. He turned quickly at a peculiar sound a short distance away. It was low in pitch, so much so, he felt his stomach tense at the sound, and after a time he recalled where he heard it last. It was when he had rested that night above the Ord, he had awoken to this sound. Walking towards it, he drew the dirk he carried and stared out over the firth. He was not afraid but leaned over the bank, staring down into the midnight blackness of the waters and frowned as only his own reflection, darker and more mysterious, stared back.

He was about to leave the shore and return to his friends when he noticed his reflection seemed to grow, and the dark strong eyes became clearer and clearer as the face moved towards him. And while it was his eyes that stared, unblinking, from the water, it was not his face. He pushed himself backward, away from the creature and snatched the flasks before he rushed to his companions, unwilling to talk to them of what he had just witnessed.

A Dream or a Premonition

Tain stretched before William as he stared across the gentle recline of the hill. For a day now he had sat and watched, waiting for Ensign John Mackay to leave the town. But he had waited in vain, for the ensign had never appeared. Drawing the pistol from his belt, he looked thoughtfully down at it. The adventure which had followed from his first encounter with the two cousins had led him through great heartache and hardship. He had parted with his heart when he said farewell to Catherine Kintail, the woman he had loved for so many years but whose family would never accept him. While he had laughed at Donald Mackenzie for his clumsy manners and his lovelorn regard for Annie, he had held the man in a great regard. As highly as James had, in his own way. To William, it was not that the man had died which caused him to seek for vengeful justice, but that he had been killed in such a way. Degrading the great man and abusing his gentle kindness.

He turned at the sound of movement behind him and gave a slight smile as he found himself regarding the same gaze he faced in the mirror. The marten cocked its head slightly before it ran past him and stared down at the town as a company of men began walking out. There were two dozen of them but, even from this distance, William could recognise Mackay. He lifted the pistol he held and pointed it towards him, but the distance was too great to shoot. Moving down to the road he stopped, waiting for the men to come into view. The seconds seemed to last for hours before the column marched past and he raised his weapon once more. He followed the line of the gun to Mackay's chest and was about to tighten his finger on the trigger when he felt someone strike the side of his head and he stumbled sidewards. He looked at his assailant, who was a stocky man clad with a fur around his shoulders, and William felt his breath catch as he realised it was made of marten fur. He rose to his feet, and was about to advance, but stopped as his assailant lifted a gun of his own and pointed it at William's heart.

William did not feel afraid. He had travelled to Tain with the notion, though not the intention, of dying. Only, he had hoped he might deliver Mackay the same fate first. The single emotion that did seize him, however, was one of sheer confusion as an enormous dog leapt at his attacker, tearing the gun from his hand. Finally, with its front paws on the chest of his opponent, it tipped its head back and issued a prolonged howl which carried through the hills to the mountains beyond. William stared at the wolf while it returned his gaze through blue eyes.

"No," William gasped as a shot sounded and he watched as the wolf collapsed at his feet, while his assailant lowered the fired pistol and glared across at him. He felt a hand on his shoulder and turned, trying to confront this new attacker, but his movement jolted him awake and he stared into the face of the man who knelt beside him.

"Caledon?" William whispered. "Was that the dream or is this?"

"That was," James said softly.

"There was a man," William muttered. "He had killed my Eile. Then he killed Donnie's."

"Enough," James replied firmly, but without malice. "It was only a dream. We can't choose what we dream."

"But it all has a purpose. He told me. Everything which happens to the Clan of Caledon happens for a reason."

"Who told you?" Malcolm asked as he crouched down on William's other side. "Donald Mackenzie?"

"No. The farmer in Tongue. Mr Gow. Nothing happens by chance to the members of the clan."

"What are you doing here, William?" Annie asked as she walked over to him. "You did not really think to combat twenty men alone, did you?"

"There was only one I was interested in combating. But now I'm not sure there isn't another."

"There is nothing I want more than justice on John Mackay," James muttered. "But I don't want to see another member of my clan fall. You can't face him alone."

William nodded slowly, but his features still held an expression of defiance. "What will we do, Jamie Caledon?"

"We'll confront him. To warn him. But until we've learnt what we can achieve in the absence of Strength, we can't fight him."

"It may not be the best idea to tell him that," Robert laughed as he offered his hand down to William, helping the taller man to his feet. "If John Mackay intends to reach Golspie tomorrow he will be leaving Tain soon."

William watched as Annie and Malcolm walked down towards the road, followed by Robert. James did not follow them but waited until William turned to face him.

"Caledon, how did you find me?"

"Annie saw you. She knew you were moving south, and she knew the only reason you would have for doing so. What's troubling you, William?"

"What do you mean?" William asked flatly. "I came here to have satisfaction from the man who killed Donnie. That is all."

"Why did you follow me, William?"

"What?"

"You were the first to swear your allegiance to Caledon after Donnie. Why did you do it?"

"You helped Catherine to safety, at great expense to your own. You had a determination to live and succeed which I hadn't seen in an individual for so long. And you had unwavering support from your cousin, and loyalty too. I wanted to fight for something I could believe in because it was worth my allegiance."

"But you fought at Drumossie."

"I fought against what the Stuarts brought, not in favour of the Hanoverians. I joined you because I wanted to fight *for* something." William stared into James' strong watery eyes and took his sleeve. "Caledon, I don't understand what it means but I'm certain it means something. I saw Donnie."

"Enough, William," James whispered, gently freeing himself from the man's grip. "It was a dream. Nothing more."

William watched as James shook his head and walked away in the direction the others had gone. For almost two weeks the image of Donald Mackenzie walking out from the waterfall had haunted him. He was conscious of Mr Gow's words but afraid of what the implication could be, that only he had seen their dead companion. It meant something, he knew, but he could not understand what it might be. Reluctantly he walked down to the rest of the clan and listened as James outlined his plan. He could feel Robert's gaze resting on him but, as he met the sharp eyes of Zeal's wildcat, all he could think of was the wolf's failing gaze in his dream. Lowering his face, he turned toward the road and snatched James' arm.

"They're coming."

An Old Enemy Under a New Skin

For ten days John Mackay had been staying in Tain, and for almost every minute he had hated it. On the first day of his stay he had been introduced to the reason he had been sent there. Now, as he rode out of the town, the man he had been sent to collect rode beside him. He had seen nothing to recommend this man to him. He was arrogant and foolish and seemed to live in the glories of the past. He had not raised arms in the uprising but had since claimed several rewards, hunting and capturing the fleeing rebels. While this action in itself did not offend Mackay, the fact he had joined neither side but made money from both in the aftermath, angered him. The promise of today had kept Mackay civil. He was anxious to return to Mary and felt a certain contentment at the closed chapter of the Mackenzies.

They were barely a mile out of Tain when his horse threw up its head, snorting loudly, so he had to lean forward and calm it. As he was doing so, trying to ignore the amusement of the man beside him, his gaze took in a single figure on the edge of the road before him. It was this man who had caused his horse to start and, as he stepped into the centre of the road, Mackay drew the pistol that he carried.

"James Og," he began. "I trust your cousin isn't with you."

James did not seem concerned by Mackay's taunting but walked forward, his eyes locked on the ensign's. "I'll make you pay for the death of Donald Mackenzie."

"You?" Mackay laughed. "You're alone. Where are your loyal band of criminals?"

"They're here," James replied, forcing a cryptic smile onto his face.

"And who is your friend?" William began, stepping out from the verge and moving over to the only other man on horseback. "I know you," he whispered, pointing his pistol at the man he had seen in his dream the night before.

"I have no memory of you," the man replied indignantly.

"That's quite a stole you have."

"William," James hissed, uncertain what the other man was trying to achieve.

Noticing this, Mackay laughed slightly. "Your men are a little unruly, James Og. Or, rather, your man."

"I came here to warn you," James continued. "As a courtesy, such as Mary showed me."

"Mary?" Mackay whispered and lifted his gun, but his grasp failed as a pistol shot struck the weapon from his grip and Malcolm stepped forward. "You're revealing your full hand, then."

"Caledon," James replied as Malcolm walked through the ranks of Mackay's militia, "has many sons and many daughters."

"Please spare me your words," Mackay snapped as he holstered his pistol once more. "I hear the repetitive sound of Donald Mackenzie's pathetic voice in them."

James felt a rage burning through him at these words and tried to keep his face calm, but John Mackay was only beginning.

"Five hours. That is how long he repeated those same words, over and over again. Can you imagine, James Og? Five hours of listening to a grown man professing to be a child of Caledon." He glared at Malcolm, William and James in turn before he added, "I think I did the world a service by eliminating such a creature."

"You took away the only balance I had to my blind rage," James snapped. "You will pay the price for it."

Whatever words might have been spoken next ended abruptly as a churning, low-pitched sound groaned out from the firth. Only James and Mackay did not turn to look at its cause, their eyes remaining locked on one another's. There was nothing to be seen, though the agitated soldiers had lifted their muskets to defend themselves, while the other man looked almost excited by this unusual occurrence.

"Remember these men," Mackay announced, pulling the attention of his men back to the outlaws before him. "I will give one hundred pounds to any man who brings me any one of them."

"You can kill us, Mackay," Malcolm announced. "But you don't know how many others there are to replace us."

A shot sounded from the undergrowth at the left side of the road while another rang from the right. Malcolm stepped into the ferns beside the road, while James disappeared at the other side. William stepped back to allow the column to continue on its way but never turned his gaze from the other man who kicked his horse forward, an amused expression on his face, as though he viewed this interchange as nothing more than a light-hearted entertainment.

"You seem to have quite a battle on your hands, Mackay," he began that evening as they sat by a fire in a small house at Lairg. "Who were those men?"

"Fools. James Og claims he's Caledon and has united a small band of outlaws to follow him through all his deeds."

"Was his cousin one of them?"

"Yes." Mackay drank to the bottom of the beaker in his hand and looked across. "I left him hanging from a tree with orders I should find him there on my return. Pathetic boy," he spat. "But the Mackenzies are gone from this land now."

"And the other two men? Who were they? One spoke with an accent of an Englishman and the other wore the ragged remains of the Hanoverian uniform."

"I don't know them," Mackay replied softly. "What is it to you? He knew you, didn't he? William, Og called him. How do you know him?"

"I don't."

John Mackay gave no answer but to scoff, proving he did not believe this protest and was finding him only more irksome. He withdrew to his bed without sharing another word with him.

The following evening found the column of men finally arriving at Golspie. Mackay smiled across at the farmsteads and, although he would never admit it, felt pleased to have returned to the town where he had established his home. The man beside him looked thoughtfully around, no doubt weighing and measuring the buildings for all he could make and take from them.

"Are we to journey to Dunrobin at once?" he asked.

"You can clean up at the hall first," Mackay replied, but the smile which had rested on his features slipped as he regarded the empty branches of the tree where he had expected to find the remains of his enemy. "I'll have them flogged," he muttered.

"Who?"

"I left two men here to guard this place and neither of them are here and nor is the quarry."

"Donald Mackenzie?"

"Yes."

"I think after the display we were witness to outside Tain, it would be safe to assume James Og removed his cousin and those guarding him."

"I'll find that fool," Mackay muttered, kicking his horse forward once more.

They reached the drill hall without further conversation and Mackay ordered one of his men to show the guest where he might make himself presentable. Walking over to his house and opening the door, he turned his back on the world. The room was warm and welcoming, made more so by the appearance of his wife from the door into the bedroom.

"John," she whispered, relief evident on her face. "I thought you might be Jamie returned again."

"James Og has been here?" he demanded.

"Almost as soon as you had left. But I sent him away and I have not seen him, nor heard anything of his cause since."

"I'm afraid he's not given up yet. I saw him on the road."

"Did you complete your duty in Tain?"

"Yes, I've brought him back, and you and I should join him at Dunrobin tonight. But," he stopped quickly as he held Mary to him, noticing for the first time how tightly he could hold her. "The child?"

"Our daughter," Mary replied as she kissed his cheek. "She also arrived almost as soon as you had left." She took his hand and guided him back into the bedchamber where she leaned down to lift the tiny babe from the hooded cradle.

"She's beautiful," John whispered, his hand trembling as he reached out to stroke her cheek. "She's so perfect."

Mary watched him with a sudden guilt. She had not been prepared for such a show of affection. She had told herself giving the child away would be easy, for she should still see her daughter, but she had not taken into account the profundity of love she witnessed in her husband.

"Have we named her?" he asked softly.

"Yes."

"What's her name?"

"Seona. My mother's name." She handed her daughter to him and felt the sickness intensify as he lifted the child so that he could kiss her forehead. "We'd better get ready to go to the castle," she muttered.

John ordered the best of care to his daughter before he escorted Mary out of the house and to the hall next door. Here she was met by the man they were to take to Dunrobin and introduce to the Earl of Sutherland. He took her hand and kissed it while she took in everything she could about him.

About his broad shoulders he wore a stole of fur which looked so soft and warm she became quite jealous of it. He had a tanned face which spoke of a life lived almost exclusively outdoors and his sharp blue eyes burnt into her.

"Mrs Mackay," he began softly. "It is more than an honour to meet you."

They walked up to the castle where they were admitted almost at once. Not one of them spoke while they waited in a large room decked with books and hunting trophies, which the guest studied intently. All three turned as the door opened and the earl entered, a slight smile turning up the corners of his mouth.

"Mackay," he began. "I see you were successful in your mission."

"Indeed, my lord," John answered and stood back slightly. "This is your new bailiff, Andrew Polson."

"You come highly recommended, Mr Polson. In these tumultuous times I need a man who can both be trusted and be effective in the role of bailiff."

"I like to believe both things are true of me, my lord," Polson replied.

"Your name sounds familiar. Have you family hereabouts?"

Polson pointed to the rug on the floor and smiled slightly. "My grandfather brought that wolf down. He was a hunter, my lord, and would seek out any prey he was asked to find. As will I."

"Now," the earl mused. "Why would you say that?"

"We encountered three men on the road here, didn't we, Mackay?"

"James Og, my lord," John answered, glaring across at Polson.

"He still goes on," Sutherland laughed. "I thought the example you made of one of his men might have deterred him."

"He will stop at nothing," Mary whispered.

"I believe congratulations are in order, my dear."

"Are they, my lord?"

"You have a child now, haven't you?"

"Yes, my lord," she whispered, a slight smile on her face. "She was born the day after my brother's death."

"I'm sorry to hear of your brother's death," Polson began but stopped as Mackay glared at him and Sutherland laughed. "Your brother was Donald Mackenzie?"

"Indeed, Mr Polson," she said caustically. "And while I'm sad he's dead, I'm not sorry, for the path he had chosen could only lead to his ruin."

Angered by this berating, Polson turned to the earl and smiled slightly. "I shall be true and effective in my role, my lord. And furthermore, I shall hunt down James Og who masquerades as Caledon and shall bring a singular justice upon each of his men."

"If you can do this, Andrew Polson, you shall be given the highest position in this county. James Og and his band of miscreants have been a thorn in my side for too long. Mackay, ensure Mr Polson has all he needs. We might be rid of this rogue if he is all he claims to be."

"In my experience," Mary retorted, hurt on behalf of her husband. "Men claim a great deal and so rarely deliver, my lord."

The evening concluded with Polson and Mackay vying for the attention and appreciation of the earl, while Mary witnessed the exchange of words with a burning anger toward each man in the room. Time could not pass quickly enough, however much she tried to persuade it.

For his own part, Andrew Polson hated to be made a fool of. He felt certain John Mackay sought only for a way to humiliate him and this riled him further. He was given a small room in the drill hall until a more permanent arrangement could be made, and he was relieved to be left by Ensign and Mrs Mackay, from whom he had received barely one civil word.

Sleep claimed him almost at once and, in his dream, he stood before a tall castle. It seemed familiar, yet he knew he had never been there before. There was a heavy drawbridge which was being lowered and, as he stood and watched, a thousand torches became visible from the courtyard beyond. For the first time, he questioned the queer light of the location. Hundreds of tiny rainbows scattered the ground with colour, and a shaft of sunlight seemed to be coming from the tall castle beyond.

"Why are you here?"

He looked at the man who walked across the bridge to him, and felt a frown cross his features. It was a young man with black hair, tangled and in disarray over his ruddy face. He wore a philamor about his waist, but it trailed behind him like a wide, flat tail. There was little wonder at his poor presentation, for his hands were tightly bound before him, and a second cord was fastened about his neck, the excess following him as the philamor did.

"Why are you here?" the young man repeated. His voice was concerned but soft, and Polson felt himself lower the gun he had not realised he was carrying.

"I don't know where I am. How can I know why I'm here?"

"You're claiming to continue the work of your grandfather."

"You're not Caledon. I've met James Og. He is taller, thinner, more aggressive than you. But you do look familiar," he continued, reaching out to snatch the long cord which hung from the noose. "You're Donald Mackenzie. I've met your sister."

The other man did not look concerned by the fact Polson held the hemp which had taken his life. He lowered his head slightly so his scratched cheeks were no longer visible as he continued talking.

"Mary is no longer a Mackenzie. But you didn't come here to speak of Mrs Mackay. You came here to seek the glory your grandfather sought. But I must warn you against it."

"He spoke of beasts he could never bring down. I will succeed where he failed."

"You will not kill the Eile, Andrew Polson. Greater men than you have died trying."

"You're afraid," Polson replied, harshly. "What could a man who has passed through death be so afraid of?" He pulled on the rope in his hand causing the younger man to stumble towards him, clutching at his throat with his bound hands. "I don't care for your sister, nor her husband, but you are my enemy as you were for them. Caledon will not escape me as he has John Mackay. They'll all suffer the same fate as you." He pulled fiercely on the rope and watched as the fire in the man's eyes began to fade until they stared into the shaft of light which poured from the castle, but saw nothing.

Polson stumbled backwards as something leapt at him, and before he could reach his gun or knife to defend himself, he felt a set of strong teeth grip his shoulder and powerful jaws shook him. Donald Mackenzie's eyes stared down at him, but now they were in the angry face of a wolf, and the lifeless form of the man he had just killed had vanished. The giant dog tipped its head back and gave a long, drawn out howl. All the torches in the courtyard were extinguished and the shaft of light blinked out of existence.

Andrew Polson awoke, back in the hall at Golspie, and clutched his shoulder. There was no blood there, and no wound, but the pain from his dream lingered on. He lay awake for some time, unable and unwilling to return to sleep for fear of what awaited him there. It was not possible. His grandfather had shot dead the last wolf in this land, but there was the constant reminder of how alike Donald Mackenzie's eyes were to those of the wolf in his dream. What had he become involved in that such witchcraft and sorcery caused him to dream and imagine these confusing subjects?

"There are no wolves here anymore. It's all nonsense," he whispered into the silent room and, little by little, he began to believe it. The dream faded and the pain in his shoulder subsided and, after several minutes he felt content enough to fall asleep. He rolled onto his side before he sat up quickly. He was not asleep, but he had certainly heard that. He snatched the fur and wrapped it about his shoulders, walking out into the night. And there it was, once more. Distant, and made only more mysterious in the moaning of the unfelt breeze, echoed the solitary howl of a wolf.

Part Eight:
The Reason to Fight

A Storm in the Still Sea

June arrived in Sutherland, bringing the thaw of the final snow in the hills. The month had passed with surprisingly few incidents. The clan had moved further into the mountains, but the bothy they had inhabited since last autumn remained empty. Despite this, as movement was now easier between Golspie and Lairg the four men had chosen to retreat. Initially Annie had felt indignant about this, but, as time wore on, she began to recall the beauty of the simple life she had led before Donald Mackenzie brought James Og to her door.

Leaving behind Annie had been difficult for James, and his mood reflected this as he trudged up the mountainside toward the three remaining members of his clan. William rose to his feet and smiled across.

"Any news of where we should be going?"

"Not yet," James replied as he sat down beside Malcolm and Robert. "Perhaps we should return to Golspie."

"Going back to Golspie isn't sensible," Malcolm muttered. "We have to find a stronger unity before we're ready to face Mackay. The meeting at Tain proved in the least that we're each known to the members of his militia."

"Who was the man travelling with him?" Robert asked. "You seemed to know him, William."

"No," William whispered. "I only know he is a man without mercy."

William turned from them and looked at the pin he pulled from his pocket. It was Donnie's, of course. He had tried to banish the peculiar image he had witnessed at the waterfall when he first picked it up. But, as he stood a short distance away listening to his comrades discussing their next moves, he heard once more the words of Mr Gow, the farmer in Tongue.

"I'm sorry," he began in a sharp tone which suggested he was not at all sorry for the interruption. "I've got to tell you."

"Tell us what?" Robert whispered, rising to his feet. "You did know him, didn't you?"

"It's not that. It was at the waterfall. The day we lost Donnie. I saw him."

"Then who is he?" Malcolm asked. "He did not have the look of a soldier, but carried a gun and had a stance which proved he was not unused to using it."

"No, I didn't see *him*," William muttered, and turned to look directly at James. "I saw Donald Mackenzie. I saw him, Caledon. He walked out from the waterfall."

"What?" James stepped over to him and looked levelly into his eyes.

"Wait," Malcolm said quickly, rising to his feet and placing a hand on the shoulder of both men. "Caledon, subside the anger in your eyes. William has said nothing wrong. Only what he believes he saw."

"I did see him."

"I don't rebuke you," James whispered softly. "At times I imagine I see him myself."

"You don't believe me." William handed the pin to James who looked down at it but remained silent. "I'm sorry I spoke such harsh words to you, Caledon, and to all of you. But you must believe I saw him. I would know that oaf anywhere."

"But we placed him in the water," Robert began. "He did not emerge from there."

"I can't explain it, any more than I can explain how I knew that man. But this man will seek to destroy us, Caledon. That much I know."

James nodded slowly. "I do believe that."

James glanced north to the smear of light on the horizon and willed himself to believe his cousin was still alive somewhere. He could not escape his guilt and the burning hurt Mackay's scornful words concerning his cousin's death caused within him. Donald Mackenzie had been as loyal to James as any man could be even when, at times, he had not deserved it. To hear William talking of him in such a way, he who had called Donnie an oaf, scorning him in so many ways, stabbed at James' heart.

"I need an answer," he whispered toward the fading light in the north. "I need to know what I'm doing."

Malcolm watched this silently while William noiselessly walked a short way down the hillside. Robert folded his arms across his chest and tried to remind himself of the reason his beloved brother had chosen to remain. It was true he loved his land, perhaps more than any other man there, but he was unsure whether his comrades were beginning to lose the zeal which he should have represented in the clan.

He turned as he felt a gaze burning the back of his neck and stepped toward where he believed the eyes were. He had taken barely ten steps when his gaze linked with his own eyes and the wildcat pulled its lips back in a sneer. Robert knelt down and reached his hand forward but withdrew it as the animal lashed out its own claws and whipped its razor-sharp knives across the back of his hand. Looking down at the three wounds he watched as the cat stalked towards him. He wanted to turn and walk away, but he found he was rooted to the spot, mesmerised by its eyes which read each page of his soul. He could see himself as it saw him, perhaps in the reflection of its eyes, perhaps as an embodiment of his very being. It stopped beside him and began licking the bleeding cuts on his hand.

"Robert?" Malcolm called, and the young man turned to face his half-brother. When he turned back it was to find his Eile had vanished and he looked down at his hand to see if he had imagined this whole meeting. Blood continued to trickle down to his wrist, a painful reminder of the reality of the situation.

"What have you done?" Malcolm continued as he walked over to Robert and snatched his wrist. "What happened?"

"I don't know," he whispered, looking across at William and James who both stared at him with expressions which might have meant anything. "But I'm fine." He pulled his hand back and looked at all of them in turn. "Actually, I'm not. We have lost the last two months. We've almost run out of the French gold. *Your* gold," he added, pointing his bloody hand at Malcolm. "I lament Donnie Mackenzie's death, but we're doing nothing to respect his sacrifice."

James stared across at the young man who lowered his hand and at once blood rushed from the scratches. Robert looked down at it, too, and felt his head go light. William snatched him as his knees buckled, before lying him down on the mossy ground. Malcolm knelt beside him and lifted Robert's bleeding hand, wiping the blood away.

"Three?" he muttered. "Three cuts in perfect lines?"

"A cat," William whispered.

"His cat," James agreed. "He's right. I have wasted too much time considering the past and ignored the present plight of the people of Caledon."

William took some strips of fabric Annie had prepared for them before they had left, insisting they should be ready for the repercussions their antics would bring, and began bandaging Robert's hand while Malcolm followed James, who walked away. William did not need to follow them to hear their hushed voices in the still night but listened to each word they spoke.

"Caledon," Malcolm hissed. "What happened?"

"I'd lost sight of my goal through personal grief. I can't afford to be James Og any longer. I can't lose sight of Caledon, and Zeal was sent to remind me."

"Must it cost you such injury to remember?"

"It cost Donnie his life," James choked. "If I had been more Caledon and less James Og, he would still be here."

"It's not your fault. What happened to Donald Mackenzie is no more your fault than it is mine or

Annie's or William's or Robert's. We all knew the dangers and the enemies we faced in swearing allegiance to Caledon."

"But he did it because of me."

"You cheapen your cause if you think that. From my understanding Mackay had a feud with Donnie long before you declared yourself Caledon."

"It doesn't make it any easier to bear. But I will not allow my grief to overcloud my judgement. If we are to be a clan, we must unite as a clan. Tomorrow we will return to Lairg and, along with Annie, we'll go wherever we are sent. Robert was right. I've ignored the sacrifices each one of you has made."

James placed his hand on Malcolm's arm before he walked to where Robert sat, supported by William.

"We're leaving tomorrow."

"I'm sorry, Caledon," Robert muttered while William watched on silently, unsure he was sorry at all.

"You were right, Robert. I'm only sorry you were injured before I came to my senses."

James watched as his clan prepared to sleep, Robert clutching his bandaged hand to him, Malcolm muttering the words of prayer and William sitting cross-legged, gazing southeast. Jamie stared up at the stars above as they began to appear as tiny specks in the pale sky, and he tried to draw the strength he needed to continue his quest. But it had been his cousin who had given him the strength to believe in himself.

"Don't be foolish, Jamie."

James looked around him and found he was standing on the wide bridge which led to Castle Caledon. His cousin was beside him as he stared into the chasm. James stepped back, feeling the abyss cause him to go lightheaded, and turned to face Donnie.

"Foolish? You don't think I was going to jump, do you?"

"I'm quite sure it would make little difference if you did. I mean you're being a fool to think you can't go on with the quest without me."

"How do you know what I was thinking? I talked to Malcolm of it but otherwise those thoughts have been confined to my mind."

"And where do you think I live now?" Donnie sighed and looked down at his bound hands. "You're wasting time, Jamie. You've let a new enemy in, and he has set his sights on something far more sacred than Mackay took."

"Who?"

"Some things seem so clear to me now, Jamie. Some things I failed to see before, or chose to ignore. William knows. He knows more about the Eile than any of you."

"I dare not trust everything William tells me."

"Jamie, they're your clan. You have to trust them." Donnie met his cousin's gaze and sighed again. "William knows what this man is capable of and what he seeks to do."

"Did he really see you?" James asked bluntly, ignoring the words of his cousin.

"I don't know," Donnie whispered. "All I know is that I saw him, as I saw you all this evening when Robert's Eile delivered him his warning, as I see you now."

James tucked his fingers beneath the noose which Donnie still wore about his neck. "I won't lose sight of it again."

"Of course you will," Donnie laughed. "But your clan will be there to focus you each time. Just trust them, Jamie. Trust them as you trusted me and as I trust you. Even William." He watched as James lifted his bound hands and nodded. "Good," he continued. "Jamie Og, you have a new direction. You must travel east, Caledon. There is a treasury ship sailing north. It's a German ship carrying bullion, and the English are waiting to relieve it at the northern cape."

"How do you know this?"

"Will you not take direction from me, Jamie Og? You must meet the ship at the harbour of Latheron. Create a storm, bring it in to you."

The more Donnie spoke, the less his voice was his own. James turned to the waterfall which continued to run behind him, and realised it was the neutral tones of the supernatural falls he was hearing. He turned back to try and find his cousin, but Donnie was gone.

"Go to Latheron, Caledon," the waterfall commanded. "You have slept too long. Your people are being massacred as the Butcher hacks his way through your lands."

"To Latheron?"

"Why will you not listen to your cousin? He is here because of you."

"Living in my mind," James whispered and nodded. "I'll go to Latheron. But in future, do not show me my cousin." He turned to look at the huge castle and swallowed hard as he considered he had seen his young cousin for the final time. "I have to learn to continue without him."

The waterfall remained silent, except for the continuous pounding of the forceful water.

"But how can I draw a boat into the harbour?"

"You must know by now that you are Power, Jamie Caledon. Use it."

James would have confronted the waterfall on the meaning of its cryptic words, but he was awoken from his dream by a hand on his arm. He turned to look directly into Malcolm's gaze and quickly sat up as he saw the expression on his face.

"What is it?"

"We should leave this place, Caledon."

"Why?" James asked, tossing the long tail of his philamor over his left shoulder.

"It's running," Robert announced as he rushed over to Malcolm and James. "There was only one."

"One what?"

"Wolf."

"We must leave anyway," James began as he collected his pouch and belted it around his waist. "We must get to Latheron with all the haste we can muster. But first we must go south to find Annie. Our clan has been divided for too long." He watched as Malcolm and Robert readied to leave, and turned to see William staring out in the direction Robert had come from. He was shaking his head as he gazed out, as though he could see something in the peculiar twilight. "William!"

"Caledon," William replied. "I believed the wolves of Sutherland had been slaughtered fifty years since."

"Yes," James agreed. "But the last remnants of the pack clearly still live on. There was talk of wolves by Forres. Perhaps they have run from there. Fleeing as we flee."

"We have direction?"

"Latheron. But we must go first to Lairg and collect Annie."

It took the four of them until the evening of the following day before they stood on the cliff to the south of the inlet harbour of Latheron. Annie had been reluctant to join them on such a mission, but Malcolm had persuaded her to for the sake of Caledon. She had not been sure whether it was James Og or the embodiment of Caledon which had compelled her to join them on the mission, for it was becoming harder to recognise one from the other. She had watched Jamie as they journeyed on, walking in the centre of the column and, the further they walked, the stronger and more assured his stance became. He never spoke of the events the clan had endured, he hardly spoke to her at all, but discussed everything with Malcolm. William he trusted to navigate their way and Robert he watched over as though he were his own son. But in the absence of his cousin, James confided more and more in Malcolm.

That evening the five of them sat around a fire which they had lit only to keep the insects at bay, for the night was warm and still. Robert was priming his pistol and continued to point it toward something in the distance, pretending to shoot before he rubbed the barrel once more. Malcolm poked at the fire while William smiled slightly.

"Poor Oaf. I missed him sliding down the hillside. It's a funny thing."

"I see very little to laugh at," Annie rebuked.

"Then you will never recover from it," William retorted. "He's out there still."

"Enough," Jamie said quickly, but without hurt or malice, only a wish not to consider the words William had shared some days earlier. "The ship will appear soon, and I was told to create a storm, but the air is so still."

"Were you not advised how to do it?" Malcolm asked.

"I am Power. Use it."

"Caledon!" Robert shouted. "The ship!"

James walked over to the edge of the cliff and stared out at the faint lights of a distant vessel. It was moving gracefully over the unusually placid water at a distance of perhaps three miles. All the power of all the kings could never create a storm to shepherd the ship in.

"Annie," James muttered, reaching his hand out to her without taking his eyes from the ship. "Annie, I need to talk to you."

"What is it, James Og?" she said softly, stepping over to him.

"Annie," he whispered, lifting her hand and stroking his thumb across her knuckles. Eventually he turned his gaze to her strong, sharp eyes and smiled nervously. "You are my Wisdom and I need wisdom now, more than I ever have before. What must I do?"

"I am no wiser than William or Robert and far less knowledgeable than Malcolm. You chose me poorly, James Og."

"No, Annie. You know me better than any of them, for you knew what I was. What does it mean to be Power."

Annie faltered for a moment, trying to understand what he meant. Finally she closed her eyes and tried to recall the bond she had felt when her Eile dispelled the crows from her kinsman's body, and saw William travelling south. "When I saw through its eyes, I focused on what I needed to know and do. My wisdom came through the raven."

"But I don't know my Eile. How do I reach it?" He glanced back at the other three who stood watching the pair expectantly. "Donnie said," he paused as he heard the words he had just spoken. Annie followed his thoughts and kissed his hand, which she still held.

"What did he say?"

"That William knew more of the Eile than any of us. But I don't dare trust him."

"Close your eyes, Jamie Caledon," she said softly and waited until he did as she said. "There is something missing. Something which has always been missing, even while your cousin lived. That is your Eile. Call it."

James tried to follow her instructions and felt tears tug at his eyes, overcome by the burst of emotions which coursed his veins. But little by little he found the raw power of these thoughts knitted together. At once he felt as though he was moving at a great speed, racing a vast distance, water pushing back on him from all sides. He opened his eyes and stared out at the white foam that began to form on the previously still, calm sea. Feeling overwhelmingly powerful, he looked across at the ship which was being driven toward the coast. A low, moaning sound churned his stomach as he watched, joined now by the other three who gazed over the sea.

"I heard that at Tain, too," William muttered.

"What is it?" Robert whispered.

James did not answer them but remained staring out at the sea, willing the ship landward. Somehow, he could see its keel as it approached the rocks, bound to the creator of the localised storm. He gave a slight laugh as he shared in its exhilaration at being out in the open waters and the feeling of freedom it gave to him.

"We should get down to the harbour if we are to relieve it of its cargo," Malcolm said quickly, rushing down the slope. James reluctantly turned from the view before him and nodded. The low noise became louder and louder and Malcolm turned to James who followed behind him.

"What is that?"

"His Eile," William called as he skipped nimbly down to the harbour wall.

"What in hell's name…?" Robert began as he stumbled forward.

At that moment the boat was struck with such force it battered into the cliff face a little to the south. But it was not the boat which the clan all gazed at or Robert's words reflected. A head, as big as a man, protruded from the whipped-up waters, topped with a crown of cold fleshy scales. It turned directly toward them and James felt a smile catch his features. It stretched its unending neck forward and gave its long low cry, causing the rocks to tremble beneath their feet. James watched as the force and power of the sound struck the earth and a portion of the cliff face crumbled and avalanched down into the sea. After this, the serpent plunged into the deep once more.

James turned back to the other four who met his gaze with uncertainty. For his part, he knew his face showed a self-confidence which only grew as he beheld the four stunned faces looking back at him.

"There's a lot of gold to carry from here, and without Donnie we must manage as best we can."

"Perhaps it would be wise to make ourselves known to the inhabitants of this village," Annie suggested, struggling to find her voice after such a display. "They certainly will not have missed this."

"But they're Hanoverians," Robert hissed.

"They're people of Caledon," Annie replied, glancing quickly at William who was now the only Redcoat in their clan.

"Annie," James whispered, staring down at the embodiment of Wisdom and feeling invincible as, for the first time, he had truly learnt what his Eile was. "You underestimate yourself."

He watched as her cheeks flushed before she and Robert rushed toward the nearest house. James glanced at Malcolm and recalled where he had last witnessed the expression of awe. It had been at Loch Arkaig when, through blind anger and sheer power, his giant assailant had been pulled into the water. His smile faltered slightly as he turned to look south towards the wrecked boat. Were the Eile always to cost life?

Repaying the Debt

Having the child in the house had given Mary great contentment. Seona was becoming more observant and aware with every day which passed so she was the pride of her mother and the adoration of her father. Mary would watch, often unseen, as John held his daughter and increasingly her choice to give up the child seemed harder and harder to accept. She had made the bargain without any notion of what it was to be a mother, and without ever considering the pain it would bring to her husband. At the last new moon she had walked down to the beach on Loch Fleet and tried to persuade Beauty and Fortune to allow her to keep the child, but they had rebuked her harshly.

"When she is seven you shall see her once more," Fortune had snapped. "You made this bargain, Mary Mackay. Should you break it, you will pay far more dearly than your mortal spirit can imagine."

Beauty had barely spoken a word to her until shortly before they parted from one another.

"It was a pity what happened to your brother," she said softly. "He was handsome beyond any man I have known. And, in my youth, I knew a great many."

"Enough," Fortune interrupted.

"I'm sure he is far less handsome now," Mary whispered, a trapped feeling gripping her stomach like a hand of ice.

"I have sought him," Beauty whispered. "But you created a creature from him which has great strength and, since his death, has no focus for that strength."

"My brother fulfilled his purpose," Mary answered coldly.

"Donald Mackenzie's role in this story is concluded, Beauty," Fortune ordered. "Leave his corpse to rot."

Mary picked up the lantern and turned from them, trying to dispel any guilt she suffered as she considered the young boy she had known, and tried not to imagine how her parents would have felt to know the end she had orchestrated for him.

"Time," Fortune said sternly. Mary turned back to her. "We shall collect the child from you."

"How am I to conceal this from my husband?"

"You are a woman to whom concealment seems to come naturally. But we shall come at a convenient time for your daughter."

Two weeks had passed since this meeting and, though it weighed upon her heart, it was not the foremost thought in her mind as she regarded the man who stood in her house. She had not offered him a seat, though two chairs stood empty. She trusted him less than she trusted James Og, Fortune or Beauty, for she could not understand his motive of such a strong hating jealousy.

"Where is your husband, Mrs Mackay?" Polson asked flatly.

"He is out. I don't know where he goes." Mary repositioned Seona in her arms and glared at the man before her. "I heard one of the farms had a fire two days ago."

"It's what becomes of those who fail to pay their rents."

"A rather messy way of dealing with it," Mary muttered before she rose to her feet and walked over to him. "For a huntsman, you leave a lot of debris in your wake."

"But I always find my quarry, Mrs Mackay. Your family would do well to recall that."

Mary was startled by his words, unsure how to take them, but forced herself to look straight into his cold eyes. "You should return later, Polson, when my husband has returned." She opened the door and watched as he walked through it into the June sun, before she leaned against it and sighed. Seona wriggled in her mother's arms and gave a slight laugh as she reached her fat arms toward Mary's face.

"I wonder what your uncle would have thought of you," Mary whispered. "But the price he paid will make you a hundred times stronger than he could ever have been."

She carried Seona out into the sunshine, intending to walk only a short way but, as she passed the castle and walked along the flat sandy coast, she could not stop. Her feet seemed eager to walk and the sun only encouraged her. Without meaning to, she found herself at the mouth of the River Brora and here she sat down upon a grassy hummock and held the baby close to her, laughing as Seona tried to catch her loose hair and smiling down into the face of the only person she trusted.

What happened next, she was unsure. A hand snatched her throat and tightened its grip so she could not call out. She tried to slow time, but her racing mind would not allow her to utilise this skill. Instead, as she felt someone strike her head, the moments which stretched while unconsciousness took her seemed to last an eternity. She felt as though she was falling through water, labouring to reach the surface, to draw breath. These panicked thoughts made her consider how Donnie must have felt as the cord tightened on his throat, blocking the last spark of life and hope of breath. Finally, a host of sun bright stars shot towards her eyes and a sickening blackness filled her vision, where everything was equally dark, although she felt certain the black was spinning.

"Mary?"

She sat up quickly, gasping for breath and surprised to find she could absorb air. Clinging to the hand which was offered down to her, she turned to face the last person she had expected to see. Her cousin's powerful grey eyes stared back into her own and he smiled slightly.

"Mary, what are you doing here?"

"Where's Seona? What have you done to her?" Mary's voice became frantic and she struck out at James.

"Who's Seona?" he asked, catching her hand, and pulling her to her feet.

The sky was darkening, she noticed, and as she turned a full circle she found two other men stood close by, one with fiery eyes and a bandaged hand and the other with a stance suggesting complete authority. He looked a little familiar and, as she recalled the last time she had seen him, she scowled.

"James Og," she stated, trying to regain her calm. "Where is my daughter?"

"Mary," James whispered softly. "You were alone when we found you. You can't think I would take your child. Not one of us knows the first thing about children."

"It was Fortune then," she sobbed, stumbling away from him.

"How long have you been here?"

Mary ignored his question but struck him repeatedly before she felt someone take her arms and pull her back.

"I warned you," she shouted across at him, ignoring the man who still held her. "I warned you as I warned Donnie. You should both have run and kept running. I will have revenge on you for what you have done, James Og."

"Mary," he began while she shrugged out of the hold her captor had on her. "I have done nothing to your daughter, and I would have given my life for Donnie."

"Well, you were too late," she snapped back, recalling the ridiculous loyalty her brother had exhibited. "He died for you instead. Son of Caledon? What foolish nonsense you filled his simple head with. The pathetic boy was too blind to see through it. And now you have taken my child from me, too. John will make you pay for this."

"As he made Donald Mackenzie pay?" interrupted the younger man, his eyes flashing as he stepped forward.

"He suffered only because he would not speak. He might have died a swift and peaceful death if he had not shared your childish ideals."

"Did you shed even one tear for your brother?"

"I shed all those he deserved." She felt the web of time slow down as she moved over to the impertinent boy and struck him across the face with the flat of her hand. With a speed which surprised her he retaliated, and she stumbled back from the action.

"Enough, Robert," James snapped.

"How courageous your men are, Caledon," she whispered as she rubbed her stinging cheek.

"I listened to your brother speaking about you," Robert continued, pacing forward so Mary continued to move backward, until Malcolm snatched his wrist and pulled him back. "He all but worshipped you."

"Enough, I said," James interrupted sternly. "Zeal has a place, but so does compassion. Mary, let me take you safely back to Golspie."

"Without Seona? I will not leave here without my daughter. What have you done with her? Given her to that shifty man, no doubt."

Malcolm smiled slightly while Robert laughed out loud. "She means William," he laughed.

Mary's eyes flashed and she marched forward to Robert. "William, indeed. He stole from my brother's corpse, your friend William. What manner of man does that?"

"Stole?" Malcolm muttered, while James felt his eyes narrow at her words.

"He had the Mackenzie pin which was placed through the hemp when he died."

"Here, Mary," James said softly, producing the pin William had given him. "It's yours by right, if you want it."

"It was my brother's. It should have been buried with him. But I don't even know where he is buried. Do you, James Og?"

"I know where these two men laid him to ground. But he's not there now."

"Then throw the pin wherever you threw him."

"Mary," he whispered. "Blame me as much as you wish, but don't blame Donnie."

"I blame him for choosing you." She spat each word into his face, having to stand on tiptoes to do so, before she rushed away from them.

It was five miles to Golspie, and she had covered almost one of them by the time James caught up with her. He was alone now, and the temptation to use the sgian dhu she carried grew and grew. But his men would be close at hand and, though hidden from her, would certainly be watching.

"What do you want from me?" Mary demanded. "Haven't you taken enough already?"

"It might seem strange to you, but I want you to be safe."

"I wish you had stayed away. I wish you had died at Drumossie, and you would have died a hero to me, my father and my brother. Let me make one thing clear to you and your ridiculous cause. My husband may have ordered the rope on my brother's neck, but you prepared the path which led him there. You're a coward, James Og, and no title of a long forgotten age will change that. You lead your band of miscreants and impressionable fools to their death while you sit safe in their sacrifice."

James let her walk on a few paces before she felt him take her arm.

"Leave me be!" she snapped. "Fortune has favoured you, I see that now, far more than she ever smiled on me. Now leave me to lament my daughter as you left me with only laments for my brother."

She walked on and, though she felt certain Jamie continued to follow her, he did not interfere with her movements anymore. The remaining distance felt unbearably long and the night had closed in when at last she collapsed through the door of her house. Almost at once her husband appeared and helped her over to one of the chairs.

"Where have you been, Mary?"

"I walked to Brora," she sobbed, clinging closely to him. "But I was ambushed by James Og and two of his men."

"Ambushed?" John repeated.

"They took Seona. I was attacked from behind and, for all I know, they have drowned her."

"Seona? My daughter?"

There was a quietness to his tone for which Mary was not prepared and, as she blinked back the tears she felt at his loss, she began to feel afraid.

"I'll find that coward and flay him," John continued, his voice still remarkably quiet. But his eyes sparkled as his anger fought the sorrow this news brought. He snatched the long musket which rested in the corner of the room but stopped and turned to her. "But you escaped him?"

"To carry this bitter news to you."

"Did he hurt you?"

Mary paused, seeing an opportunity to further fuel her husband's rage, before finally she shook her head. "Not beyond ensuring I could do nothing to protect our daughter. Please don't go out tonight, John. He knows this land, every incline of every hill. You won't find him and he'll kill you. Stay here with me."

He lowered the gun and knelt down beside her chair. Neither of them spoke for a time and Mary began to feel unsure which was comforting the other. This feeling only intensified as the evening concluded and she went to bed, with dry eyes. John waited until he thought she was asleep before she watched as he sat on the edge of the bed, leaning forward to rock the empty cradle as his shoulders shook with noiseless tears.

Drawing out the Quarry

The fire in Annie's hearth never died. Because of her role as a baker she never let the ovens fade and if, as was often the case, she needed to be away she would ask one of her neighbours to oversee it. James had never welcomed it more. June was not a cold month, in fact all the other members of the clan were beside the open window playing cards for their share in the gold they had acquired. It made little difference for the fund belonged to Caledon, but they laughed and joked at each other's losses, celebrating their own wins as though they were going to buy a castle with it.

Annie walked over to him as he huddled close to the stove.

"Have you any space in your thoughts for company?"

"Is Mary right, Annie?"

"I needed to talk to you of Mary Mackay, Caledon. But I'm afraid to raise such thoughts."

"What is it?"

"When her daughter was born she spoke of Donald Mackenzie's death."

"It was the same day, Annie."

"I know," she said in a tone which made it clear she had not finished making her point and did not wish to be interrupted again. "But she knew details she should not have known if she was as innocent in the affair as she claimed. And then yesterday. She spoke of the pin in the hemp cord. She could not have known that if she had not witnessed it. And if she witnessed it and said nothing, she was almost certainly responsible for it."

"That is a vast chasm of doubt you have built your assumption across," James hissed. "Mary kill Donnie? That makes no sense. He would have done anything for her."

"But more for you," Annie continued, wishing she had not raised her concern but knowing she had to. "Don't you remember when we saw Donnie's end played out before us? He spoke of you saving someone's life after they had been shot. That could only have been Mary."

"I remember him saying you were never his. I remember him saying repeatedly that he was a son of Caledon. And I remember feeling as though I couldn't breathe as the cord tightened in the image and the crows flew toward his faded eyes. But, no, I don't remember Mary at all."

Annie felt tears roll down her cheeks as she nodded slowly, trying to dispel the memory of the haunting scenes. "You told me I was your wisdom. Why won't you trust me?"

"Mary is bound and blind in her grief, Annie. She would never have harmed Donnie."

Annie nodded slowly but felt only more certain than ever. "He was right, you know? I was never his. But I am entirely yours, James Og."

"Jamie Caledon," he corrected her, laughing mirthlessly.

"No. James Og. He knew I loved you, that's why he knew I was not his."

"But he was yours, Annie."

"No, Jamie. He was *yours*."

James watched as Annie walked to the back door and stood staring out over the rising hill and into the starry sky above. He tried to reconcile with what she had said but no amount of Annie's wisdom could lead him to believe Mary had killed her own brother. And such thoughts only drove a greater and greater hatred of Ensign John Mackay in his heart. He moved over to Annie and wrapped his arms around her, placing his head close to hers. She let him kiss the salty tears from her cheeks while Robert and William cheered to witness this embrace.

"It seems the baker has her mind filled with other things, and is forgetting her duties," William laughed. "Something smells of burning."

Annie gave a laugh so girlish that Robert and James joined in her laughter, but William's gaze took in Malcolm's anxious expression as he rushed to the other window.

"That's not a loaf of bread."

"God in heaven," Annie whispered as she ran to the front door and walked out onto the dusty street. Away to the south, the smell being carried on the faint breeze, was a blazing inferno on the hillside.

"Whose farm is that?" James asked.

"A tenant farmer, Brock," Annie replied. "We have to help them, Caledon. A fire like that does not grow by itself."

Annie tucked her skirt in at her waist and began running forward. Robert and William were only a step behind her and they overtook her quickly as they rushed on. James was about to follow but turned as Malcolm placed a hand on his arm.

"Be careful, Caledon," he muttered. "Annie's right. A fire like that does not start itself, not in the heights of summer. Someone is drawing us out."

James nodded but did not offer any words as they both rushed toward the burning beacon.

Far from being the only people to go to the Brocks' aid, some twenty people were gathered around the family, shielding the children from the sight before them. Annie, clearly known to these people, comforted the mistress of the house. The farmer, Alec Brock, was bring held a short distance from the crowd by two men while a third stood before him. In spite of Malcolm's warning and all the sense James knew it carried, he burst through the gathered people and felt relief beyond measure to find Malcolm stood to his right and Robert to his left.

"What is this man's crime?" James demanded, drawing the attention of all the gathered people.

"Wrecking and theft."

"Who claims it?"

"The bailiff. And furthermore we found a chest of foreign gold in his house."

"Indeed you did," Malcolm announced. "That was my money. My gold. And it was French gold, not German."

"Who is the bailiff?" James asked. "I thought Mackay oversaw these lands for the earl."

James turned as the joists of the building collapsed causing an explosion of tiny sparks. Malcolm turned too while Robert, who stood close to the building stumbled backward. When James turned back it was to find Alec Brock being marched away by two of the men. But it was the third man who James stared at as the soldier pointed a pistol into his face.

The sound of gunfire echoed from the northern hills and James blinked in confusion as he rubbed his hand across his face and looked down at the blood on his fingertips. Annie rushed forward but Malcolm snatched her wrist and held her back. James turned his bloodstained face towards where William lowered his gun.

"His name is Andrew Polson and he is a mercenary and a hunter, not a bailiff."

William walked over to the corpse of the man he had just shot. He crouched down and took the loaded pistol from the dead man's grasp.

"We have to go after them or Alec Brock will be hanged for concealing our gold," Malcolm began, releasing Annie and walking to stand in front of James. "And because of our actions at Latheron," he added.

"We should go at once," Robert agreed.

"Wait," Malcolm hissed and looked up the hillside. "I was correct, Caledon."

Annie watched on in confusion as Malcolm pointed his gun towards the silhouette of a long-legged dog as it tipped its head back and gave a long howl. Robert looked across at William whose expression became anxious, and James watched as the Hanoverian stood in front of Malcolm's gun.

"Wait!" William pleaded. "The three of you should go after Brock. Don't shoot the wolf, I beg you."

"What are you doing?" Robert asked as William turned at the second howl from the creature, pointing the two guns he carried toward where it stood on the hillside. "You just told us not to shoot it."

"Go after, Brock," William replied without turning back to them. Instead, he waited until the three men had begun moving away in the direction of the arrested man. Annie, along with many of the other bystanders began retreating to the village. William rushed up the hillside without lowering either of the two guns he carried, toward the wolf, but searching instead for the man he knew would have his own gun focused on the animal.

James, Malcolm and Robert stopped as one as gunfire sounded further up the hillside. Without checking the movements of the other two, all ran towards the sound. Robert, perhaps fired by the zeal which coursed his veins, overtook his leader and his brother and flung himself at the man they had encountered on the road at Tain. He pulled the knife from his belt and gripped it against the man's throat. This was how Malcolm and James found him.

"Who are you?" James asked as he looked at the blood which seeped from a wound on the man's forearm. "Who are you really?"

"This is Andrew Polson, Caledon," William muttered as he walked over to join the other three members of the clan. "And he has his sights set on a far greater prize than the one hundred pounds on each of our heads."

James felt his forehead crease as William lowered his trembling hand and tucked the pistol he carried into his belt. "What prize?"

"The wolf to begin with," William replied, but before he could explain further, the four of them turned as six soldiers appeared over the ridge of the hill.

"You will be dead men," Polson began, "if you do not let me go free."

"We're dead men if we do," William's voice whispered.

"Let my men go free," James said quickly. "It is I you have quarrel with, not them."

"You've nothing to bargain with, James Og."

"We can disappear into these hills in the blink of an eye, Polson," James continued. "You will not find us."

"Shoot them!" Polson shouted but, as true as James had promised, Robert, Malcolm and James disappeared at once, and William was only a moment behind them.

Out of Sight, Not Out of Mind

Each of them knew to gather at Annie's house and Annie stood at the door, waiting anxiously. Malcolm reached the house first, relating to her the events which had caused them to become separated. She listened with widening eyes before she watched as James stepped through the back door, at which point she folded her arms and sighed deliberately.

"It is like having a house full of children, looking after you all." She clung tightly to James and smiled up at him. "You frightened me, Caledon. I thought you'd been shot."

"I have to meet him, Annie. Donnie said he is an enemy with a higher goal than Mackay."

"Donnie?" Robert asked as he stepped into the house. "But Polson arrived after Donnie's death."

"William," James corrected himself, unwilling to explain his cousin's presence in his dreams and the frightening way in which the waterfall used him to deliver direction to him. "Where is William?"

"Here," replied a flat voice from the corner of the room. "But Caledon, don't meet with Polson. He's remorseless."

"How do you know him?"

"You would not believe me if I told you. But he follows no code and will stop at nothing to obtain what all others have failed in."

"What is that?" Annie asked bluntly.

"I wish," William began but stopped as he rubbed his eyes.

"What?" Malcolm began.

"Catherine."

"Catherine?" Robert echoed. "Who's Catherine?"

James let go of Annie and rushed over to William, pulling back his jacket and pushing aside the protests of the man. William's head lowered as he tried to look at the wound on his shoulder where his shirt was stained red.

"Catherine would have made light work of it," William laughed slightly while Annie rushed to draw fresh water and Robert eased the coat from the wounded arm. Malcolm stood behind William, supporting his head as it lolled from side to side as though it was too heavy for his neck. James pulled the shirt back and ran his thin fingers over the gunshot wound, causing William to return sharply to his senses for only a moment before his head dropped to his chest. Annie stepped back into the house and carried the basin of water over to William's side.

James and Robert watched on as Annie tended their friend, assisted by Malcolm. Robert turned to look across at James and spoke softly.

"Who's Catherine?"

"His sweetheart. As loyal to the Stuarts as you and I."

"Does it not seem strange to you, Caledon, that we fought so fervently against them, yet it is the two Redcoats of our clan who have given their blood for your cause. I always thought any man who raised arms against the Stuarts fought against Scotland, but Donnie and William are as true sons of Caledon as any of us."

James nodded slowly. "There are many reasons to fight."

Both of them turned as Annie rose to her feet and washed William's blood from her hands while Malcolm dragged his unconscious form over to the bed. Annie turned to look at James' wide-eyed gaze and smiled slightly.

"He will be well, Caledon. The shot passed straight through his shoulder."

Robert gave a relieved sigh and glanced across to share a smile with his brother, but Malcolm's face was set hard. The older man looked sternly across at the gathered clan and shook his head.

"William has never been caught out like that before. Nor has he ever been as pleading as he was about the wolf."

"Do you think he's hiding something?" Annie whispered, feeling once more her mistrust toward the solitary clansman.

"I'm certain of it," James muttered as he looked across at the sleeping form of the man he knew so little of. "I would like to know how he knew who Andrew Polson was and what he believes Polson wishes to obtain. But for now, I intend to honour my word. I shall send a message to our bailiff and tell him to meet me in the house of Alec Brock. First, though, we have an invitation to deliver."

Sleep was slow to reach James the following night as he tried to strengthen the frail plan he had made. It was not until he heard the continuous noise of driving water that he realised he had fallen asleep. It echoed behind him as he walked towards the castle, seeming strange to be in this place alone, and at once he felt as though he were a trespasser. He stood on the high bridge over the ravine below and questioned whether he should go forward. After several minutes he walked into the courtyard, ducking under the heavy portcullis which hung at a lowered height. The air was still and the castle was dead. He walked to one of the doors which opened into the castle and stepped through.

He had entered a large hall with a giant staircase crafted into the stone and an elaborate chandelier which hung squint on two ropes, the third having been eaten through by the rats and mice, whose existence was evident by the scratching and scampering sounds. Away beyond him, at the other side of the room, was a shuttered window. Intrigued by what view awaited, he walked to the window and pushed open the shutters. At once daylight flooded into the room in an explosion of rainbow hue as the waterfall filled his view.

"What do you want in this place, Jamie Caledon?" asked the unemotional voice.

"I got the gold at Latheron, and it has cost the life of an innocent man and the health of one of my clan. Why did you tell me to take it?"

"You met your Eile there. And without the Eile it would not solely be Stealth that suffered."

"What do you mean?" James was met with silence. "If you will not answer me that, then tell me who Andrew Polson is."

"He has come to continue his grandfather's work. Beware him, Jamie Caledon, for he will stop at nothing to preserve his family's legacy. Do not trust him."

"Where is Donnie?" James demanded, recalling his cousin's words of warning about the man.

"You did not wish to see him, Caledon. His spirit has joined his body. You shall not find him here again."

James, without realising, gripped the pin which had been his cousin's heirloom and he looked down in surprise as the sharp point stabbed into his hand. The waterfall had gone, and the window faced onto a wall of solid stone. The sunlight and the rainbows were gone, too.

"I'm so sorry, Donald Mackenzie," he whispered, overcome by his foolish decision to banish Donnie from this place. Tears stabbed at his eyes and he struggled to hold them. He jumped as he felt a hand dip into his own and lift the pin from it. He spun around, hoping to find Donnie's gentle face, but he was alone in the castle, and there was no sign of either the man or the heirloom.

He walked silently out of the ruined hall and through the courtyard. As he ducked under the portcullis, he looked over the bridge to where a tall dog stood. It looked weary, its eyes were red, and it panted as though it had run a great distance. James lifted his pistol and began walking toward it. At the sight of the gun, as though it recognised the threat, it gave a deep growl. Pointing the pistol, Jamie pulled the trigger, too late to realise William now stood before the dog and James' shot struck the other man's chest causing him to collapse to the floor. But as James rushed forward both the dog and William simply vanished.

"William!" James called out.

"I'm here, Caledon," William said, amusement in his voice.

James looked about him and realised he was awake once more in Annie's house in Lairg. The waterfall, the castle and the wolf all faded into the realms of sleep. William was sitting on the edge of the bed, gripping his right shoulder. Malcolm was at the table, as was Annie. Robert walked into the house and scowled across.

"I did it. It doesn't sit well with me, though."

"She is a smart woman, Robert," James laughed. "And she is the only person we know we can trust."

"What have you planned, Caledon?" William asked, rising uncertainly to his feet. "And how long have I missed?"

"Only a day," Annie said softly.

"What happened?" Robert asked, his sharp gaze watching as the Hanoverian sat down at the table. "I didn't think anyone could catch you unaware."

"He knew the wolf would be there." William looked down hungrily at the bread which sat on the wide window ledge. "And he knew I would stop him shooting it."

"You seem quite attached to this wolf," Robert laughed.

William scowled across, cutting Robert's laughter short. "What plan have you made? And, please, Annie, let me eat some of that bread. I'm starving."

Annie smiled slightly and nodded while Malcolm pushed the butter down the table toward him.

"Moira is to oversee the transfer of the German gold into Polson's house while Jamie meets him in Brock's house," Robert said in a voice suggesting he did not approve. "And to deliver a letter to Mackay as soon as the gold has been planted so Mackay believes Polson is responsible."

"Don't meet him," William said quickly, turning to James. "He does not adhere to a code of honour. He is a hunter and will not lose sight of his quarry for anything."

"Malcolm will join me, William," James said softly. "I'll be safe, and Mackay will arrive in time to arrest Polson."

"What will Robert, Annie and I be doing?"

"Robert will be our lookout, and ensure the gold we worked so hard for will not fall into Mackay's hands. Annie will be here. Looking after you."

"I'm well," William protested. "If you are going to face Polson and Mackay at once you will need all the help you can get."

"Very well," James said, watching as William placed the crust of bread down on the table in his left hand. He handed his pistol to William who took it in his right hand and grimaced at the pain such an action caused. "That's why you're not coming."

William nodded slowly and listened as the other three men planned the events of the morning. Each were to wait at Insh to ensure Polson made the journey alone, after which Robert was to leave for Golspie to retrieve the gold while James and Malcolm went on to the Brock house. Malcolm would wait outside and give a sign to James to let him know when Mackay arrived.

William watched as, with the premature dawn, Malcolm, James and Robert departed. James held Annie close and kissed her brown hair. She tried to hide her anxiety but gripped him tightly.

"Be careful, Jamie Caledon. Remember what rests on your shoulders. Not one of us could continue this quest without you."

"I will be safe, Annie, and if I do not return you must all go to the waterfall and it will direct one of you in how to continue. Look after William, and don't let him talk you into letting him leave the house. He'll try, I know."

"Don't worry about William, just be safe."

She clung to his hand, reluctant to let it go, but forced to as he walked out. William walked over to the window and watched as the three of them disappeared into the landscape. He turned back to Annie and frowned.

"He'll be killed."

"Don't say that," Annie snapped back.

"Annie, you have to let me go. I know Polson will have a trap waiting."

"You'll risk everything if you go. For once, William, be content with your orders."

William scowled across at her and watched miserably as the sun began to climb and shuffle lazily toward her midday position. The morning had reached its peak when he finally left the window and walked over to the table, kicking his feet like a sulking child. Annie placed the salted fish on a plate and tipped a handful of nuts beside it.

"I'm not happy about it either," she confided. "But we all have our part to play."

"You're Wisdom for a reason," William began, smiling across at Annie.

"I've got some honey," she said softly. "There should be enough for us both."

"Oh Annie," William sighed as she rose to her feet to fetch the honey. He rose too and walked over to her. "I'm sorry."

"Sorry?" Annie whispered. "Sorry for what?"

"This," he replied, spinning her round and clapping his right hand over her mouth and wrapping his left arm about her neck. She tried to struggle, but even with his wounded shoulder she was no match for him. "But I am Stealth for a reason, too."

He pushed her into the larder and dragged a chair over to secure the door long enough to rush out of the house. He wasted no time as he ran toward the burnt-out shell of the Brock's farmhouse and nor did he stop until he had reached it. His arm throbbed as he leaned against the corner and, with great discomfort, primed the pistol he carried. He walked sedately round to the doorway and he stepped in, pointing the gun before him.

"Well, if it isn't the ferret."

"You won't succeed in killing Caledon," William replied. "Greater men than you have died trying."

"I've heard those words before," Polson remarked, sitting down on the floor and motioning for William to do the same. "From a man with a noose about his neck and death clinging to him."

"Donald Mackenzie?" William muttered before he had checked his words which brought a faint smile to Polson's face.

"Mackay may waste his time with each one of you but, so long as the Eile live, the threat will remain." He placed his gun across his knees and smiled across. "And no one knows what the sixth Eile is. But I'd wager you know."

"You will not draw Jamie's Eile out."

Both of them turned as the sound of footsteps approached the house and William watched as Polson picked up his pistol and directed it towards the door.

"Jamie, stop!" William called out and the footsteps ceased at once.

Polson rose to his feet quickly and pointed the gun at William. "That was foolish."

"Foolish?" a commanding voice questioned from the doorway. "Foolish is swapping loyalty for hireling. You do not understand, Andrew Polson," continued Malcolm as he stepped into the house and fired a shot at the pistol in the man's hand, causing the shot to ricochet into the room. Both Polson and William ducked, but Malcolm continued to advance. "But Caledon protects one another beyond gold and silver, beyond uniforms and armies. That is why you will never catch Jamie Caledon. And you," Malcolm added as he pointed to William. "You have only proved that."

"Be seated, Andrew Polson," James continued as he stepped into the roofless house. "I promised I would speak with you, and here I am."

Malcolm picked up Polson's gun waiting until the other man was seated, before he sat down on the floor, facing him. James never looked once at William but waited for the bailiff to volunteer words.

"You are mighty bold when you are three against only myself, but it shall not stay this way for long."

"You mean the militia," James said with a smile. "Did Nobility not tell you that hirelings were a mistake? I would take the loyalty of five over the wages of five hundred. And I'm sure you've seen the extent of my men's loyalty. Your militia will come, but they will come under the banner of the law and they will come to arrest you."

"Arrest me?" Polson laughed. "Even Ensign Mackay would not be so foolish."

"There are no limits to that man's folly," James replied calmly.

"Yes," Polson muttered. "I saw what he did to your cousin."

"Donald Mackenzie paid a dear price for his loyalty," James replied in a detached manner which caused William's eyes to narrow. "But that was months ago."

"Caledon," William whispered as he rose to his feet and pointed to the window. A stag stood a short distance away, staring directly at them. Malcolm rose quickly and turned to James.

"Mackay."

James followed Malcolm to the door but turned as Polson snatched William's pistol from him and rushed to the window. William threw himself at the man, gripping his arm to redirect the gun he carried and both Malcolm and James crouched down on the ground to try and avoid the aim of the pistol. The stag had bolted now and, upon seeing this, William felt his strength fade and he relinquished the man, dropping to the ground. Malcolm stepped forward and guided the dazed William from the house while James led them up into the deep heather of the higher ground. Here they crouched and listened as Mackay and his men arrived at the house. Mackay dismounted from his horse and walked to the door where he was met by Polson.

"You're here to arrest me," Polson stated. "You're a damn fool, Mackay."

"How dare you?" Mackay demanded.

"He was here. With his two men. He's set us both up. What did he tell you I'd done?"

"Who are you talking about?"

"James Og," Polson replied, and a look of vehement hatred caught Mackay's features. "He was here, minutes ago. What am I supposed to have done?"

"The gold taken from the Latheron wreck was all found at your dwelling."

"Well isn't that convenient?" Polson remarked with a weighted sarcasm. "If I had plundered the king's vessel, I would not be so stupid as to conceal the bullion in my own house. You have been played for a fool, Mackay."

"No more than you." Mackay turned to his men and ordered them to secure Polson.

"Your wife can confirm I was in Golspie too soon after the wrecking, for she was there with your daughter when I visited to find you. You are playing into his hands."

Mackay stepped forward and gripped Polson's throat in his hand. "The only reason I haven't killed you already is that I would rather see James Og condemned for this crime and suffer the end his cousin endured. But if you so much as whisper a reference to my daughter again nothing will stay my hand on the trigger."

He released Polson and watched as the men marched him away towards Golspie. He lowered his head and James realised, as he watched his turned back, that John Mackay was trembling with sorrow, not anger. This display, though brief, lingered with James as he turned to William, whose eyes were as like a marten's as James had ever noticed.

"I told you to remain."

"I knew you had underestimated him. Now you've seen what he is, what he wants."

"The Eile," Malcolm muttered, feeling a fear within him at how close he had come to losing his.

William nodded.

"Where's Annie?" James asked, helping William to his feet.

"In the larder," William answered sheepishly with a faint smile, while Malcolm laughed openly.

They walked back, feeling great contentment at the successes of the day, and extending back weeks and months. When they reached the house, they found Annie sat at the table. She glared at William as they entered.

"What he did was wrong," James began before he kissed her. "But he saved my life. I would have walked directly into a pistol shot if he had not been there."

Annie gave an indistinct sound which could have meant anything. While the four of them sat about the table, talking and laughing, there was a tension to them all which did not abate until Robert returned later that evening. Begrudgingly, he had to admit the plan had been a success. He and Moira's father had secured the gold which was now safely hidden beneath the floor of the kirk.

James felt an uncertainty at how well the plan had unfolded and, for the first time in two months, he began to feel he had achieved a great victory despite the absence of his cousin. He placed his hand into his pocket to take out the Mackenzie pin and frowned as he realised it was not there. At once he recalled feeling the hand in his dream take the pin and he choked on tears as he recalled he had asked not to see him anymore. Malcolm smiled sadly across at him while Annie poured out beakers of mead and Robert gave one to each of them.

"To Caledon," Robert began, lifting the beaker in a toast.

"To her people," Malcolm agreed, raising his vessel.

"To Donald Mackenzie," Annie added softly. Each of them bowed their heads slightly as this poignant toast fell upon their ears.

"To the Eile," William added.

"To the Clan of Caledon," James concluded. "My clan."

The Quest of Caledon
will Continue